Critical acclaim for Zane and
THE HEAT SEEKERS

"The sexy, uninhibited wordplay between the characters will make your toes curl. A perfect freaky bedtime story."

—*Vibe*

"The novel is warm and engaging, stressing the importance of personal responsibility and attesting to the power of hope while delivering the clever banter and sizzling sex scenes that Zane's (many) readers have come to expect."

—*Publishers Weekly*

"A cheerfully lusty contemporary tale with raw energy to spare."

—*Kirkus Reviews*

More Praise for Zane

"Zane's writing warms me, heats me up, satisfies me with a passion. This woman does incredible, erotic things with words. Read with a lover nearby."

—Eric Jerome Dickey, author of *Thieves' Paradise*

"At a time when much of African-American fiction has fallen into formulas and mediocrity, Zane has lifted the bar of literary standards. . . . The sista can write!"

—Robert Fleming, author of *Wisdom of the Elders* and *The African American Writer's Handbook*

Books by Zane

Addicted

Shame on It All

The Heat Seekers

The Sex Chronicles: Shattering the Myth

Gettin' Buck Wild: Sex Chronicles II

The Sisters of APF: The Indoctrination of Soror Ride Dick

Nervous

Skyscraper

Afterburn

Edited by Zane

Chocolate Flava: The Eroticnoir.com Anthology

Gettin' Buck Wild

Sex Chronicles II

Zane

ATRIA BOOKS

New York London Toronto Sydney

ATRIA BOOKS

1230 Avenue of the Americas
New York, NY 10020

ISBN: 0-7434-5701-3
        0-7434-5702-1 (Pbk)

First Atria Books trade paperback edition October 2003

10   9

ATRIA BOOKS is a trademark of Simon & Schuster, Inc.

Manufactured in the United States of America

For information regarding special discounts for bulk purchases,
please contact Simon & Schuster Special Sales at 1-800-456-6798
or business@simonandschuster.com

This book is dedicated to my Aunt Rose. Even though you are eighty-four, you understand that everyone needs to get their freak on from time to time. Thanks for your continuous support throughout the years. For all the sweet potato pies, the twenty-pound pound cakes, the living room furniture set when I needed it so badly, the black-eyed peas, the baked chicken, and the reminders to get my behind up and go to church. I could think of no one who deserves this book dedication more than you. I love you.

Acknowledgments

Each time it comes down to this, I always worry that I will leave someone important out. So let me say up front that everyone who has ever crossed my path in life is important to me. Whether it was lending me an ear to talk into, a shoulder to cry on, or a hand to hold in the down times, it has meant the world to me and you have my deepest gratitude.

First, as always, I have to thank God for His blessings, for giving me the opportunity to tune my visions and do what it is I love to do for a living. I must thank my parents for their undying support, for standing by me no matter what and for having the patience to guide me even when I didn't want to be guided. To my children, you are my everything, my entire world, and every single day inspires me to make you proud of me.

To my husband, Wayne, what can I say except I love you more than I love life itself and I am grateful for your love, patience, and understanding. I appreciate the pampering, the romance, and yes, the hellified sex.

I would like to express thanks and appreciation to my immediate and extended family members: Charmaine, Carlita, David, Rick, Jazmin, Arianna, Ashley, Aunt Rose, Aunt Neet, Aunt Margaret, Percy, Ronita, Trey, Franklin, Renay, Bo, Alex, Alan, Brittany, Dee, Dana, Janet, Karen, Miss Maurice, Uncle Snook, Beverly, Fran, Aunt Cle, Aunt Jennie, Aunt Barbara, Carl, Jr., Phil, Mom Bettye, and everyone else in the extremely large family tree. That includes my honorary family members in Kannapolis, North Carolina.

Sara Camilli, thank you for being the greatest literary agent of all time. Every gesture that you make on my behalf, both professionally and personally, shows how thoughtful and caring you truly are. Pamela Crockett, Esq., thank you for being the greatest entertainment lawyer of all time. With both you and Sara in my camp, I could never go wrong. Tracy Crockett, thanks for holding down the fort in New York City for me.

Malaika Adero, thanks for being such a wonderful editor and for being so personable. Demond Jarrett, thanks for keeping me informed and updated on a regular basis. Judith Curr, Louise Burke, and Karen Mender, thanks for being such wonderful and supportive publishers. I look forward to a long future with ATRIA and Pocket Books. Tracy Sherrod, thanks for taking the initial risk on me and allowing me to prove myself. I would also like to thank my publicist, Staci Shands, for her relentless efforts on my behalf and for getting me tons of media exposure.

Thank you to all the distributors and bookstores that have supported my books and recommended them to readers. Especially the African-American distributors and bookstores like Culture Plus, A and B, and Seaburn.

Thank you to David Kirkpatrick of the *New York Times,* Carol Mackey from *Black Expressions, Black Issues Book Review, Quarterly Black Review, Publishers Weekly, Honey, Essence, Vibe,* AALBC.com, Mosaicbooks.com, Timbooktu.com, NetNoir.com, BET.com,

RAWSISTAZ.com, Bookremarks.com, The Nubian Chronicles, and all the other Web sites, magazines, newspapers, and book clubs both on- and off-line that have supported my books.

To the Strebor authors, your journey has just begun but it will be a great one. Darrien Lee, V. Anthony Rivers, D.V. Bernard, Mark Crockett, Laurel Hanfield, Destin Soul, Nane Quartay, JDaniels, Shonell Bacon, Rique Johnson, Michelle Valentine, Mallery Basher and Indigo Moon, you are all forces to be reckoned with. To the other authors who have supported me, the list is far too long to mention but know that you are all loved dearly.

A big shout out goes to all of my sisterfriends: Lisa Fox, Sharon Johnson, Gail Kendrick, Destiny Wood, Aliyah Bashir, Vicki Tolbert, and all the rest of you chicas.

I could sit here for three days and still come up with people I need to thank but I have a deadline. Thus, I just want to say thank you once again to everyone who supports me. I love you and may God bless you and yours always.

Contents

Wild

When Opposites Attract

"You have an eight-thirty meeting with the board of directors about the five-percent projected increase in the fiscal budget, a ten o'clock meeting with the legal team about the impending lawsuit from the Grayson Corporation, a lunch meeting with Ronald Jackson about his transfer to the Hong Kong office, and a three o'clock conference call with the regional managers from Los Angeles, Dallas, and Atlanta."

I could hear my secretary, Shelly, running off my daily schedule, but I was looking past her out of the floor-to-ceiling window. She had greeted me at the door, mug of steaming coffee in her hand, two creams, one sugar, just like she did every morning. She was a pretty sistah—tall, graceful, beautiful skin, perfect smile—but she always seemed so stressed out. I often wondered why she let her executive assistant job get to her so much. Granted, I was stressed out all the time as well, but I had more to lose. Unlike me, Shelly earned no more than $889.95 after taxes, every two weeks, no matter what her work performance.

I glanced up at her, standing rigidly like she was preparing for a military drill. "Shelly, can I ask you a personal question?"

A nervous expression shadowed her face, causing me to wonder if she was afraid of me. We were the exact same age but had never bonded. I was the vice president of corporate development, pulling down 250K a year plus bonuses. She had barely finished high school.

"Sure. Go ahead," she finally responded.

"Do you ever just go out and have a good time?" I redirected my eyes to the window. There was not a cloud in the powder blue sky. "I mean, just let it all go, hang out with friends, party hearty?"

She giggled. She was gleaming at the mere thought of it. "My friends and I all go to this club over in Brooklyn every Friday night for happy hour, and sometimes we go to a reggae club on Saturdays."

"Reggae, huh?" It was my turn to giggle. "I can't even imagine you dancing to reggae music."

Shelly sat down facing me in one of the leather wing chairs across from my desk. I couldn't remember the last time she had actually taken a seat, other than to take dictation. I was pleased. It felt comfortable, like two sistahs shooting the breeze.

"What about you, Maylia? I mean, Ms. Kincaid."

"Maylia is fine," I responded. "You don't have to be so formal all the time."

"Thank you."

I didn't know whether to be flattered or offended by her thank you. Did she think I was so high-falutin' she had to show appreciation for calling me by my first name?

"So, what about you, Maylia? Do you ever just hang out?"

I pondered her question. I wasn't sure that attending business dinners with clients or boring social engagements at the country club with my parents constituted hanging out.

"Shelly, to be honest, I really don't know," I answered. "I go a lot of places, the finest restaurants and theaters in New York, but I can't remember the last time I actually had fun."

I gazed deep into her eyes and recognized something I hated: pity. I was pitiful. I needed to face facts. All the money, power, and security that I had in my life meant nothing unless I was enjoying the ride.

My parents had groomed me to take my place in high society, pure and simple. My father made his millions in international trade while my mother spent her days shopping in Macy's, Saks, and various boutiques on Fifth Avenue. I went to school at Yale University, graduated with honors, and nabbed a job with McMillan and Associates before I could even move out of my dorm good.

There I was, in my corner office on Fifty-ninth Street overlooking Central Park South, wondering what the hell I was doing with my life. Shelly did not have much money, but she had freedom. She could leave the office at five o'clock and do whatever she wished. I had to play negotiator over soft-shell crabs or spend my nights going over stacks of reports. I truly envied her.

I jumped up from my desk, startling Shelly. She jumped up too and waited for my instructions, assuming her military position again.

"I'm going out," I announced.

"Out? What about your meeting?"

"Cancel it!" I walked toward my private bath, grabbing my purse off my desk on the way. "In fact, cancel all of my appointments. I'm taking the day off!"

"But, but, but Ms. Kincaid, I mean Maylia," she stuttered, "what am I supposed to tell everybody?"

"Tell them I'm sick or something." I swung around to face

her. "Isn't that what people usually say when they play hooky from school or work?"

Shelly shrugged her shoulders. "I guess."

I was about to close the bathroom door in her face when a lightbulb went off in my head. "Shelly, after you cancel all of my engagements, take the day off as well."

"Are you serious?" She put her hands on her hips, striking a sistahgurl pose. I fell out laughing. She looked good like that.

I put my purse on the vanity counter and struck the same pose. "Yeah, gurl, I'm serious!" I exclaimed in my best ghettoized accent.

"Well, *aiight* then." She giggled, enjoying our little scene.

I walked back out of the bathroom and raised my left palm. "Give me five!"

She slapped me a high five and laughed so hard that she was practically crying. "I guess I'll see you tomorrow, then?"

"Maybe. Maybe not," I chided, knowing good and well taking two days off in a row would be pushing it. They'd probably send the police to my penthouse to make sure I was still breathing.

Shelly strutted out of my office with more pep in her step than I had ever seen and closed the door. I went back in the bathroom and gazed in the mirror. Now, I was glowing. I felt so, so, so invigorated. The mere thought of actually shucking my responsibilities for an entire day was thrilling.

I took a good look at myself and decided I appeared to be more like fifty than my actual thirty years. My hair and makeup, not to mention the stuffy, conservative suit, put age on me. I pulled the clip out of my ebony hair and let it fall down across my shoulders. It had been so long since I physically and symbolically let my hair down.

I took off the blazer of my Donna Karan suit, unbuttoned my sleeves, and rolled them up to just below my elbows. I looked younger already. I turned to the side so I could see the profile of my body. My breasts were as pert as ever, and my ass was just as firm and round as it was in college. Too bad I didn't show off my assets more often.

I had no idea where I was going to go or what I was going to do today, but I was determined to savor and enjoy it. Then I thought about the park. Every day, I looked down from the twenty-fourth floor at the ant-size people Rollerblading, strolling, or riding bikes through Central Park. I didn't know the first thing about Rollerblading, and I hadn't been on a bike since my first year in high school, but I did know how to stroll.

The three-inch leather pumps I had on were not made for walking, though, so I dug through my closet behind the bath-room door and retrieved my gym bag. The same workout clothes had been in it for more than three years. I had every intention of hitting the corporate gym on the seventh floor—I really did—but time constraints just never allowed it.

I opted out of changing clothes completely, but I did take off my thigh-high stockings so I could put on my white crew socks and cross trainers. I had often laughed at the women walking down the street or catching the train in work clothes and tennis shoes. It looked so silly. But I was content to look silly for just one day.

When I emerged from my office less than five minutes later, Shelly was nowhere in sight. Her phone console had been for-warded to the night message, and all the papers I had seen strewn across her desk when I came in were neatly stacked in her in box. Girlfriend meant business about her day off. Now it was my turn to escape the madness.

I managed to get down to ground level in the elevator before someone began to question me. The security guard, Fred, wanted to know if I needed him to call a company car. I told him no thanks, that I would be taking a morning walk in the park. He looked at me in stunned disbelief. I left him sitting there at the security desk with his mouth wide open and swiveled through the revolving door into the brisk morning air.

I sucked air into my lungs, and it felt wonderful. I went to the corner and waited for the light to change before crossing the street and entering Central Park. People were laughing and enjoying themselves. They had lives, unlike me.

I walked down a path for a long time. The muscles in the back of my calves began aching, and I realized I needed to start working out. Not because of weight issues—I was only carrying about 133 pounds on my five-six frame—I was just out of shape, *period.*

I spotted an ice cream vendor and grew excited. I had not had an ice cream cone in years; just fancy desserts like biscotti, compote, and slices of cheesecake that cost more than having a pizza delivered. I half-ran over to the vendor and whipped out a five, asking for a double scoop of chocolate on a waffle cone. I licked my lips while he hand-packed the ice cream onto the cone. I paid him and then turned around just as a big-ass basketball appeared from nowhere and knocked the cone into me. Luckily, the ice cream was so hard that I only ended up with a brown circle over my left breast, but I was still pissed. My ice cream was on the ground. *What idiot would be so careless?*

I glanced up and saw the idiot coming toward me. I wanted to spew out a bunch of ugly words at him, but I could not. I was reared up better than that, and people do make mistakes. He was average-looking and I envisioned what type of woman would date him. Certainly not me.

He frowned. "I'm sorry. Did you get hurt?"

"No, I'm fine." I smiled at him and pointed to my shirt. "Just a little stain."

"Well, let me buy you another cone. That's the least I could do." He picked up the cone from the ground and tossed it into the nearest receptacle. "You should let me pay to have your shirt cleaned also."

"None of that is necessary. Really."

He wasn't paying attention. He was already digging into the pockets of his athletic shorts, searching for money. He paid the vendor for another cone.

"Thank you," I said as he handed it to me.

"You're welcome." He glanced back over to the basketball court, where three other men were standing, looking mighty impatient. "I better get back to the game. Have a nice day."

"You, too."

I decided that my best strategy was to find a bench and eat my cone. I did not want to risk someone bumping into me while I was walking and causing another mess. There was a bench on a hill about thirty feet from the basketball court, so I grabbed it seconds before a man in a suit with a bag lunch got to it.

I was sitting there, licking the hell out of my ice cream cone, when I started surveying the rest of the men on the court. One of them stood out from the rest. Not just because of his height, though he had to be at least six-five—he stood out because he was the finest man I had seen in ages. Sepia skin, ebony eyes, and some seriously lickable lips. None of them had on a shirt, but his muscles put the rest of theirs to shame.

"Damn!" I heard myself exclaim out of lust.

Before I finished my cone, I was in heat. The ice cream did nothing to cool me down. I was sitting there fantasizing about that man's hands, tongue, and whatever else all over me. Once I finished my cone, I did not budge. I was mesmerized. How fool-ish, I finally said to myself. This is so unlike you, Maylia.

That may have been true. In fact, it was completely unlike me, but that did not keep me from following the brother when he threw his shirt back on and started walking away.

I had no idea what I hoped to accomplish by following him, but I kept my distance. I was sure he had absolutely no idea that I was trailing him until . . .

"Why don't you just walk beside me?"

Was he talking to me? Unfortunately, he was. He had stopped dead in his tracks and turned around, staring down at me.

"Excuse me?" was the only response I could come up with.

"I said, why don't you just walk beside me?"

"Why would I want to do that?" I asked, feigning innocence.

"It's better than following me." He grinned. "You are follow-ing me, right?"

"Don't be absurd!" I could not believe his nerve. Even if he was right about me following him, he did not need to point it out. "What are you, some sort of narcissist or something?"

"I have no idea what that means."

"A person who's egotistical, full of themselves."

"Now, I do know what that means, but I'm not that." He pushed a loose hair away from my face and I felt faint. He was turning me on so much that it was scary. "I am flattered, though."

"I can't imagine why," I replied, determined to keep some composure.

"I saw the way you were checking a brotha out on the court."

"Oh, were you just playing basketball back there?" I asked the question with a straight face. "I wasn't paying attention. I was too busy eating my ice cream cone."

"The way you ate it was a treat in itself." He licked his lips. I wanted to lick them for him. "It made me wonder if you devour everything else like that."

"You're nasty."

He came a step closer, and I could smell his sweat. Even that was turning me on. "And you're fine."

"I'm also well-bred. I don't tolerate men speaking to me in such a fashion." That much was true. I was not used to men addressing me like that. The majority of the men I had dealt with felt like they had to impress my parents first, so they always went out of their way to be completely proper. That was why my sex life had been so drab. "I only hold conversations with gentlemen."

I could tell by the way his eyes narrowed that he was offended. "Then why don't you converse your ass back in the opposite direction?"

"This is a free country." I stepped around him and started walking. "I can go wherever I please and do whatever I want."

He grabbed my arm and swung me around. "What do you want to do right now?"

"For starters, I'd like for you to let go of my arm." I tried to free my arm, but he overpowered me.

He started walking, pulling me along with him. "Come on, let's go."

"Let's go where?" I asked out of curiosity. I was being accosted in Central Park, and instead of screaming for help, I was asking questions. Bad sign.

"My place, of course. It's not that far. Unless you'd prefer me to sex you down right here in the park."

His place? "You're a lunatic!" I lashed out at him.

"And you're fine."

I could not help but blush. After all, that was the second time he had called me fine.

He stopped walking, let my arm go, and eyed me seductively. "I bet you wear nothing but the finest, sexiest lingerie. Probably silk or satin thongs and lacy, revealing bras." He crossed his arms and cupped his elbows, looking me up and down. "On second thought, I don't see you in thongs. I see you as a French-cut bikini type of sistah."

"Hmph, you don't know me," I stated.

"But I'd like to know you." He raised his eyebrows and looked me up and down some more, making me feel totally uncomfortable. "Back to my analysis. I bet you wear expensive perfume, two hundred dollars an ounce and up. You bathe in milk and honey and go to the salon once a week to get your hair done and your nails and toes tended to."

"Are you done?" I was insulted because 90 percent of his statements were true. Was I so artificial that a complete stranger could read me like a book? "Since you think you know so much, why don't you join the Psychic Network?"

"I'd rather do this."

He leaned down and slipped his tongue in my mouth. I backed away and slapped him across the cheek.

"How dare you?"

"How dare I not?" He chuckled, rubbing his cheek. "I'm sorry, but I'm one of those people that realizes just how short life really is. To just let you walk away from me and risk the chance of never seeing you again is asinine."

I'll be damned if he was not making sense to me. "I see you know some big words after all."

"Besides, you were following me for a reason."

"For the last time, I wasn't following you," I stated vehemently, determined not to be classified as a stalker. "I was just on my way to, to, to . . ."

"Yes?" He smiled, awaiting the answer we both knew I could not supply.

"Oh, never mind. I don't have to explain myself to you. You're a complete stranger."

"Just answer me two questions, and if you still want me to, I'll walk away and never look back."

"Fine." He better not just walk away from me, I thought. "Go ahead."

"Are you seriously involved with anyone right now?"

I saw no harm in answering that particular question. "No, but that's because I work all the time, and—"

"A simple yes or no will do."

I rolled my eyes at him. "Your other question?"

"Has any man ever made you feel the way you imagined it would feel like in your dreams?"

How did he know I had sexual dreams? Damn him! "What makes you think I have dreams?"

"That's answering a question with a question. Play fair." I rolled my eyes at him again. "Everyone has dreams."

"But that doesn't mean everyone dreams about sex," I countered.

"Most women do."

"See, there goes that psychic ability of yours again." I chuckled. "Did you take an official survey or what?"

"Don't you want a man that asks you what you need, what you crave, what you yearn for, and actually cares enough to try to give it all to you?" He started playing with my hair, fingering it gently. "A man that not only talks the talk but walks the walk?" His fingers moved to my lips and started tracing the outline of them. "A man willing to move heaven and earth to make sure you get just as much pleasure out of making love as he does?"

"Stop it!" I squealed, stepping away from him. "Just stop it!"

"I can't." He closed the distance between us again and put his arm around my waist, using his other hand to hold my chin up so that I was forced to look at him. "I want you, and I don't even know your name. You don't even have to tell me if you don't want to. Just come with me. Take a chance. Do something totally uncharacteristic in your normal life."

"I've already done that once today by just being here in the park," I said, wondering how far I was really willing to take this. "Twice in one day might be pushing it."

"Life is about pushing past limits." He gave me a peck on the lips and then drew my bottom lip into his mouth, suckling on it for a few seconds before letting it go. "Life is about doing everything you want while you still have a chance. Tomorrow is guaranteed to no one."

I debated all of five seconds before I started tonguing the living daylights out of him.

His place was a dump. I was halfway afraid to even walk through the front door. He lived in a public housing complex, the projects, the type of place I had never been anywhere near in my entire life.

His one-bedroom apartment was dark and dank. As soon as he turned on the living room light, roaches scattered for cover.

"Um—I think I better go," I whispered, turning around in hopes of making a quick exit.

He grabbed my elbow. "Don't tell me you came all the way here with me just to leave?" He saw the way I was surveying his place. "Ah, I get it. You hate my home. You think you're above all this." He let go of me. "Well, take your prissy ass on then. I thought you were ready for a *real* man."

"I'm not prissy," I stated defensively. *I just hate being called out.* "And your place is lovely." We both knew I was lying. "I'm just not comfortable being here with a stranger. No one knows where I am. This is like something out of a movie."

"Not yet, but it can be." He grinned seductively at me. "I don't have a camcorder, but I do have a Polaroid. Want to take some pictures?"

"You're insane."

He pushed me up against the open doorframe and palmed my breasts through my blouse. "I'm not insane. I'm just horny. I want to spend the rest of the day getting to know your body and committing every single inch to memory."

His lines were getting rather corny, but that did not prevent my panties from getting wet.

"Have you ever been tied up?"

He was insane! "No, I never have, and I never will be."

He smirked. "Still don't trust me, huh?"

"Still don't know you," I replied crudely. "Besides, I wouldn't let you tie me up if I'd known you my entire life. I trust no one that much."

"Well, I trust you. I'll let you tie me up, if you want to."

"Are you serious?"

He started unbuttoning my blouse. "I'm very serious."

"You would actually let me tie you up?"

"Tie me up." He lowered my blouse off my shoulders, along with my bra straps. "Blindfold me. Whatever pleases you, pleases me."

Now I had been with enough men in my life to know that most women wait decades to hear a man say something like "Whatever pleases you, pleases me." I had never heard anything close. Maybe that was why I had never had a man turn me out, dick-whip me, make me yearn for him every second that he was away. That was it! That was the second I knew I was not leaving his apartment without getting the dick.

I started helping him with my clothing, and within a few seconds, I was nude from the waist up. He rubbed my hardened nipples between his thumbs and forefingers while I hiked my skirt up. I wanted to provide easy access when he was ready for the goodies below the waist.

He gazed into my eyes, and my breathing became heavy. There was something about the way he looked at me. It was clear that he was a man about his business and that I was in for one hell of a sexual experience. I was ready for him to lead me to bed, but he shocked me by letting me go.

"I need to take a quick shower. I'm all sweaty from playing ball."

I started to say, I don't give a damn! "Okay, but make it fast," I heard myself demand.

He grinned. "Don't rush it. Good things come to those who wait."

I watched him walk toward the bathroom, stripping along the way. He kicked off his shoes and bent down to yank off his socks. Then he lost the shirt. His back was well defined, and I imagined digging my fingernails into it in the throes of passion. He let his shorts drop and stepped out of them, revealing form-fitting black briefs. Damn, what an ass!

He stopped a foot shy of the doorway and turned to me. "Why don't you come in? You can help me scrub something. Possibly everything."

I did not respond. I just stared at him, wondering how I went from eating ice cream in the park to contemplating joining a stranger in his shower. Life sure is full of curveballs. I knew all along that I would join him in the shower, but I wanted to play hard to get, so I gave him a five-minute head start to make him wonder about my next move.

When I entered the bathroom, the steam was so thick that I could barely make out the glass door of the shower. I took off the rest of my clothes and slid the door to the side. There he was, with hot water cascading over his ripples. The brother was seriously cut. We seductively eyed each other for a few seconds before I directed my eyes down and targeted his dick. His large, juicy dick. Nice and round. Thicker than most. I licked my lips reflexively.

"See something you like?" he asked jokingly.

"Maybe. Do you see something you like?"

He reached out and ran his damp fingers through my hair. I moaned. I do not know where that came from, because I am usually not a moaner.

"Come here, sexy lady." He pulled me into the shower with him. "I adore everything I see."

He lifted me up and placed my back against the tile. I straddled my legs around his waist and slipped my tongue into his mouth. He eagerly accepted it, and I found myself moaning again because his kissing was all that.

Once we broke the kiss, he lifted me higher and licked a trail across my right breast with his tongue. He drew my nipple into his mouth and sucked on my black pearl. I do not think my nipples have ever been as hard as they were at that exact moment.

He took a breather and announced, "I'm a breast man!"

"Damn! I can see that!"

We both started laughing as he let me back down. He handed me a loofah sponge. "Can you get my back for me?"

I was disappointed. What happened to the breast sucking?

I scrubbed his back for him and could not help but whip his ass into shape while I was back there. His body was admirable. I tried to recall the last time I had seen such a magnificent specimen of a man and quickly deduced that I probably never had. He did not seem like he would turn around any time soon, so I reached in front of him and began to caress his stiff dick with the sponge.

He moaned, and I dropped the sponge on the floor so that I could work my hand up and down his shaft. He finally turned to face me and buried his tongue into my mouth again. His kisses did something to me, and I do not know if it was only them or the fact that I was finally letting go of the inhibitions that came from being reared by my bourgeois parents, but I was suddenly motivated at that point. Motivated to indulge in the fuck of a lifetime.

I caressed his chest and placed small kisses all over it as I got down on my knees in the shower. My hair was doused with water, but I did not care. I *definitely* would not be returning to work that day. It had been years since I even had the craving to suck a dick, but the mere thought of taking him into my mouth made me tremble. I gazed at his dick, surveying every inch and vein.

"You look delicious," I told him.

"Well, don't let me stop you."

He tried to push my head toward his dick, and I pulled back. "Whatever pleases me, remember?" I said coldly, staring up into his eyes. "I don't like it when a man instructs me. In my own time. In my own way."

That seemed to intrigue him. He grinned, and though it seemed impossible, his dick became even harder inside my hand.

I stuck my tongue inside the head and sampled his essence. "Umm, that is delicious!"

Before he could respond, I took him deep, and he pressed his hands against the walls to keep his balance. The water made it easier to slide him in and out, and I kept taking in more and more, relaxing my throat until I could feel the tip tickling my tonsils. I used one hand to hold his dick in place so that I could deep-throat it and teased his balls with the other one.

He began to shiver, and I sensed that he was about to explode, so I released him from my mouth and started licking up and down the shaft. He was a stranger, and allowing him to cum in my mouth was out of the question, no matter how much I yearned to taste it. I finished him off with a few seconds of handiwork, and when he came, we both watched it trickle down the center of my chest with delight.

"Damn, woman! I knew you were something when I first saw you!"

I did not comment. I just stood up and told him, "Your turn."

He did not hesitate to get on his knees, place one of my feet on the side of the tub, and bury his tongue in my pussy. I threw my head back into the stream of water, raised my arms, and grabbed the showerhead so that I would not slip.

My pussy had been an entrée a few times, but never an all-you-can-eat buffet. Not until that day. He ate me until I came all over his tongue. *Twice!*

We were washing each other off when the hot water finally ran out. We giggled as we leaped from the shower, struggling to share the same towel to dry off and not freeze. I finally yielded the towel to him and ran into his bedroom, burying myself under his black comforter.

He jumped into bed beside me. "Let me have some of that."

"You have the towel." I leaned over and kissed his shoulder. "And you can have me, too, if you want me."

"Oh, you know I want you."

He climbed on top of me and started sucking on my neck.

"There is one condition," I said, trying to refrain from laughing because I am ticklish on my neck.

He looked at me. "What's the condition?"

"You have to wear a raincoat. The last thing I need is to catch something. Especially pregnitis."

He chuckled. "Pregnitus?"

I slapped him gently on the chest. "Yes, you know what I mean."

He got up and retrieved a condom from his top dresser drawer. I sat on the edge of the bed, opened it, put it in my mouth, and secured it on his dick. He was impressed with me, and so was I. I had wanted to apply a condom like that ever since I saw it on cable television. In my humble opinion, I did one hell of a job.

I pulled him onto the bed and straddled him. "I want to be on top," I said.

"Whatever pleases you," he said.

I leaned down and gave him a kiss. "Just what I wanted to hear."

I guided his dick into me, and it filled me up. I had to pause a moment to let my body get used to the size of his invasion. Then I started moving slowly as he palmed my breasts and squeezed. I lowered them to him so that he could suck on my nipples and got into a rhythm.

After that, we did not speak another word for an hour. Not while I was riding him. Not while he took me from behind and pulled me back deeper onto him by grabbing my hair. Not while we pleased each other orally again. Not while I dipped my fingers into myself and let him suck my pussy juice off them. We just immersed ourselves in the experience.

He fucked me to sleep, and by the time I awoke, I could see the sun setting from his bedroom window. I glanced at his alarm clock, and it was after seven. I felt behind me, where he should have been, and found emptiness.

I got up from the bed, wrapped a sheet around me, and walked out into the living room. His hand was buried in my purse.

"What are you doing in my purse?" I lashed out at him.

He turned around, startled. "Nothing."

I stomped across the room and grabbed it from him.

He laughed uncomfortably. "Do you honestly think I would try to rob you after what just happened between us?"

"No."

I dropped my eyes to the floor and set my purse down. I suddenly felt ashamed because that is exactly what was running through my mind.

"Go ahead," he insisted, picking my purse back up and shoving it at me. "Check and make sure nothing's missing."

I set it back down and caressed his cheek. "I apologize for sounding accusatory. I'm just a bit nervous about all of this."

He pulled away from me and plopped down on the sofa. "I'm sorry to hear that. I was hoping you would be totally relaxed."

"I am. I mean, it was great. You were great."

"Great enough to see again? To see on a regular basis?"

There it was. The dreaded question that I had hoped would not surface.

"I can't," I replied, deciding honesty was best. "You and I are from two different worlds, and people in my world just wouldn't understand."

"Why does it matter what they think?"

I sat down beside him and pondered on that. "Good question."

He took the sheet off me and teased my nipples. "Tell me your name."

"What's in a name?"

"My name's Julian."

Part of me wanted to tell him my name, my history, my goals, my desires. The other part, the sensible part, told me to just seize the moment. So, I did. I seized the moment, and I seized his dick, taking it into my hand and rubbing the shaft to prepare it for round two.

"Let's do it again, Julian." I lowered my head to his dick. "Maybe this time I'll tie you up."

I never saw Julian again. I went back to my daily grind, working on overload and staring out at the people enjoying life in the park. He had placed his telephone number in my purse that day. I guess he had sensed that I would not be a woman to take chances. He was my complete opposite, and it never could have worked. It was still pleasurable to have just one day without judgment. It was still pleasurable to find out what happens when opposites attract.

Come In from the Rain

He'd been out there for more than an hour, messing under his hood. He seemed well prepared, but he was obviously lacking one thing: a cell phone. The rain was coming down in sheets, banging against my roof like bullets. There was no lightning or thunder. Just the rain, but the rain was more than enough to make the situation extremely uncomfortable.

I couldn't see him that clearly as he hopped in and out of his car every five minutes or so, probably trying to warm up before trying something else to get his car moving again. One thing was for sure: he was built. He had on a white muscle tee that was hugging his body something fierce. I could make out his physique thanks to the street lamp about twenty feet from where his Ford Mustang had broken down. Lickety-split, the man was thick.

I felt kind of guilty. I have no idea why. I'm sure most of my neighbors saw him stranded out there as well. As quiet as my neighborhood is, something out of the ordinary rarely goes unnoticed. Still, the fact that the brother was out there struggling on one of the worst nights, weather-wise, of the year didn't sit right with me. What harm would it do to offer to let him make a phone call, loan him a flashlight, or let him warm up by my gas fireplace for a moment?

I had on nothing but a knee-length flannel nightgown, a present from my mother, who was always worried about me catching colds even though I was well into my thirties and had been independent for more than a decade. I went to the closet in my foyer and found my London Fog overcoat, quickly throwing it on and sliding my feet into a pair of rubber rain boots.

I was about to open my door when the phone startled me. It was like something out of a horror movie, the loud ringing serving as some sort of warning not to go outside, or the Boogie Man might get me.

I snatched the receiver up on the third ring. "Hello."

"Hey, Kimmie, it's me!"

"Me who?" I asked coldly. I knew it was my ex-boyfriend Mike but played dumb anyway. I didn't want him to think that he could phone me at will and get me excited.

"This is Mike."

"Oh."

"Oh? Is that all you have to say to me?" he asked.

"What else would I have to say?" I replied. "I haven't spoken to you in weeks."

He laughed into my ear. "Kimmie, I haven't called because I figured you needed some time to calm down. That immature tantrum you threw the last time I saw you was totally uncalled for."

Now it was my time to laugh. "Immature tantrum? I'm not the one that tried to bring some *Jerry Springer*–type drama into the mix. You had some woman calling my office demanding that I stay away from you."

"I didn't tell that tramp to call you," he said with disdain. "I don't even know how she got your number in the first place."

"Obviously, she got it from you. Even if it was indirectly. I'm just glad she didn't find out my home phone number, because it really would have been on."

"Forget her." He got quiet for a few seconds; without question trying to strategize his next move. "I made a mistake, Kimmie. I had a weak moment. What can I say? I'm all man."

"Is that the best you can do?" I yelled into the phone. "What can I say? I'm all man?"

I moved the curtain aside on my front door to see if Mr. Built was still out front. He was, poor thing.

"Kimmie, how about I come over?" Mike asked. "It's raining cats and dogs, and I know how horny you get in bad weather."

He was right. I was horny, but not desperate enough to allow him back into my temple. "Why don't you call your piece on the side? I'm sure she's down, the way she was sweating you."

"I don't want her. I want you."

"Too bad."

I slammed the receiver back on the cradle and grimaced so hard out of anger that I got an instant migraine.

I'll show his ass, I thought. I swung the front door open like a woman on a mission. I stomped across my front porch and right down my steps, pulling the back of my coat up over my head to protect my recently permed hair from damage.

"Excuse me!" I yelled out from the sidewalk on the opposite side of the street from where the brother was parked. He looked in my direction, and I could finally make out his face. I was not disappointed.

"Hello there!" he responded loudly. "Bad night!"

"Yes, it is! Do you need to use the phone or something?"

He came closer to me, and once he got within a few feet, I

knew I wanted to fuck him. I'm typically not whorish, but there's a first time for everything.

"A phone would be nice."

I turned around and went back up the steps. "Follow me."

Once inside, I asked him, "What's your name?"

"Randall. Randall Davis."

I reached out to shake his hand. "I'm Kimmie Thompson."

"Nice to meet you, Kimmie, and thanks in advance for your hospitality. I kept hoping that someone would be generous enough to offer a brother some help. You guys sure don't get much street traffic around here."

"No, it's rather quiet." I took in every inch of him with my eyes. The tight white shirt was damp and exposing every single muscle. He had short dreads, a dark complexion, and long, sexy eyelashes. "You could have just knocked on someone's door."

"Well, Kimmie. I thought about knocking on a door or two, but in this day and age, you never know what you might find. Most people are so suspicious, especially of us brothers, that I didn't want to cause a ruckus."

"Most of the people around here are extremely friendly."

That statement was true for the most part, with the exception of "Queen Bitch" across the street. I have never seen a nosier woman in my entire life. Talk about not having a life. I had a cookout once, just once, because I am not big on having functions at my house. People don't appreciate or take care of your shit, and I can't afford to have people messing up all the stuff I work so hard to pay for. Anyway, the bitch across the street took it upon herself to sit outside on her porch with a pair of binoculars and peep everything that was going on. She went up and down the street with a pen and pad writing down license plate numbers and made all of my guests nervous. I won't go so far to call her a racist, but she is white. I have seen my other neighbors—all white—have events, and she wasn't out there record-ing information. If Randall had mistakenly knocked on her door, she might have called the police on his ass—for real—and re-ported a prowler.

He looked like he was freezing in his wet clothing, so I asked, "Randall, would you like a blanket or a dry shirt?"

"A blanket would be fine. As petite as you are, I doubt I could fit into one of your shirts." I thought I saw a flicker of lust in his eyes as he said that. At least, I hoped I saw lust. "Unless your man has a shirt I can borrow."

I blushed. "I don't have a man."

He flashed a smile. "Oh, come on. A sexy young woman like you has to be taken. I'm quite sure you don't live in this big old house all alone."

"Actually, I do." He started trembling even more. "I'll be right back, Randall. Let me go grab that blanket right quick."

I ran up the steps to get a spare blanket out of the linen closet. While I was there, I decided to do some quick coochie maintenance. A woman always has to be prepared for any kind of sex, including oral sex. No man wants to get down there and wonder about your hygiene practices. I freshened up with a towel and soap and hit it with three sprays of feminine deodorant until only a fresh powder scent invaded my nostrils.

When I got back downstairs, Randall was standing by my mantel, checking out the photos of myself and my family.

"Here you go," I said, handing him the blanket.

"Thank you." He wrapped the blanket around his shoulders and then pointed at the pictures. "You must come from a very large family."

I giggled. "Yes. There are eleven of us altogether."

"Where do you fit in the chain?"

"Right smack in the middle. I'm number six, so I have five

older siblings who think they know everything and five younger siblings who think I know everything."

Randall laughed. "I bet you had one hell of a childhood."

"Between all the bickering, jealousy, and competition, it had its moments." I pointed to one picture of myself and three of my sisters, dressed alike. I was about twelve at the time. "Momma always had this thing about us wearing the same exact clothes to church on Sundays. We hated it because it took away our individuality."

"I bet you all rebelled before it was said and done."

"Boy, did we!" I pointed to another picture of myself in college with hair so short that you could almost see my scalp and an earring in my nose. "You see how I spent my college years, don't you?"

We both laughed.

"Very sexy," Randall commented and then gave me *that look*.

I turned away from him; I didn't want him to see the desire in my eyes. I was beginning to have second thoughts about fucking a complete stranger.

He must have sensed the tension. "Kimmie, can I make that phone call now?"

"Sure. I'll get the phone."

I went to retrieve the cordless from the kitchen. When I came back, Randall had turned on my gas fireplace. He looked over at me and said, "I hope you don't mind?"

"Not at all," I replied, handing him the phone. "Make yourself at home."

Our fingers touched, and we both let the contact linger for a moment. There was electricity between us.

"Why don't I go make a pot of tea? Be right back."

I went into the kitchen to put the kettle on while Randall made his call. I heard him fussing at his automobile association.

Apparently, they were understaffed and had several other motorists in the queue ahead of him. When I returned with a pot of tea on a tray with two mugs and some vanilla wafers, Randall looked disgusted.

"Didn't go the way you wanted, huh?" I asked.

"They have a sorry-ass company. Can you believe they told me it could take as long as four hours to send someone?"

"Wow, that is a long time."

Randall looked at his watch. "I don't want to impose on you that long, so once I drink my tea, I'll go wait in the car."

"No!" I exclaimed, regretting the desperation in my voice. "I mean, you don't have to go wait out in all that bad weather. You're welcome to hang out here until they show up."

"Sure you don't mind?"

"Positive."

Randall and I hung out for the next few hours and got to know each other better. It turned out that he was a guitarist in a hard rock band. I couldn't even imagine listening to hard rock, rather less playing it, but Randall managed to sway me a little bit. He turned to a cable station and encouraged me to watch a few hard rock videos. Even though I couldn't make out half the things they were saying, it wasn't half bad. I have never been one to plop down in front of the television and watch music videos anyway. I always find myself disgusted at the rap videos that feature women demeaning themselves. I often wonder what their parents think when they appear ass-out on the TV screen. I doubt that they felt even a hint of pride.

Randall looked at his watch for the fiftieth time. "I guess they'll be here soon."

"I guess so. Sorry that you had to spend so much time with me, but I have appreciated the company."

He took my hand in his. "To be honest, I keep looking at my watch because I don't want them to come anytime soon. I've really enjoyed tonight, and I hope we can see each other again."

I used my free hand to rub up and down his thigh. "I was hoping you would say that."

He gazed into my eyes. "Kimmie, I have to be honest. I'm kind of torn right now. I'm extremely attracted to you, partially because you're so nice, but mostly because you're fine. I must admit that nothing would please me more right now than laying you down by your fireplace over there and making love to you."

I moved my hand farther up his thigh and started caressing his dick. "Then why don't you?"

He tried to keep his composure, but a moan escaped his lips just the same. "Because I don't know what tomorrow might bring."

"Tomorrow is guaranteed to no one."

"This is true, but I have this band thing going, and hopefully something will materialize soon, which would mean traveling a lot. I'm not so sure a relationship is in my best interest right now."

"Randall, we just met. I'm not trying to hook you for life or anything. Who knows? Tomorrow we might wake up and find out this was all a dream." I started to unzip his pants. "All I know is that I want you."

I pulled his dick out and ran my fingertips over the head of his dick. It was every bit of eight inches long and had just the right thickness. I admired Randall's dick so much that I told him, "Your dick's beautiful."

He threw his head back in laughter. "I've never had a woman tell me that before."

"Well, now you have," I said as I got down on my knees. "Just relax. I invited you inside from the rain. Now I'm inviting you inside of me."

"Umm, I can't wait to get inside of you."

I tugged on Randall's pants, and he helped me out by lifting his hips slightly from the chair.

After I had him naked from the waist down, he pulled off his still damp shirt to show me what he really had, and all I could think was *wow*. He was truly a sexy-ass man, and my hormones were suddenly raging out of control.

I took all of my clothes off and then climbed on top of him on the chair. I placed my hands on his shoulders and took my time sliding my pussy down on his dick. Then I locked my feet on the bottom rungs of the chair so I could get some better leverage.

I rode him gently at first. We gazed into each other's eyes, and there was a connection. The fire made things heat up even faster, and before we knew it, sweat was trickling all over our bodies. The phone rang, but I ignored it.

Randall stopped pushing up into me for a second and asked, "What if it's the auto club?"

I drew his bottom lip into my mouth, sucked on it, and then bit it gently. "What if it is? Do you really want to leave tonight?"

He laughed. "Hell, no!"

"Then shut the hell up and fuck me."

"Damn, I love it when a woman takes control."

"Then relax and let me take the dick."

"Umm, take it."

We fucked for a good hour on the chair alone and then took it to the floor by the fire. Randall turned me on my side and then entered me from behind. It was a strange angle, but once he got his dick in, I figured out that he was a man of much experience. The shit felt so good as he plummeted his dick in me. I fingered my pussy with one hand and reached behind me to caress his balls with the other.

I sensed that he was about to cum, but he pulled out suddenly.

He leaned down and kissed me on the cheek. "Can I sample a little something else?"

I knew he meant the ass, and while I'm normally against it, I wanted to see how he would handle my most prized possession. I didn't reply, but he knew I was down when he started rubbing the tip of his dick up and down the crack of my ass and I elevated it a little so he could get to it better.

It took a little effort, but he finally got his dick in me and started exploring with it. I clamped my hand around his neck and pulled him closer so I could kiss him on the mouth.

"I want to see you again," I readily admitted.

"I want to see you again, too." He swept my hair off my face and placed it behind my ear. "I want to see you every damn day if I can."

We both chuckled, and then all conversation stopped. We were too busy enjoying one another. Randall came in my ass, and I loved it. I wanted to go grab a shower together and go for it again, but the damn doorbell rang.

"Auto Club!" we heard a man shout from outside. "Hurry up, because I've got half a dozen other calls tonight!"

Randall stared at me lovingly as he pulled his dick out of my ass. "I better go see about the car. I can get them to tow it, and I can still stay."

I grabbed his face and kissed him with as much passion as I could muster. "Hurry back."

I was pissed off when I found out that Randall would have to actually go with the driver when the car was towed. Apparently, they had new regulations. I planned to write his crappy auto club the next day and complain. We shared a brief intimate farewell at my door, and he was gone, just like that.

Fortunately, he came back the next day, and we picked up where we had left off. Thirteen months later we are still picking up where we leave off every morning when we both leave for work. Yeah, we're shacking, and it is a good thing. I hope to get a ring soon, but I am patient and will let things happen in their own time. Just like things happened the night I met Randall.

Fuckastrated

Six months without sex. Felt like six damn years. I never knew I was a sex fiend until I had to go without it for a spell. Davon and I had broken up after a four-year serious relationship, and I was determined not to throw myself on just anyone. A sistah does have to be selective in this day and age.

Sure, the propositions came flooding in as soon as the infamous split hit the grapevine in our little Kansas town. That was my first damn problem: being single and living in Kansas. There weren't exactly a ton of eligible brothers in Kansas, if you get what I'm saying. Finding a decent black man in Kansas is equivalent to hitting the lottery.

At first I was disappointed. Then I was frustrated. Ultimately, I ended up "fuckastrated." I made the word up for those who have to go without sex when the rest of the world is getting their freak on.

Ironically, Davon wasn't all that in bed in the first place. I was just used to having him around. He was familiar and comfortable, like a favorite pair of holey jeans on a Saturday morning or a favorite coffee mug. He had become a daily factor in my life, and once he was gone, something felt missing.

The way the breakup came about was partially my fault. Okay, it was entirely my fault. Davon had continuously warned me not to talk about our private matters in the streets; especially when there were only four stoplights in the entire town. But I just couldn't help myself. I was sitting around the water fountain in the town square, kicking it with my two oldest girlfriends, Stacy and Allison, when it simply slipped out. I didn't mean for it to happen. I really didn't.

Anyway, as soon as Davon found out that I had told them about his experimentation with my underwear, he hit the roof. What kind of man wants to parade around the crib in his woman's panties and bras? He came storming into the little two-bedroom rental house we'd been shacking up in and went from his normal blue-black to cranberry before laying into my ass with a vengeance. I really didn't think it was that big of a deal, but to him it was *everything*. His male friends had apparently gotten wind of the situation and teased him without mercy.

Once Davon packed up his shit and rolled out, I was semi-relieved—it had become painfully obvious that the relationship really wasn't going anywhere. We were definitely not compatible in any way, shape, or form. I liked football. He liked basketball. I liked horror films. He liked comedies. I liked to have sex three times a day. He liked to have sex three minutes a day. It just wasn't working out.

Yet and still, I did miss the companionship. That's why I made the decision to make the fifty-minute drive to the state university three nights a week to take a night class about business development. I had always wanted my own business but had never gotten around to starting one. I figured if I ever did, I would at least know the basics.

The first night of the class was straight-up boring. Professor Taylor spent half the class time bragging about all of his accomplishments. I was thinking to myself, Yeah, right! If you've accomplished so damn much, why are you teaching night school instead of sitting on the beach somewhere collecting 20 percent?

After he finally finished yapping, he let us spend the rest of the time introducing ourselves to the other classmates. Since my name is Shameika Zales, I knew I had plenty of time to gather thoughts in my head so I'd sound intelligent when I did run my little bio down.

At twenty-six, I was actually younger than most of the class, which totally surprised me. Most of them were in their late thirties, forties, or fifties. Either that, or some of them looked old as shit. I swear one man had to be a hundred ninety, maybe a hundred ninety-one.

One thing I ascertained from listening to them all speak was that they had been out in the corporate world, worked their asses off to build up someone else's corporation, and were just damn sick of making money for other people. I guess it just took them some time to realize it. I decided right then and there that I wouldn't find myself in that situation ten years down the road—wishing I had made a change earlier on.

When they got to the *P*'s, I perked up in my seat as this finer than fine brother stood up to give us the 4-1-1 on himself. If they were giving out awards for sexiness that night, he would have won hands down. He was about five-nine with caramel skin and a bald head that was glimmering under the overhead lights. I could just imagine rubbing his dome in the heat of passion.

He grinned directly at me, and I almost creamed in my bloomers. I had taken to wearing big-ass granny bloomers since I was manless. No need to ruin the good stuff on myself.

Anyway, he grinned at me and then faced Professor Taylor.

"My name is Thomas Phillips," he said. "I'm the vice president of marketing for a start-up technology company based here in Kansas. I'm originally from Detroit, and I've been living here for about a year. I hope to gain some serious knowledge in this class because knowledge is definitely the key to success."

And your dick is the key to my success, I thought wickedly to myself from my third-row seat. I should've known that his ass wasn't from Kansas; they didn't grow men that fine. I stared at him throughout the rest of the introductions until it was my turn.

I almost missed hearing my own name when the professor yelled it out. I came around and stood up. I suddenly became conscious of my appearance, and I straightened out the back of my skirt in case it was wrinkled.

"My name is Shameika Zales, and I currently work for the government as a human resources recruiter. However, my true ambitions lie in starting my own company." I glanced over at Thomas. "I really want to get into the technology field, since that seems to be the wave of the future."

I sat back down in my seat, knowing good and well that technology had never crossed my mind before that night. But I had contemplated opening a catering business, since my ass can burn some damn food. I had considered opening a restaurant but figured a smaller-scale business like catering would be better. Then there was my nightclub idea. I asked around about it, and people scared the shit out of me when they started talking about kickbacks for liquor licenses and payoffs to the mob so they wouldn't set your place on fire in the middle of the night. No, thank you, I said. That would not be the move.

Much to my dismay, class ended too soon. I was enjoying checking out Thomas Phillips. I lingered for a minute as people poured out of the classroom, hoping that he would mosey on over my way and holler at a sister. It didn't happen, though. He got bum-rushed by these two women who looked like they were my age when my mother was born. What a damn shame it was that they were throwing themselves at him like that. He was surely older than me—probably in his mid-thirties—but he was young enough to be one of their offspring.

I gave up and walked on out to my car, Nicki. I called the Pontiac that because it was banged up with nicks all over the hood and trunk. There wasn't a single mark on the sides of the car, but the top of it looked like someone had just taken a knife and tried to punch holes in it.

I got in and tried to start the engine, but it just pooted and died.

"Shit, not now!" I screamed at myself.

It was the dead of winter. At least, what you would call the dead of winter in Kansas. Every time it got cold, Nicki would start tripping. I popped the hood and got out to get a bomber jacket out of my trunk.

I decided to try again to get Nicki started. If I failed, I planned to head back inside and see if the professor was still around. I didn't seek him out for help at first because I hated the thought of listening to his mouth if he had to assist me with my car. But I had no intention of spending the night out there in the middle of the parking lot.

There were a few cars still scattered around, and I wondered if one of them belonged to Thomas Phillips. He seemed like a sports car kind of brother. There was a BMW Z3 in the corner slot, and I pegged that one to be his. Start-up company or not, the brother was dressed in some serious gear and carried himself like he had some sense.

I turned to get back in my car, and there he was, standing so close to me that I could see his eyelashes.

"Having car trouble?" he asked in his sexy-ass voice.

"Actually, I am. Stupid thing won't start," I replied.

"Would you like me to take a look?"

"I'd appreciate that."

"Not a problem."

We gazed in each other's eyes, and it was definitely a heated moment. In fact, I wanted to jump his bones. Finally, he broke the stare and chuckled.

"Mind popping the hood?"

I giggled. "Oops, I guess that would help."

"Tremendously."

I opened my door and reached down to disengage the hood.

"Wow, look at all these dents on your hood," he commented as he lifted it. "Were you caught in a hailstorm someplace or something?"

I was so embarrassed. "No, I don't know what it is, but my car seems to get nicked all over the hood and trunk for some reason."

"Just a stroke of bad luck, I guess."

I stood beside him as he bent over the hood. *Damn, what an ass!*

"What was your name again?" he asked.

I started to cop an attitude but recognized that my name was not exactly a common one. Peeps often had to hear it a few times before they caught on.

"Shameika Zales."

"Aw, that's right. I'm Thomas Phillips."

"I remember," I said seductively and licked my lips, even though he couldn't see them.

"You're interested in technology, right?"

"Oh, yeah, very interested," I lied again.

"Cool. Maybe I can show you around my operation sometime."

"Or maybe you can just operate on me."

He stood erect and faced me. "Excuse me?"

I lowered my eyes to the ground. "Damn, did I say that out loud?"

He chuckled. "Yes, you did, but it's cool. I like aggressive women."

I was up to that challenge and did something totally out of character for me. I reached out and caressed his dick through his pants. "Is that right?"

He jumped for a second and then relaxed. "Yes, that's right."

"Can I be completely honest with you?"

"Please. Feel free."

"I came out of a long-term relationship about six months ago, and I haven't had the benefit of sex since."

"Aw, poor baby," he replied. "I haven't had any sex in a while myself."

Yeah, right! I thought to myself. A while for men means two weeks instead of months, like it does for women.

A few more people came out of the building, including Professor Taylor, but I still didn't let go of the dick. I simply moved closer to him so nobody could make out what we were doing.

"Good night, students!" the professor yelled from across the lot as he made his way to the Escort. Yep, he sure was accomplished.

We both waved at him, but I *still* didn't let go of the dick. I used my free hand.

The professor pulled off, followed by the two older women who had earlier accosted Thomas. They were in a Camry, and I could see their eyes rolling from fifty yards away. That's what they get for trying to pull up on a man so much their junior. The parking lot was now empty, which was just fine by me.

"Shameika, I have a proposition for you."

"Really?" I asked, full of curiosity. "What might that be?"

"There's nothing I'd rather do than take you home with me and sex you down right now."

I drew his bottom lip into my mouth and sucked on it. "Sounds like a winning plan to me."

He startled me by pushing me away and forcing my hand off his dick. "However, I have certain rules that must be followed."

"Rules? In the game of life, there are no rules," I challenged.

"In my life, there are plenty of rules, and rule number one is that I get to know the women I become intimate with before the act and not after."

Okay, I must admit that I was stunned. On the other hand, it was kind of arousing to have a man insist on getting to know me. Especially considering the way I was willing to give up the drawers.

"Fine," I responded. "I'd like to get to know you first also."

"Let's just leave your car here and head over to town to grab a late dinner."

"I could use a bite."

"Great!"

He slammed my hood closed, and I grabbed my purse and locked my car.

"You learn something new every day," I commented as we waited for our food to arrive at our table.

"What do you mean?" Thomas asked.

"I had no idea there was a bona fide chicken and waffles place in Kansas. I've heard of them in Los Angeles and Atlanta, but here in Kansas? Stop the madness."

He laughed. "I was shocked to find it here myself."

The waitress delivered the platters of fried chicken wings and gigantic waffles to our table along with large glasses of fresh lemonade. Let's just say there was no shame in my game. I threw the hell down on that food.

Thomas and I had a wonderful conversation throughout dinner. He shared his background, and I did the same. We had a lot in common. By the time the apple crisp à la mode we ordered arrived at our table, the conversation had turned to sex.

"Shameika, I must admit that I tend to get kinky in bed."

I raised an eyebrow. "Kinky? Do tell."

"Well, I like to experiment."

"Experiment with what?"

"Just some of the gadgets I've either designed myself or helped to design over the years."

Now my interest was really piqued. My days of being fuckastrated were about to be over. Thomas was a straight-up freak. What luck!

"Well, are you going to tell me about these gadgets?"

"I'd rather show you," he said, eyeing me seductively.

I knew what time it was. "What happened to your rule about getting to know a woman before you become intimate?"

"Rules are made to be broken." He chuckled. "Besides, I realize this might sound strange, but it seems like I've known you for a long time. You ever get that feeling?"

"From time to time."

"Do you feel that way right now?"

I was about to answer when my eyes landed on the door and the couple entering through it. No, the hell Davon wasn't up in there with another woman, I thought—a straight-up slut at that. Now I might have had a tendency to wear hoochie momma clothes on certain occasions, but sisterfriend had issues. She had on this tube top in the middle of the fuckin' winter with thin-ass leggings and sandals. Who the hell wears sandals in January?

Granted, Davon and I were splitsville, but he had no business bringing that whore up into an establishment that he had never brought me to. I didn't know whether it was his first time there or if he was a regular, but it didn't matter.

"Earth to Shameika," I heard Thomas say as he snapped his fingers in front of my face.

"Sorry about that," I stated sullenly. "I saw a ghost from the past."

Thomas glanced toward the entrance. "Old boyfriend?"

"Something like that." I reached across the table and took his hand. "How about we blow this joint so you can show me some of those gadgets you keep bragging on?"

He grinned at me. "I wasn't bragging, but now that you put it that way, some of them are quite spectacular."

I slipped off my loafer, lifted my foot up between his legs, and commenced with a quick foot job. "I bet your dick is spectacular also. I could tell you were holding when we were back there in the parking lot."

"I can handle mine," he replied with a blush.

Davon's eyes zeroed in on me as they were led to a table on the other side of the room. I wanted to scream out, "Yeah, I'm here with a *real man,* you panty-borrowing, sissified mutha fucka!" Looking back on it, that was some truly sick shit. He rolled his eyes and smacked his lips in my direction. I returned the favor.

Even though the foot action was turning me on and Thomas was getting this glassy look, it was time to roll out. I slid my foot back in my shoe and rose from the table.

"You ready?"

"Yes, just let me drop some cash on the table."

Thomas peeped the check and then plopped two twenties down. As we were walking out, I made a point to make it clear that I was on a date. I grabbed Thomas, stood on my tippy-toes, and kissed him passionately on the lips. He got into it, because the next thing I knew, he was slipping a sistah the tongue. It was thick and juicy and tasted sweet from the syrup.

Before I knew it, Davon had jumped up from his table and was headed straight for us. "Shameika, what the hell is this? Why are you throwing yourself on some man in the middle of a public place?"

I frowned at him. "Are you my daddy? Matter of fact, are you anything to me? Mind your own damn business."

Thomas stepped in between us. "Look, buddy, we don't need any trouble. The lady and I are leaving, so why don't you just go and enjoy the rest of your meal."

Thomas made the mistake of placing his hand on Davon's shoulder, and Davon knocked it off. "Don't touch me!"

"Whatever! Just go sit back down."

"I'll sit down when I fucking get ready to sit down!"

That's when I jumped back in. "Hmph, no you didn't take issue with me kissing in public when you're standing here cussing."

"Shameika, get your ass outside! I need to talk to you. *Now!*"

I laughed at him. "You've got jokes." I pointed over to his date, who looked like she'd rather be anywhere else but there. Nothing is worse than being pushed off for another woman in public. "You need to go over there with the skank hoe and let me be."

I could see smoke come out of her nostrils from across the room. Then she got up. She must've run track in high school, because she was at our table in a matter of seconds. "What did you call me?"

I got up in her face. "I called you a *skank hoe!*"

She picked up a glass of lemonade from the table next to the one we'd just vacated and tossed the contents on me. The sistah seated at the table went off. "What the hell is this shit?"

I went for her date's coffee and threw the hot liquid on the skank. She went for a waffle, as did I, and we both hit each other in the face at the same time with them. The next thing I knew the scene descended into complete madness. Someone yelled, "Food fight!"

Five minutes later, the restaurant was in a shambles, some people were having the time of their lives, and others were trying to beat each other to death. You can do a lot of things, but don't mess with black people's food.

We heard sirens approaching, and Thomas and I managed to navigate our way through the crowd to the door. I glanced back and saw the skank hoe beating Davon in the head with somebody's purse. It was a sight to remember. He was in for a long-ass night. I hoped he would get locked up.

Thomas and I made a mad dash for his Beemer and took off just in time as a paddy wagon and several police cars pulled up in front.

After a moment of seriousness, we both fell out laughing. Thomas was so overwhelmed by the moment that he had to pull over before he lost control of the car. He and I both laughed until we were in tears.

We went back to my place because it was closer than his. I would have to peep his gadgets at a later date—I needed a shower and a change of clothes. I could take care of one thing at his place, but not the other. Besides, there is nothing like using my own shampoo and bath gel. It took me years to find the ones I like the most.

I looked in my bathroom mirror, and I was a mess. There was syrup and bits of waffles and chicken plastered to my face and hair. After inching out of my sticky clothes, I turned on the shower. The warm water was invigorating against my skin, but getting all the food out of my hair was quite a chore. Thomas planned to take a shower after me. I found that amusing. We both knew that we'd end up slapping skins that night. It was as inevitable as the sun rising the next morning.

I wasn't looking my sexiest now, and neither was he. I thought back to the food fight at the restaurant and couldn't help but relish the thought of Davon getting locked up for the night. If anyone deserved to be arrested up in that bitch, it was him. I was a bit jealous that he was dating someone else. But, on the other hand, I had found me a possible soul mate, so it was all good.

I got out of the shower, wrapped myself in a pink satin robe, went out into the living room, and told Thomas it was his turn. I handed him some towels, and he headed for the bathroom. While he was showering, I decided to light scented candles and spray lavender water into the air.

I turned down the paisley comforter on my queen-size bed and put on a slow jam compilation CD. There was but one thing missing, so I headed to the kitchen to retrieve two flutes and a bottle of champagne. Thomas came out of the bathroom, wearing nothing but a towel. His muscles were in all the right places.

"Do you want me to rub you down with some body oil?" I offered, hoping he would say yes, so I could feel him up real good.

"Sure, as long as you let me return the favor."

We treated each other to the most sensual of massages for the next thirty minutes or so—full-body massages that awakened every inch of our beings. Thomas had the most incredible hands, hands that could bring me pleasure night after night after night. Being nude around him seemed so natural it was almost scary.

"So what did you think about the first night of class?" he asked me, breaking the silence.

"It was cool, but the professor seems a bit egotistical."

"You can say that again." Thomas chuckled. "If he has it going on so much, why is he teaching night school?"

"My thoughts exactly."

We both snickered.

"Thomas."

"Yes."

"Can we not discuss class or *him?* I'm trying to stay in one zone, and the mere mention of all that is kind of killing it for me."

"What zone might that be?"

I licked my lips, dipped my index finger into my pussy, and then placed it in his mouth so he could taste me.

"This zone," I replied seductively, dipping my finger again before tasting myself.

"Damn, I've never seen a woman taste herself before," he whispered in awe.

I laughed. "Think about it. Most women like for men to taste them, right?"

"Right."

"So why should we expect a man to partake of something we're not willing to sample ourselves?"

Thomas grinned. "Makes sense." He reached out and fondled my breasts. "So do you like to be eaten out, Shameika?"

"Is the sky blue?" I replied.

"I'll take that as a yes."

"Do you like it when a woman goes down on you?"

"Is the grass green?"

"Only in good neighborhoods," I replied.

We both fell out laughing.

"Seriously, some grass is rather dry. Even in Kansas." I placed my hand on top of his, prodding him to squeeze my breasts harder. "I'll tell you what's never dry, though."

"What's that?"

"My pussy. Especially not now."

"And why is that?"

"Because you excite me."

"That goes both ways."

I reached for the champagne. "I was going to pour this in glasses, but I think I'd rather just lick it off you. Is that cool?"

"That's more than cool."

I poured about an ounce of the champagne on his chest and traced a path from his breastbone down to his belly button with my tongue. The mixture of the cool liquid and the flavored massage oil was delicious. Thomas moaned in delight as I poured a little more right on the head of his dick and then sucked it off.

"I want to taste you, too," he said, running his fingers through my hair.

Without letting his dick go, I maneuvered myself until my pussy was on top of his face and we were in the sixty-nine position. Thomas wasted no time going to town on my pussy. He started eating me and inserted a finger into my ass, increasing the sensation.

The way we went at it, you would have thought neither one of us had eaten in days, much less the bomb-ass chicken and waffles.

I reached into my nightstand to remove two black drapery tassels. Thomas's eyes widened. "What are those for?" he asked.

"I know you said you have some *innovative* toys at your house. Well, I have some of my own." I took his left wrist, slid it through a tassel, and then attached it to one of the headposts. "Sometimes everyday household items can be sexy as well."

Thomas grinned. "You have a little freak in you, huh?"

I eyed him wickedly. "I have a lot of freak in me."

I secured his other wrist and then got up off the bed, headed toward the living room.

"Where are you going?" Thomas yelled after me.

"I'll be right back."

A moment later I returned with two items that I knew would turn his ass out: a feather duster and a cordless hand massager.

"What are you going to do with those?" he asked.

"You'll see," I said as I climbed onto the bed next to him.

I tickled his dick with my yellow feather duster, and Thomas fell out laughing. He tried to get his wrists loose to no avail.

"Do you like this, Thomas?"

There was no need for him to respond verbally. He shed tears of joy, and his dick looked like it could split bricks. It was time to go in for the kill. I turned the massager on low and started rubbing it up and down the shaft of his dick. All the while I continued teasing the head with the feather duster. Thomas gave a good impression of a man strapped in an electric chair with a thousand volts going through his body.

The tiny pulsating heads of the massager did their job in less than a minute. Thomas's cum shot about two feet in the air. It was an amazing sight. I had tried that move on Davon a few times, but he never climaxed like *that*.

As I released Thomas from the tassels, he said with bated breath, "Damn, girl. I've never felt anything like that before."

"It felt good?"

He snickered. "It felt *great!*"

I kissed Thomas on the lips and gently caressed his dick. "Let's allow him to rest for a while. Then I have some other things I want to show you."

Thomas kissed me deeply. "I can't even imagine."

We both broke out in laughter.

I placed tiny kisses all over his chest. "After I show you all my goodies, maybe you can take me to your place and show me yours."

"I have lots of goodies," Thomas boasted.

I gripped his dick and said, "I already tasted some of them."

Thomas and I ended up drifting off to sleep, and we would have stayed that way if my phone hadn't started blaring. I snatched the phone up in irritation. "Who the hell is this?" I said.

"Shameika, you've got to help me," I heard a raspy male voice say on the line.

"Davon?" I sat up in the bed. "You have got to be out your damn mind, calling me this time of morning!"

He raised his voice. "Shameika, this is all your fault!"

"What's all my fault?"

Thomas woke up, rubbing his eyes and looking at me. "Something wrong?"

I shook my head no and repeated, "What's all my fault?"

"I got locked up." I fought to suppress a laugh. "I'm locked up in here with a bunch of perverts because of that shit you pulled earlier."

"The shit I pulled?"

"Yeah, the shit you pulled!" He was practically screaming into the phone now. "I'm over here at the Fifth Precinct, and your ass better get here on the double to bail me out!"

"Why not let the hooch you were with earlier bail you out?"

Thomas grinned, apparently catching on.

"She's locked up over on the woman's side."

I couldn't hold in my giggles any longer. "Davon, that's what your ass gets. I'm in the middle of getting my groove on. I'll have to catch you later."

I could hear him taking deep breaths. "You mean to tell me that you're over there fucking while I'm in jail?"

"Exactly!" I said. "And the sex is all that, too. He even cums better than you, you piece of shit!"

I could hear him calling me all kinds of names as I slammed the phone down.

Thomas rubbed my cheek. "I'll have to remember not to piss you off. That was kind of cold, girl."

"If you knew the history, you wouldn't even be saying that. That fool put me through the wringer and then some." Thomas's dick was hard again. "Besides, why are we even discussing Davon when we can be putting all this dick to good use?"

Thomas placed his hands behind his neck and propped his head up. "So use it. You want to tie me up again?"

"Nope." I shook my head. "I want your hands available for this next round." I handed him the massager and feather duster. "Now it's my turn."

Needless to say, Thomas and I had a ball together for the rest of that day, and the day after that, and the day after that. After our next class, Thomas took me back for some more chicken and waffles. We had to wear disguises—dark shades and caps. Even though it was late at night, we were surprised no one recognized us as we chowed down. Then we went back to his place—and let's just say his gadgets were a *whole* lot better than mine.

Thomas and I dated for the next year or so, but then things tapered off. He became absorbed in his business, and my interests turned to getting the hell out of Kansas. The world is such a big place, and I felt stifled there. He had just gotten to town. I, on the other hand, had been trapped in the place my entire life. I decided to take the leap. I started my own business selling, guess what, adult toys! I distribute some of Thomas's inventions along with my own I developed from common household items.

Now I travel the country giving seminars and hosting adult parties. One thing is for sure; sistahs of all races love sex, and their men love it even more. I have made a ton of money and plan to settle down one day on the East Coast someplace. New

York City is rather costly, but hey, there's no point in doing something half-ass, so that's probably where I'll end up.

Thomas often crosses my mind. He's the perfect catch for someone—*in Kansas*. It came down to making a choice, and I feel like I made the right one. But I will never forget that first night we spent together and the way his cum shot two feet in the air. Every time I think about it, I break out in a grin. This sistah will never be "fuckastrated" again.

Down for Whatever

      Chauncy and I have been living together for a little over a year. I met him in a nightclub, and as soon as I spotted him across the crowded dance floor, I wanted to fuck him in the worst way.

      I practically begged my homegurl, Nicole, to walk across the floor and get him for me. After a bunch of convincing, which included bringing up all the things I did for her in the past—like hooking her hair up and baby-sitting her bad-ass kids—she gave in.

      Whatever Nicole yelled in his ear, over the loud music, worked, because less than five minutes later she brought him back to our table.

      He is so fine, there ought to be a law against it. Chauncy is half black and half Puerto Rican; mixed together, they make butter pecan. Six-foot-two and lean with curly black hair and light brown eyes; too dayum gorgeous. We look good together because I am five-foot-ten, slender, caramel, with long, medium brown hair and big brown eyes. He sat down at the table, Nicole introduced us, we smiled at each other, and thus the sensuous love affair of Chauncy and Dawn began.

There is no shame in my game; I fucked Chauncy the first night we met. He is still here, so the sex must have been banging for both of us. In fact, it was more than banging; we fucked like beasts.

I was sort of on the conservative side when we met but thought my sex was the bomb. Most young women swear up and down they have the bomb-ass pussy, but Chauncy schooled my mistaken little butt right quick. He took me to the limit and showed me what "real" fucking is all about.

Now I am out there, *way* out there, and sitting here pondering the question: Can I honestly think of a thing I haven't tried or am not willing to try sexually? It's like this, I am down for whatever. Simple as that.

Let me guess! You think I am a freak, right? A slut? A hoe? Not hardly. But people thinking I am one is not terribly surprising. Sexual repression explains a person every time who would look down on sexually uninhibited women like me. Funny thing is, the women talking all the critical shit are the same ones sitting at home alone on the weekends, wondering why they can't get or keep a man. Peep that!

Anyway, back to what I was saying in regards to my baby. Chauncy is twenty-six, and I'm twenty-three. Both of us had stable upbringings and the benefit of a higher education. Both of us have good-paying jobs and in general have our shit together.

I often call Chauncy my "twin" because his sexual appetite mirrors my own. That explains why I will never leave him, not ever. We understand each other's needs, and the willingness to fulfill each and every sexual desire is mutual. This includes sexual activities with other people. But mostly it's all about the two of us. Sometimes we incorporate toys, and at other times the wild shit we do is downright dangerous.

When I first met Chauncy, I had the basics covered. I sucked a mean dick, and my pelvic muscle control was above par.

Chauncy has taught me never to be ashamed of anything that feels good, which is why I am always down for whatever sexual situations he proposes. My girlfriends claim I allow him to dominate me; they call me his "sub." But I don't see it. If anything, we alternately dominate each other.

It is true that he is more likely than me to improvise and incorporate creative ideas into our sex lives. But that's because I am still a baby to sexual freedom. The fact remains that I love every minute of it.

Like the time three of his best friends came over to our crib to watch a college football game. Chauncy asked me if I wanted to experience a train. I told him he was out of his fucking mind, went in the bedroom, and slammed the door. I was furious.

Once I calmed down and contemplated it, though, the thought of having four men wear my ass out made me extremely horny. The decision to go for it was a big step for me.

I went back into the living room, stood in the middle of the floor, blocking the screen, and slowly took off my clothes in front of all of them. Surprisingly enough, the fear I naturally assumed would be present was nonexistent. On the contrary, I did it with no hesitation at all. Chauncy motioned for me to come sit between him and his friend, Robert, on the couch, by patting the spot with his hand.

After I sat down, Chauncy lifted my right leg, which was closest to the side he was on, and pulled it up over his thigh so my legs were spread open. Robert lifted my left leg and placed it over his. My pussy was exposed as if I was about to undergo a gynecological exam or birth a baby.

Chauncy and I began tongue-kissing while Robert sucked my left breast. Chauncy undid his pants so I could rub my right hand up and down the shaft of his hard dick, and Robert started finger-fucking me, still sucking on my nipple the entire time.

Chauncy rubbed my right breast while Alex and Sean, his other two friends, just watched for a while. Then Sean came over and got on his knees in front of the couch, moved Robert's hand out of the way, and started eating my pussy, which was so wet.

They discussed it among themselves and decided there was no way all of them could fuck me at the same time, so Chauncy and Robert decided to go first. They took me in the bedroom, and the whole experience was quite enjoyable.

They both got naked, and Chauncy lay on his back, resting his head on a pillow. I got on my knees and sucked his dick while Robert ate my pussy and ass from behind. Robert fucked me doggy-style in the pussy. Chauncy kept cumming in my mouth, and as always, his cum was scrumptious.

After Robert came all over my ass cheeks, I turned around and sat on Chauncy's dick with my back to him. He fingered my ass while I rode his dick and gave Robert, who was on his knees with his dick dangling in my face, a blow job. Then I lay on my stomach, and they both took turns fucking me in my ass.

I was exhausted, and it was only halfway over. Hoping the pulsating warm water would rejuvenate me, I hopped in the shower. Before I was able to squeeze a drop of shower gel into my palm, Sean joined me in the shower. I wanted to pass the hell out when I saw his dick. He must have been sporting at least ten inches.

He asked me if I could handle it but didn't bother waiting for a response. He picked me up, with my legs straddled around his waist, and fucked me up against the shower wall.

Sean was busting a nut when Alex joined us. Sean knelt down, put one of my legs over his shoulder and ate my pussy while Alex stood behind me and fucked me in the ass. I was able to maintain my balance by reaching behind my head and holding on to the nape of Alex's neck. I came all over the place, as we all did.

Half of me feared the night would never end, and the other half feared it would. I never understood what people meant by the term "pleasurable pain" until the four of them tore my ass up in such a fashion. But even when it was all over, said and done, I was one happy camper.

Chauncy and I have experienced many other things together, and in due time we will experience a hundred more. The only limitations to sex are the ones people set for themselves. The only way to know how far is too far is to actually go too far. I can't wait for Chauncy to take me there.

Life Is Crazy

My mother always told me that when the time was right, good things would come to light. Well, after waiting twenty-eight years to find a decent man, I began to wonder if Mr. Ideal Mate would ever appear. Men always talk about sistahs being rude and having bad manners, but what about them?

Case in point. I went out with this brotha named Antoine, and everything was everything until we got to dinner and he broke out a jar of deodorant. Yes, I said deodorant. Now how come men start tripping when we apply makeup at the table, but they don't see a damn thing wrong with doing nasty shit like that? What made it even worse was that it wasn't the kind you just roll on. This Negro had the kind you actually have to dip your fingers in and rub on. His reasoning behind it? Check this out. This might not be verbatim, but it's close.

"Hey, Tenage, you don't mind if I handle a little hygiene issue right quick, do you?"

"Hygiene issue?"

"Yeah. I took a shower and all that before I left the crib, but I forgot to put on my deodorant."

"Hmph, thanks for telling me."

"Naw, for real. You know a brotha can't be going around with that au naturel thing going on."

"So, you have some on you? Just go to the bathroom and put it on right quick."

"Actually, I can sneak it on right here. Nobody's looking."

I couldn't believe it. That nashy fool—and I do mean "nashy," because he was way beyond nasty—put on his shit right there at the table and then had the nerve to wipe his fingers off with a white linen napkin and then reach for a pumpernickel roll. I knew right then that he didn't stand a chance in hell of climbing up into my sugary walls. That shit was just simply out of the question.

There are three things a sistah should always realize. First, if a jacket doesn't fit well in the shoulders, put it back on the rack. Two, it doesn't matter how raggedy your checked luggage is as long as your carry-on bags are fly. Three, a "nashy" man will end up bringing something home you weren't planning on. While you're sitting there expecting to dine on lobster and shrimp, you might end up with crabs—of the pubic variety.

Yes, I went there because that fool went there. I told him that he was a fool, too. It went a little something like this.

"Antoine, that is hands down the nashiest thing I have ever seen, and I've seen a lot."

"Nashiest?"

"Yes, nashiest."

"Is that a word?"

"It is now, because nasty just doesn't do you justice. You have a lot of fuckin' nerve. Sitting up here in a classy restaurant, surrounded by decent people, putting on your funk control."

"Hey, hey, watch your damn mouth. I didn't even have to

bring your ass here. I was just trying to do you a favor. Break you off with a piece of hellified dick a little later on."

"Hellified dick? First of all, what made you think I wanted you to break me off with a damn thing? Secondly, I doubt you have anything to break me off with. From what I hear around the hood, you're not holding much."

"Yeah? Well, from what I hear around the hood, your shit is like a car wash. You can run through it and get wet but never touch anything."

I picked up my piña colada and threw it in his face. "You mutha fucka!" I screamed at him.

"Oh, I got your mutha fucka!" he screamed back before throwing his beer all over my expensive black sheath. Okay, maybe the dress was only twenty bucks on clearance, but after I ripped the tag off, it became a hundred-dollar dress again.

Antoine and I went to scrapping right up in the restaurant. I yanked at his mustache like it was glued on, trying my best to rip it off. He tried to get a good grip on one of the tracks in my head, but I wasn't even having it. I smashed my three-inch stiletto heel into his suede shoes and then kneed him in the groin for good measure. Needless to say, we were "escorted out," but I was 1 and 0 when I left up out that bitch.

After my Antoine fiasco, I chilled for a minute and took a quick inventory. From what I could determine, there wasn't a damn thing wrong with me. I wasn't at the top of my game career-wise, but I wasn't trifling either. I had a decent job, but I hated my boss, Mr. Jenkins. The entire time I had been a night auditor at the hotel where I worked, he was displaying the typical behavior of a male chauvinist pig. Mr. Jenkins was straight-up disgusting, not to mention ugly as all hell. This man actually thought someone would fuck him to get ahead. *Puleeze!* Ain't that much getting ahead in the world.

Jenkins was ugly, stank, and had gray teeth. He tried to use his stubs—he didn't have fingers—to feel up any sistah that crossed his path. He was getting away with that shit too, until one sistah called his wife and gave her the 4-1-1. His wife came up there and opened a can of whup-ass on him at about three in the morning during one of our nightly shifts. I had heard rumors of women committing acts of domestic violence, but seeing it was truly enlightening. I never knew a woman could get down like that. By the time she took a breather, ole boy had two black eyes and four cracked ribs. Sistahgurl was not even playing. While I am not a supporter of violence in any way, shape, or form, I have to admit that the shit was mad funny.

Anyway, after the ass-whupping of all ass-whuppings, Jenkins never tried to cop another feel. However, he was still harsh on the females, pretending like we were beneath him in some way. That in itself would have been a feat because he was so short, a sistah would have to slither on the ground to actually be beneath him. My job was so-so, but it paid the bills. I had a nice little crib in Northeast D.C.

Most of my girlfriends were on lockdown. Their men would make them answer fifty questions and sign an I-shall-not-cheat-or-even-get-my-freak-on-dancing agreement before stepping foot out of the door. It was difficult for them to hang out with me on the weekends, which meant I had to often venture out onto the club scene alone.

It was during one such adventure that I ran across Black. Trust me, he was black in every sense of the word. His skin was black, his hair was black, his eyes were black, and he was wearing all black. He was so black that I almost didn't see him approach me at the bar. All I could see were the whites of his eyes. At first I was scared and ready to run. But after he flashed his pearly white teeth at me—the only other feature visible in the dim lighting—I realized his ass was fine as frog's hair.

Scratch that! He was finer than frog's hair. The fact that he was extremely tall was an immediate turn-on, considering I am five-ten myself. He had to be around six-eight, and that was right on time.

"Excuse me, is anyone sitting here?" he asked, pointing to the seat beside me.

"No, I don't see anyone," I replied.

"Well, mind if I sit down?"

"I don't own this club."

He plopped down beside me and waved the bartender over. "You're funny."

"Thanks. I'll take that as a compliment."

"Maybe you'll take what I'm about to say as a compliment also. I think you are the finest lady in here tonight."

I glanced at him, and his eyes almost had me hypnotized.

"Is that right?"

"Yes, you have a very exotic look about you."

"That's ironic, because I was thinking the same thing about you." I smirked at him, because I knew he was full of it. "What's so exotic-looking about me?"

"Let's see. I'm going to describe you like you're a stranger to yourself, and then you can tell me whether you sound exotic or not."

"Sounds like an interesting game."

The bartender finally made it over, and Black ordered a Bacardi Silver. "Would you care for anything, Miss Fine?"

"No, I'm cool. Thank you, but I'm still nursing this Pink Lady."

He looked down at my glass on the bar. "That sounds and looks like a very feminine drink."

"Men who don't have hang-ups about their masculinity drink them as well," I said.

The bartender returned with Black's drink.

"Hey, I'll also take a Pink Lady," Black told him before he could take off again.

The bartender looked at him funny and then chuckled. "Sure, I'll be right back with it."

I leaned over closer to Black. "So is that your way of proving that you're a *real* man?"

"No, that's my way of trying out a new drink that I've never heard of that looks interesting."

I slapped him gently on the arm. "I like that answer. Now go ahead and describe me."

"Okay, but it would help if I knew your name."

"Oops, that might help. My name is Tenage."

"Gorgeous."

"What, my name?"

"You and your name are both gorgeous. By the way, I'm Black."

I couldn't help but blush. "So describe me, Black."

"Tenage is about five-ten with smooth skin the color of the finest mahogany wood in the world. Her eyes are like black pearls, and her hair is like silk. Her facial features are perfectly placed, and she has this little mole on her left shoulder that's incredibly sexy."

I was speechless for a second before saying, "Damn, you do make me sound exotic."

We both laughed.

Black and I danced the night fantastic until it was time for the club to close. He asked me to go home with him, but I explained to him that my pussy wasn't as readily available as some. I needed to be wined and dined and mesmerized before I gave up my most precious jewel.

He seemed to be digging that and asked if I'd hang out with him the next day. I didn't have anything else to do, so I said, "Sure."

The next morning Black picked me up in a burgundy Infinity SUV. It still smelled new, and it was right on the money. There's nothing like cruising in a smooth ride. We cruised down to Haines Point. He had a prepared picnic. He won major brownie points for that move, because I had never had a Negro take me on a picnic, much less prepare the food himself. This was the real deal all right. I can tell store-bought food anywhere. I know some sistahs that sneak over to this local soul food shack to get their vegetables for Sunday dinner, go home and throw a chicken in an oven, and pretend that the greens, black-eyed peas, and collard greens are homemade. Some of them even get away with it, too.

Black had laid it out: po'boy sandwiches with Havarti ham and smoked turkey covered with Swiss cheese, and carrot raisin salad. It was incredibly delicious. He also served fruit salad sprinkled with sparkling apple cider. He had a thermos full of Bellinis, my all-time favorite, for us to drink.

Haines Point used to be the ultimate hangout. People rode around in circles for hours to see who they could see. My sister met her husband that way. The D.C. police had put a stop to that years ago—shit got out of hand. But our picnic was peaceful. We laid out a blanket down by the statue. The breeze coming off the water was great. I spotted someone fishing on the Potomac, which surprised me because fish often roll up to the shores belly-up.

Black and I discussed everything from A to Z. He told me about his childhood in Jamaica. Surprised me, too—he didn't have an accent. He said that he had moved to America when he was ten and made a gallant effort to speak like the people around him.

I had grown up in D.C. and didn't consider that a damn thing to brag about. Like most Washingtonian natives, I had never really experienced all the museums or landmarks because it was taken for granted that they would always be there.

Black was a restaurant manager. His job had transferred him from Richmond, Virginia. That meant he often had to work long hours, and he made sure that I knew that up front. Apparently, he'd had problems in previous relationships because the women felt he was neglecting them for work. I told him that, as a night auditor, he had to be even more understanding about my job. He said that was cool.

The Bellinis started kicking in, and I was beginning to feel kind of frisky.

"Hey, have you ever been out to the Bay Bridge?" I asked him after our stomachs were full and the conversation had finally tapered off.

"No, can't say that I have been. Like I said earlier, I've only been in the District for about a year."

"Well, that's where the view is truly beautiful. I know a little private spot on the beach that is practically always deserted. Want to go check it out?"

He shook his head. "I don't think I should drive that far. I'm kind of tipsy."

"Me, too, but not too tipsy to drive. I can take us if you don't mind me driving your car."

"I don't mind at all."

Forty-five minutes later we were parked on the sand. The sun was setting over the bridge, and the view was spectacular. Black laid the blanket out, and we sat side by side.

"This is beautiful," he said to me.

"I told you so."

Black caught me off guard by kissing me. I knew it was coming at some point, at least I hoped that it would, but I wasn't quite prepared for it to happen so suddenly.

He was a good kisser, which is always helpful. If a brotha can't kiss, I'm not trying to kiss him, period. I dated one man for two years and never kissed him after the first time. He was a decent lover, but I simply couldn't force myself to go there as far as kissing.

Black's kisses were so arousing that I could feel my panties getting damp. Black reached over and fondled my breasts through the sheer fabric of my cotton sundress. Our kiss grew in intensity, and I pushed him on his back and climbed on top of him. All that shit I said the night before about not giving up the drawers fast evaporated. I wanted him, and I wanted him right that second.

I pulled my dress over my head and unhooked my bra, lowering it off my shoulders and exposing my breasts. I took a quick look around to make sure no one had snuck up on us. The coast appeared to be clear. I stood up just long enough to take off my panties. Black used that opportunity to get undressed as well.

We were naked on the blanket, just staring in each other's eyes.

"Are you okay with this, Tenage?"

"I'm more than okay." I kissed his chest and then bit gently on one of his nipples. "I don't know what it is about you, but today has been a wonderful day, and I don't want it to end without exploring all other possibilities."

"So you think this thing with us can go somewhere?"

"Where would you like it to go, Black?" I asked him.

"I'm looking for the real thing. I'm looking for love. I'm not trying to play silly games. I was raised to believe that every good man needs a good woman behind him. He needs a good wife, and that's what I'm searching for."

I buried my head in his chest and laughed.

He lifted my head up and looked at me. "What's so funny?"

"Nothing. I'm just trying to imagine me as anyone's wife. I've never considered myself marriage material, and the fact that we're sitting here talking about this less than twenty-four hours after we met is crazy."

He flashed that pretty-ass smile at me. "Life is crazy."

"True."

"So what do you think?"

"What do I think? I mean, you're not proposing or anything now, so I guess we'll just see what's what."

Black ran his fingers through my hair. "What if I am proposing now?"

Let's just say that I sobered up *real quick!* "Black, we just met."

"So? I know what I want, and I wanted to ask you before we had sex because I don't even want you to think it's about that. From the second I saw you sitting at that bar, I knew you were the one."

He was dead serious. I was shocked. I sat up straight and looked down at him. He was incredibly fine and seemed nice enough, but *marriage?*

"How could you know I was the one that fast?" I asked. "How can you even know I'm the one now?"

He shrugged his shoulders. "I just know these things. When I was a little boy, I used to dream about the type of woman I would marry. I could see her so clearly, and guess what? She looked exactly like you."

"This is insane!" I exclaimed, expressing my thoughts out loud.

"What's so insane about it, Tenage?"

We sat in silence for a moment while I attempted to come up with an answer.

Finally, I said something that even stunned me. "Sure, I'll marry you."

He chuckled. "Say what?"

"I said, I'll marry you. If it works, it works. If it doesn't, we'll move on."

Black took my hand and started sucking my fingers one by one. "Tenage, I promise you'll never regret this."

I nervously laughed. "Let's hope not."

Black jumped up from the blanket and snatched up his pants. "Get dressed!"

"Get dressed? I thought we were about to have sex?"

"Not until after we're married."

"What?"

"It's still early. We can go find a justice of the peace and get hitched tonight."

"Whoa," I lashed out at him. "This is moving just a little too fast for me."

"Come on, Tenage. Live a little. What else did you have planned for tonight?"

As I watched Black get dressed, all kinds of shit ran through my mind. I would have to be insane to go and marry the man. Then again, what if he was the man of my dreams and I missed out on the opportunity of a lifetime?

Lawd, what a day! What a day! We were married less than two hours later in a little cottage by a justice. Just like in the old movies, his wife played the piano, and his housekeeper and gardener stood in as our witnesses.

Black wanted to go get a hotel room to consummate our

marriage, but I insisted on going back to the beach. I wanted to finish what we started.

He methodically licked every inch of my body and ended up with his head buried between my legs. He hooked my legs over his shoulders and sat up on his knees. That left only my shoulders and head resting on the sand. I had never had a man eat me out like that before and I came within a couple of minutes the first time. We made love all night on the sand. Black worked me over in a major way, and I tried to match his generosity.

After he was done with me, I did him, but I wanted to do him in the water. We went down to the water's edge and walked just enough into the waves to cover our thighs. I took him into my mouth and relaxed my throat until I could get him all the way in. His dick was sweet because of the fruit salad we had eaten earlier.

I stuck a finger in his ass while I was sucking him off. He flinched at first but then let me continue to move it in and out. He came in my mouth, and the warm liquid lined my belly. Then he scooped me up in his arms, and we had sex standing up in the water. With my legs wrapped around him, he held onto my ass cheeks and worked his dick inside me. *Yes, I loved this man I had just met. Yes, I loved my husband.*

I arched my back until the waves teased the ends of my long hair. Black sucked on my breasts, and that made the experience even more delightful.

"Let me down," I instructed him. "I want to get on my knees."

After I got on my knees in the water, Black entered me from behind, and for anyone that has ever done water aerobics, you know that the added pressure made the dick seem even bigger and more powerful. Black grabbed my ass cheeks, spread them, and played with my anus with his fingers.

"Do you want it there, Tenage?" he asked. "Tell me how you want it."

It had been years since I had anal sex, and I hated it the first time, but life is crazy, so I answered, "Yes, I want it there, baby."

Black took my ass that night, and it was ten times better than the first time. I think it was because he was so much more of a considerate lover. The blazing sun woke us up the next morning. I heard a dog barking in the distance, which immediately made me nervous. What if someone was coming?

"I think we should go," I told Black.

He yawned and looked at me lovingly. "We have so much to discuss."

"Well, we probably need to discuss it someplace else," I said jokingly. "Someone might find us soon."

"Okay, we can leave."

We got dressed in silence, gathered everything, and got in his SUV. As we were driving off, I felt compelled to ask, "Do you have any regrets?"

He took my hand and kissed it. "Not a one. Where are we headed? Your place or mine?"

I laughed. "That's a damn good question, and you're right. We have a ton of things to discuss, like where we're going to live, do we want kids, how many vacations to take a year—"

"Tenage, all of that will work itself out. I promise."

I leaned over and kissed his cheek. "Somehow, I believe you."

Peaches

I greet you at the door after a long, hard day at work. I know you are exhausted because you called a couple hours before you arrived, telling me how stressful the day had been for you. I want to do something very special for you, Boo, so I decide to pamper you and fulfill your every wish.

I open the door, and you are startled to see me in a black French maid's outfit, black fishnet stockings, and black stiletto heels. I hand you a glass of chilled Chablis and take your coat. You look so debonair in your business suit, I almost hate to see you take it off, but I know that your birthday suit is so much more thought-provoking.

I lead you to the bedroom and proceed to help you undress, doing it very slowly and gazing deep into your captivating bedroom eyes. I bite my bottom lip as I remove your pants and silk boxers, feeling my desire for you grow and my pussy beginning to cause a slight dampness in the crotch of my white satin panties.

Once you are completely unclad, I take you by the hand and

walk into the master bathroom, where your bath awaits you. I know how much you love peaches. So I have the whirlpool tub filled up not with water, but with thick cream and hundreds of peach slices in heavy syrup. You are amazed to see the high-pressured spigots swirling the peaches around in the cream.

I have the entire bathroom counter and part of the floor covered with scented candles that also smell like peaches and cream. The bath is only the beginning of my peaches theme for the evening.

I ask you to step into the tub and proceed to wash your entire body with a huge loofah sponge, starting with your back and shoulders. Then I move on to your arms and chest. I reach my hand into the cream and wash your legs, your dick, your balls, and then your feet. As I am bathing you, I tell you all the things I love and admire about you, how my love for you is unconditional, and how everything from the way you walk to the way you cum turns me on. Your dick is so hard.

After I am sure you are relaxed and feeling tingly all over, I have you get out of the tub and dry you off with a fresh, thick bath towel. I help you slip into a nice, comfy terry cloth robe I had embroidered with your initials. As we go into the dining room, where I have a feast prepared for my Nubian king, soft jazz music plays in the background.

I have prepared you some lobster, wild rice, string beans amandine, and buttery hot biscuits. The dining room has peaches-and-cream-scented candles scattered all around it. I put a bib on you, one with a picture of a lobster on it, and straddle your lap, facing you. I begin to feed you slowly, dipping the succulent lobster into some hot butter and lapping up any that trickles on your chin. While I am feeding you, I recite erotic poetry and feel your dick pulsating between my legs.

Once I have fed you the main course, I disappear into the

kitchen just long enough to retrieve the two jars I picked up at the country market up the street. One is filled with peaches in heavy syrup, and the other one is filled with peach preserves. I open the jar of peaches, and then I begin to undress slowly and seductively for you.

I take you by the hand and lead you to the other end of the table, which has no food or dishes on it, only a huge silver platter. I motion for you to sit down in the chair, and you comply. I take the jar of peaches and get up on the platter. Starting at the top of my breasts, I pour the cool mixture all over my body. It makes my skin tingle.

I lean back on my elbows and clasp my legs around your neck, using my ankles to pull your head forward between my thighs. You show your appreciation for the dessert I have enticed you with by consuming all of it, one peach at a time. The thick syrup is dripping all over my body, trickling down my inner thighs onto the platter. You take your time with me, eating and sucking and licking all of it off my body.

Then you stand up and disrobe. You make mad, passionate love to me right there, with my pussy on the silver platter. I dig my fingernails into your chest, overcome as I am by feeling the man I love more than life itself deep inside me. Our two bodies fuse together from the body-generated heat. Our bodies both spasm in unison as we cum. I begin to cry because the love you give to me is so overbearing and so intense.

We retire to our bedroom, taking the jar of peach preserves with us. I spread it all over your body from head to toe and, starting with your temples, give you a tongue bath, licking every inch of you. I lick everything from your ears to your armpits, from your chest to your ass, from your dick to your toes, all of you. Then I get some scented body oil, the kind that gets hot when you blow on it, and give you a full-body massage.

By now you are so relaxed and sexually satisfied that you've forgetten about your hard day at work. I prop myself up on a pillow beside you and let you fall asleep in your favorite position, with my arms around you and one of my tender breasts in your mouth. I listen to you snore for a while and watch your chest go up and down as you breathe. Then I fall asleep also, dreaming of peaches and my boo.

The Subway—A Quickie

It is late at night, and we are returning from a show downtown. We are on the subway, and there are just a few passengers scattered about. We hug and kiss, but no one pays us any attention, and soon we begin to get hot and heavy. You slide your hand under my blouse and begin to caress my breasts. My hand slides up your thigh and grabs at your dick.

I have on a short skirt, and your other hand begins to slide up my thigh. Soon your hand is all the way up to my pussy, and you begin to slide my panties to the side. I push your hand away and continue to kiss you; your dick is as hard as steel. I continue to rub it and then unzip your pants. You try to slide your finger behind my panties again, and I don't stop you this time; soon your finger is buried in my wetness.

Your dick is out of your pants now, and we get more heated as I stroke it and hump my hips back and forth on your finger. Then I lean down and take the head of your dick into my mouth and begin to suck on it, licking all around the head and down the shaft. You moan softly and hold the back of my head, caressing my hair with your fingertips.

I stop and begin to slide my panties down and off. Afterward, I hold them to your face. You smell the sweet aroma of my pussy as I now face you and straddle you. We find that this is uncomfortable, so I turn around with my back to you. Slowly, I let your dick part the lips of my hot pussy as I climb on top of it. Gently, you grab my buttocks and help me go up and down on the shaft.

I put my hands on your knees for leverage and get into a rhythmic motion as you push your manhood deeper and deeper into my paradise. You let go of my hips, reach in front of me, and start pinching my nipples. I start to tremble, and my excitement is uncontrollable. I look around the subway and realize that now people are watching, but neither one of us care.

I start riding your dick harder and harder, and I can feel myself climaxing at top speed as the subway train rattles along the tracks in the dark tunnel. I climax with an explosion, and you tell me you are cumming. I slowly climb off your dick, turn around, and begin jacking it off with my hand. I rub it harder and harder until you can't hold it anymore, and you explode.

We look at each other and laugh, realizing what we have just done. The few passengers left on the train start applauding us and yelling approving remarks. Quickly, we replace all our loose clothing, still gasping for air. As we get off the train at the next stop, you gather my panties from the floor—the one item I forgot to replace—and tie them onto the post of the seat where we made love, marking the spot of our transgression. Giggling and holding hands, we sneak briskly off into the night. Now that's what I call a quickie!

Under the Mistletoe

It's Christmas Eve, and we've just returned home from the burn unit of the inner-city hospital where we portray Mr. and Mrs. Santa Claus every year. We both have a great love of children. We don't have any of our own yet, but it would be a crime for us not to in due time. While we wait for the stork to deliver us a baby, we enjoy donating time to "special" children like the ones at the hospital. Seeing their faces light up, even when their little bodies are in so much pain, is a joyous feeling.

Part of the reason I married you is because of your compassion and empathy for others. It's a trait we share along with our love of travel, books, and the art of making love. I love everything about you, from the way you laugh to the way you rub your eyes like a little boy when they're tired. Which is what you are doing right now, rubbing your eyes.

I go into the kitchen to get the gingerbread cookies and put on a huge kettle of water so I can make several cups of apple cider. You stay in the living room and start a fire. Our mantel is decorated with garlands and red bows and has three stockings hung from it—one for you, one for me, and one for Subzero, our Dalmatian, who is somewhere snuggled up in a corner of the house.

The tray of cups of cider is ready, so I ask you to carry it outside to the front porch. I follow behind you with gingerbread cookies in hand and a basket of candy canes hung on my arm. We get outside just in time to see the Christmas carolers making footprints through the blanket of snow toward our house, coming from the McKenzies, our neighbors, who always give them shiny new silver dollars every season. It is a tradition in our neighborhood that we hold dear.

We make sure the walkway is shoveled and clear before the serenading begins. The carolers arrive, holding songbooks in their precious little mitten-covered hands. They're too cute for words. The smallest children are distracted from their singing, more intrigued by the way we're dressed up. You're in your fluffy red Santa suit, a silver wig and beard, black military boots, eyeglasses pushed down onto the tip of your nose, and a Santa hat. I'm in an old-fashioned ankle-length red dress covered with a long white cotton apron, black pilgrim shoes, silver wig, and white cotton bonnet.

We stand there overlooking the porch banister and watching them sing their little hearts out as the adult chaperones and parents look on. When they're done, we applaud them and then descend the steps so we can pass out the goodies we have for them. All the children are well mannered, saying, "Thank you, ma'am," and, "Thank you, sir." We stand there, with your arm around the small of my waist, waving to them as they walk away sipping on the warm cider and munching on the cookies.

We get back inside the house and you start to take off the Santa outfit. I stop there and ask you to wait a second. I hurry to the upstairs closet to get our camera, put it up on the entertainment center, and set the timer. Then I hurry into your arms so we can take a Christmas photo together. We can use the photos on the Christmas cards we send out next year to our friends and family.

Like a firecracker bursting into a kaleidoscope of light on the Fourth of July, an idea pops into my head. I tell you to have a seat by the fireplace on some floor pillows. You have a bit of trouble sitting down, with all the extra inches from the pillow stuffed in your jacket and thick towels stuffed into your pants legs. After you slowly make it down, I go to the kitchen and get you a stein full of eggnog with rum and bring it to you.

I walk over to the entertainment center and flip through our tower of CDs, searching for our *Ebonics Christmas* CD, which your friend Dave bought us. It has a bunch of hilarious Christmas rap songs on it, with kicking-ass beats. I locate it, put it in the CD changer, hit play, and then grab the camera. I hand it to you just as the first cut comes on, telling you, "Ooh, Santa, you are so sexy. Can an old woman like me do a little dance for you?"

You laugh, and with the pillow and all, it really looks like you weigh a good three hundred pounds instead of being cut like you really are. You reply, "Dance for me, baby!"

So I do. I shake my ass off in my red dress, lifting up a hemline so you can see my black pilgrim shoes, black fishnet stockings, and puffy, white cotton bloomers with elastic around my center thighs. I look like somebody's grandmother doing a hoochie dance, with the silver wig on and all.

As the beat goes on, I turn around and undo my white cotton apron, take it off, fling it around in the air, and then toss it toward you on the floor. It lands with a corner snagged on the edge of your glasses. You remove it, throw it beside you, and sip some more eggnog.

I unbutton my dress and pull it down off my shoulders, one

at a time, until it is hanging around my waist, revealing my white lace bra. I let the dress fall all the way to the floor and kick it to the side, leaving me standing there looking like Old Mother Hubbard on ginseng.

You start snapping photos, saying, "Baby, we have got to put these in the family scrapbook for the kids!" We both start giggling while I reach behind my back, unsnap my bra, and let it ease down, allowing my erect nipples to break loose.

I walk over to you, spread my legs, and start gyrating my bloomers in your face, tits bouncing up and down. You grab one of my legs, put it on your shoulder, and then bite my thigh through the fishnet stockings, causing me to shriek out, "Ooh, Big Daddy, what a big appetite you have!"

You pull me down on the floor, flipping me back on the pillows by the fire, climb on top of me, and take one nipple in your mouth, grabbing it between your teeth and tugging gently on it. Then you say, "My turn! Time for Santa to give you what the elves made for you. Have you been naughty or nice?"

I yell out, "NAUGHTY!" as you jump to your feet in the Santa costume and start break dancing and unbuckling the wide-ass black patent-leather belt around your artificial tummy.

You throw the belt at me and start taking off the furry jacket, exposing the red pants held up by suspenders, over the white undershirt stuffed with a pillow. I sit up in the Indian position, start jiggling my tits to the rhythm, and egg you on—"Go Big Poppi, Go Big Poppi, Go!"

I grab the camera and start taking pics of you while you take the suspender straps down and pull off the undershirt, letting the round pillow fall to the carpet. Times like this make me realize why I married you. You are always down to act silly with me, and that's why you will make such a great daddy one day.

You take off the stuffed pants, stepping out of them, leaving nothing on you but your black military boots, beard, wig, hat, eyeglasses, and boxer shorts that say "Ho-Ho-Ho" on them. You look so sexy, baby!

You turn the *Ebonics* CD off and switch it to some slow jams. Now there are songs we used to listen to in high school when we first fell in love, like "Fire and Desire" by Rick James and Teena Marie—back in the days we used to dedicate love songs to each other on the radio. We fell asleep at night talking to each other on the phone, sat in class all day staring at each other across the room, getting caught by the teacher as we passed love notes from each other back and forth. We carved our names inside hearts that said "2gether 4eva" on just about every oak tree in between your house and mine.

Now, in our home, I lie back on the pillows and wait for you to join me. You grab the basket of candy canes sitting by the front door on your way and sit down beside me. What a trip, looking at you with the wig and beard on. I am sure you feel the same, looking at me with a wig and bonnet on.

You lie on top of me and start kissing me as you remove the hat and wig from my head, allowing my long, thick, shiny hair to freely flow. The fiber from your beard starts to get caught in my mouth, so I pull it down around your chin, take your hat and wig off, and then straddle my legs around your back, pulling your hard dick closer in to me. I feel your dick pulsating against my excited clit through the material of your boxers and my bloomers.

We kiss for the length of two slow songs. You have always been so passionate and such a great kisser; you make me melt. You take the stein of eggnog, which is almost empty, and pour the remainder on my breasts. I begin to moan as you lick all the eggnog off my breasts, trying to catch every drop before it hits the floor.

I run my fingertips down your spine while you suckle on my nipples like a baby. You sit up for a moment and pull off my ugly-ass pilgrim shoes and then pull my bloomers down along with the fishnets until they are completely off. My freshly shaven pussy greets you, moist from the stimulation your hands and mouth have brought the rest of my body.

While you are on your knees, I sit up and pull down your boxers, helping you get them off. I pull the beard, which is still hanging on your chin, up and over your head and toss it aside, accidentally flinging it into the fireplace. You try to catch it, but it goes up in flames in a matter of seconds, and we break out in laughter.

Our eyes meet, and all the love we feel overwhelms us, both of us knowing what lies ahead. You reach over and pull a big candy cane out of the basket and stick the long part into my mouth. I take it in, deep-throating it like it is your dick, and place my hands on top of your hand, holding it as you push it in and out.

Once the candy cane is nice and sticky, you pull it out of my mouth, use your other hand to spread open the lips of my pussy, and then slowly glide it in. I start contracting my pussy muscles on it each time you stick it all the way in, leaving only the curved part sticking out. You start sucking my breasts again. I hold one for you, squeezing it so it is even more prominent, while you continue to fuck me with the candy cane.

You take the candy cane out and then lick it, tasting the mixture of the mint with my pussy juice. You utter, "Ummmm! Dayum delicious!"

You hold it up to my mouth, saying, "Taste how delicious you are." I comply by licking around the cane with the tip of my tongue, tasting my own nectar. I know how much it turns you on to see me taste myself, and your dick, which was previously just hard, turns rock hard like a battering ram.

I tell you to lie down, and then I climb on top of you, placing my pussy smack on your face as my mouth makes its way toward your beautiful dick. My mouth is still sticky from the candy, and as I suckle on the head of your dick, it mixes with the precum oozing out of it.

I feel your tongue flickering in and out of my pussy while I start licking around the shaft of your dick, grabbing hold of the base so it doesn't escape the spectrum of my tongue. I move your dick aside so I can lick your balls as you begin to shiver and moan because it is such a sensitive area.

I begin to wax your entire dick with my mouth while you part my ass cheeks and insert a single finger, which makes me flinch as you continue to suck on my sweet clit. Cum starts to trickle down my inner thighs onto your cheeks, and a drop or two even makes its way into your ear canals.

Your dick overflows my mouth, and saliva starts to trickle out the corners of my thick, juicy lips. Whenever I am sucking your dick, I feel the most close to you. It is like I am sucking the life out of you, and there is something so erotic about it.

You cum inside my mouth, and the heated substance, candy-flavored because of the candy cane on my tongue, makes a warm lining in my belly. You start pushing your finger into my ass faster and faster, pulling my pussy deeper onto your tongue until I cum also, leaving you with a smile on your glazed face.

You wanna go upstairs, but I tell you I wanna make a quick stop in the kitchen. Once we are in the kitchen, I tell you to sit on the tabletop. I go over to the counter and get one of the decorating tubes full of homemade frosting I used to make the gingerbread men. I push you back onto the table, climb on top of you, and then start squeezing the red frosting onto your chest, making a design on it. I make your nipples look like eyes, squeeze a line down the center of your chest, forming it like a nose, and make your belly button look like a mouth.

Carefully, I lick all the frosting off you. You say the words you always say to me during lovemaking, "You are so crazy, baby! But I love your crazy ass!"

"I love you, too, baby!" I tell you with a mouth covered with red frosting. I kiss you, and you lick some of the frosting off. Then I go back to the task at hand until I have licked every inkling of it off.

Then you say, "I wanna do you, too, but you know what I want to decorate."

I snicker, 'cause I know, right off the bat, you mean my ass.

I climb off you, you get up from the table, go get the tube of green frosting, and tell me, "Stand still!"

As you take a seat in one of the chairs at the square table, I get in the doggy-style position so my ass is all in your face. You start to decorate my ass like a face as well, and you even put a fancy hairdo on it. After you decide it looks enough like a van Gogh, you eat it all up while I absorb every second of the pleasure it brings.

We hear a noise, a whimper, and both of us turn our heads to see our dog, Subzero, standing in the kitchen doorway with his head bent to one side in curiosity, wondering what freaky shit his owners are up to this time. You throw him a gingerbread cookie and tell him to get. He catches it in his mouth and heads back to his cozy corner to snack on his treasure.

You sweep me up into your arms and almost break out in a run carrying me up the staircase, taking two steps at a time. You take me in our bedroom, toss me on the bed, and shut our door so Subzero won't make any more sudden appearances.

The bedroom is dark, and the only light is coming from the electric candles held by the animated miniature black Mr. and

Mrs. Santa Claus dolls. There is one in each of the bedroom windows, so passersby can see them waving as they drive down the street.

There is a single piece of mistletoe hanging in the center of our headboard, and the bed is covered with the homemade quilt we purchased from the Amish on a recent weekend getaway in Pennsylvania. It is there, on the quilt, we make our own beautiful music together before falling asleep in each other's arms.

Remember I Love You Always

Saying good-bye to him was going to be the hardest thing I ever had to do. To go away for such a long time—fifteen years. But when you break the law, someone has to pay. There is a consequence for every action, and armed robbery carries an extremely heavy consequence.

I had him meet me in our private place—the first place we had ever made love. There was no way the police could know about it. No one knew about it but the two of us. It was a little cabin on the side of the river. The mosquitoes in Alabama are eight inches long in the summer, and they were seriously attacking that night as I waited for him on the front porch.

The cabin had long been abandoned. The man who owned it had died in his sleep more than a decade earlier. He had no next of kin, and since the property was basically worthless, no one had bothered to do anything with it. The world had long since forgotten it even existed. Only Jesse and I visited it from time to time.

I saw some headlights approaching and ducked, just to be on the safe side. I wanted to make sure it was Jesse before I exposed myself. I didn't recognize the raggedy Oldsmobile that pulled up, so I continued to hide in the shadows. Then I saw Jesse get out of the driver's side. I could see the worry on his face, even in the darkness.

He cut the lights and called out to me. "Susan, are you there?"

"Yes," I responded half in a whisper. "I'm over here on the porch."

Jesse ascended the creaky steps and took me in his arms. "I've been so worried about you. Are you okay?"

"As much as I can be. Tomorrow's the big day, and I'm not sure I can handle it."

"I know I can't handle it," he said despondently. "Fifteen long-ass years."

"Seems like forever."

"And it will feel like forever."

I stood on my toes and kissed him on the lips softly. "At least we still have tonight."

"Yes, at least we have tonight."

Jesse rubbed my shoulders. "Are the mosquitoes biting you?"

"In the worst way."

He opened the always unlocked door of the cabin and pulled me inside. "Let's get you safe."

"Nothing can keep me safe after tonight."

Jesse used some matches to light the two hurricane lights on each side of the cabin. "Susan, I'd prefer if we just didn't talk about tomorrow. It's going to come soon enough, and there's nothing either one of us can do about it."

"That's true," I conceded. "You're right. Let's just not talk about it."

"Oh, shit! Are you hungry, baby? I should've bought you something to eat on my way up."

"I'm fine. I haven't had an appetite for days. Food is the furthest thing from my mind."

Jesse came closer to me and embraced me once again. "So what is on your mind?"

"Other than what's going to happen when the sun comes up?"

"Yes, other than that."

"Making love to you one last time. We've loved each other so long, Jesse. Things are just not going to be the same once we're apart."

He forced a smile, but it didn't relax me one bit. "We'll still see each other often. They have visiting hours, you know?"

"It won't be the same, Jesse!" I yelled out in desperation. "We won't be able to touch, and I need to feel your touch. I need to feel your touch all the time."

He caressed my cheek and kissed my forehead. "So imagine that I'm touching you. Imagine that I'm always around, always there for you. Just close your eyes and feel me. Feel my hands all over your body. Feel me inside you. Feel my love surrounding you." He lifted my chin so I had to look into his eyes. "Will you try to do that for me?"

"I can try. Just not sure it's going to work."

"It will work. Trust me. Have I ever lied to you, Susan? Ever?"

"No."

"And I'm not about to begin lying to you now."

Suddenly the tears began to fall from my eyes. "Jesse, just promise me one thing."

"What's that, baby?"

"That fifteen years from now, when those gates open up, we'll be together again."

"I promise you that, Susan. I promise."

I wrapped my arms around his neck. "I love you, Jesse. Remember I love you always."

"You remember the same."

Jesse dried my tears with his shirt and lifted me up so that my legs straddled his waist. He danced with me in his arms to imaginary music and hummed our favorite slow song. We twirled around and around until we ended up over by the ancient iron bed. Jesse put me down, and the bedsprings began to creak.

I laid my head on the dusty pillow that made up the bed along with an old patchwork quilt. Jesse lay down beside me.

"I wonder what the man who used to live here was like," I said aloud.

"I don't know. I never knew him. He kept pretty much to himself, from what I hear."

"I wonder who he loved. If he ever loved—and if anyone ever loved him back."

Jesse sighed. "I'm not sure, but I guess he was alone when he died. No one claimed any of his property; not even this house."

"Thank goodness for that, because this house holds so many special memories for us."

Jesse and I faced each other on the bed and became lost in each other's eyes.

"Susan?"

"Yes, baby?"

"I want you to have my baby."

I was stunned. *A baby!* "Jesse, you know that's something I've always wanted, but under these circumstances, it doesn't make sense. A child should have both parents, and that can't happen."

Jesse looked so sad. Then a grin spread across his face. "Will you still be able to birth babies in fifteen years?"

I giggled. "Hmm, I guess so. I'm twenty-six now, so that would make me forty-one, and I've heard of women that old having babies."

The despair returned to his face. "Forty-one. God, that seems like forever."

I lifted the bottom of his shirt and rubbed his flat, muscular stomach. "Let's just make love like there's no tomorrow, because there really isn't a tomorrow for us."

Jesse leaned over and kissed me passionately. I took his hand and placed it between my legs. I wanted him to feel how hot I was for him. How much I needed to be with him just one last time.

Within minutes of intense foreplay, we were both naked and rolling around on the bed like wild animals. Jesse entered me, and I cried. Not because it hurt, but because I knew it was the last time I would likely feel him inside me. Fifteen years was a long time, and there was no guarantee both of us would live to see the day.

I grabbed onto his ass cheeks as he worked his dick around inside my love canal. It was more intense than ever, and I wanted to make it last forever. I sucked on his earlobe as he came the first time. I was already ahead of him by three. Cum was all over the quilt, and most of it was mine.

Jesse turned me over and entered me from behind. I grabbed the headboard and let him enjoy the ride. He started moving in and out of me more vigorously, and I could feel his balls slapping up against my ass. It was heaven.

He grabbed my hair and pulled my pussy back deeper onto his dick.

"Susan, I hope a miracle happens tonight," Jesse whispered in my ear. "I hope something changes."

"Jesse, please." I gripped my pussy muscles as tight as I could onto him. The tears began again. This man truly loved me, and soon I would be without him. "Please don't mention tomorrow again."

We made love until Jesse fell asleep. I couldn't sleep if my life depended on it. I was too afraid that the police would find us somehow.

I got up from the bed and did something I had never even thought about doing in all the years we had been coming there. I went over to the old rickety dresser and opened the top drawer. For some reason, I felt like I needed to know something about the man who had lived there—the man who made the old cabin his home.

There was not much worth interest in the drawer. Some dingy clothing, an old pocketknife, and some Tiger Balm for aches and pains. I was about to close the drawer when something got stuck. I reached underneath the drawer and realized something was taped to it. It was tough, but I managed to rip it off.

There was a plastic bag surrounded by duct tape. I removed the tape and discovered a stack of old photographs inside the bag. There was a young black man in every single photo. They were taken in different years, but you could easily tell they were all of the same person. There was a picture of him as a baby bouncing on a woman's lap. There was a picture of him as a young lad standing beside a man holding a hunting rifle. I figured those were pictures of him and his parents. Then there were pictures of him as a teenager with a teenage girl. She was very pretty and looked like she was full of life and hope for the future. The last picture was of the same couple standing in front of the cabin, which looked recently built. They had on wedding rings and were caught up in a tight embrace.

"So he was married," I said to myself. "I wonder what happened to her."

I put the pictures back in the bag and placed them inside the drawer instead of taping them back underneath. I wondered why he would have them hidden like that. I decided to explore further and opened the second drawer. There was a knitted baby blanket on top, and underneath there was a silver spoon. I wondered if they also had a child. It is amazing what items can tell you about people who have passed on. Then I saw it: a death certificate. It stated that Abigail Lewis, age twenty-five, had died during childbirth along with her infant son.

A sadness came over me that I had never experienced. This man, the man who had resided in the place where I now stood, had gone through so much pain. He had lost his only true love at such a young age, and he had lost his child. Suddenly I didn't feel so bad about my own situation. Fifteen years was a long time, but maybe Jesse and I still had a chance. Maybe the parole board would feel some sympathy and cut down on the sentence. Anything was possible as long as we were both still breathing. The people whose lives I had just explored had no more chances. Their time on this earth was over.

Jesse stirred in the bed, and I went to him. I lay on top of him and showered him with kisses. He woke up and kissed me back until our tongues were entwined. We started our lovemaking all over again, and we made love until the sun came up.

"Jesse," I whispered in his ear. "I think it's time."

Jesse clung to me and began to weep. He had been so strong the entire time, and now he was breaking down. "No, it's not time. This can't happen."

"Jesse, we agreed that today would be the day. We can't prolong it. Things will only get worse. Right now, we're looking at fifteen years. If we don't do something now, we could be looking at a lifetime."

"I need you just once more," he proclaimed suddenly through tear-drenched eyes.

I couldn't help but succumb to his wishes. How could I deny the man I loved anything? I caressed his dick and worked it up and down in my hand. He lapped at my breasts and clung onto my waist for dear life. I climbed on top of him and quickly placed him inside me. I prayed that the moment would never end.

"I love you so much, Susan."

"I love you, too."

"God, I'm going to miss this."

Jesse pulled me down on him tighter, and I worked my pussy back and forth on his dick as hard as I could until we both achieved one last orgasm.

Jesse let me go and got up to get dressed. I slipped my clothes back on and went out on the porch. A moment later I felt his arms massaging my shoulders. "You want me to drive you into town, Susan?"

I placed my hand on top of his. "That would be nice."

We drove in silence, and I looked at the sky the entire time. It was so beautiful. The air hitting my cheeks through the lowered window was a wonderful sensation. Everything I had ever taken for granted seemed significant during that drive.

We pulled up in front of the police station, and Jesse got out to come around and open my door. Before I could even get out of the car good, the sheriff and two of his deputies were on the sidewalk. They must have spotted us through the window.

"Susan Wilson!" the sheriff yelled out at me. "Put your hands over your head and step away from the car!"

I looked into Jesse's eyes and saw pure sadness. "I'm so sorry, Jesse. I made a mistake."

"Susan Wilson! You're under arrest for armed robbery! Now place your hands over your head! I'm not going to tell you again!"

"Sheriff, I'm here to turn myself in!" I informed them. "Just give me a chance to say good-bye!"

Jesse grabbed me around the waist and kissed me. Our one last kiss.

The sheriff and one of the deputies grabbed me from him, pulled my hands behind my back, and slapped on handcuffs. They wasted no time in dragging me across the pavement toward the door.

"Remember I love you always," was the last thing I heard Jesse say before they slammed the door in his face.

June 2002

My cell was like a dungeon. The years had blended together, and time lost all meaning. Fifteen years turned into seventeen because of an escape attempt. I couldn't live without Jesse, and I needed to see him. I needed to be with him. The other two inmates who tried to escape with me were shot and killed right outside town. Dogs tracked me down, and I surrendered. Being ripped apart by sharp teeth was not the way I wanted to die.

Jesse visited me every single weekend at first. Then, after his Christmas visit in 1997, I had never seen him again. No letters came. His phone number was disconnected. My heart was broken. I figured that he came to the realization that loving a woman behind bars was not really loving one at all. He was right. I had no business trying to prevent him from leading a normal life because of my own mistakes. He deserved to be happy—to have someone to wake up to every morning and fall asleep with every night.

When the gates opened, I hesitated to even step outside them. I had no place to go and no one to see. People didn't believe in hiring ex-convicts, and finding a decent job was going to be downright impossible. I stepped out onto the street and looked both ways, having no clue which way was best to walk.

"Susan Wilson?"

I turned to face a young girl of about fifteen. I had no idea who she was—I couldn't have, because I had been locked up longer than she had been alive.

"Who are you?" I asked. "How did you know my name?"

"I've seen your picture."

"My picture?"

"Yes. Of course, you look a bit older now."

I was frozen in place. I had no idea what to think.

"Let me explain," she continued. "My stepdaddy was Jesse Spencer, and he asked me to give you something when you got out of prison."

"Your stepdaddy?"

"Yes. I've been calling on and off to see when you might be getting out. Funny thing is, I called yesterday, and they said you'd be getting out today, so I came here and waited."

"Where is Jesse?" I demanded to know. "Does he want me to come to him?"

The young girl lowered her eyes and handed me an envelope.

"I have to go now, Miss Susan. Nice meeting you."

Before I could respond, she jumped into some new kind of fancy car with a teenage boy and pulled off.

I spotted a bus bench across the street and decided to sit

there to open the envelope. Inside was a letter that looked rather old. I unfolded it and read it aloud to myself.

Dear Susan,

I know you are surprised to be getting this. I asked Bianca to deliver it to you as soon as you get out. I have no idea how old she'll be by then, but I bet she'll sure be beautiful. Susan, I never knew how to tell you that I had married someone else. Her name's Allison. She's a nice woman, but she's not you and never will be. For three years after I married her, I continued to visit you in the jail, but the deception finally got to me. It was unfair to both of you for my visits to continue. Allison deserved respect, and you deserved to be set free. Free from the disappointment of not being able to be intimate together.

I'm dying, Susan. The doctor says cancer will take me any day now, and I can feel my insides being ripped apart. I felt like I needed to write you this letter so you would know that I never once forgot your touch. I never once forgot the way you kissed me or moaned when we were making love. I have never forgotten you. I don't know what will happen to you or where you'll go when you get out, but I want you to know that I wish things could've been different. I never expressed it, but I was angry with you for what you did. Money was tight, but that was no reason to try to take it illegally. We could've had so much, Susan. If we had worked hard and had faith, we could've had everything. Instead we ended up with nothing.

I have to go now, Susan. Just remember one thing. Remember I love you always!

Jesse

The tears flooded down my cheeks as I concluded the letter. A bus had just turned the corner, and while I had no idea where it was headed, I planned to be on it. The little bit of money I had earned doing prison work would help some, but I would have to find a way to make more. I would not fail this time. I would make something out of myself for Jesse.

The bus stopped and before I got on, I looked up at the sky. "Are you up there, Jesse? Remember I love you always, too."

Wilder

A Night at the Movies

Sistahs are always complaining about not being able to find a decent man, and I was no exception. It was a terribly humid August night, and yes, I had a man, but he was ghost, as usual. JayQuan had been canceling date after date for about a month, and I was beginning to grow a bit suspicious. Scratch that! I was extremely suspicious. I'm not saying he was a man-whore like the guys from *Deuce Bigalow* when I met him, but he was surely knocking on whoredom's door. That is, until I gave him a good puddy-whipping and tamed him down a notch or two. Just like every lifelong pooch, he was destined to start chasing yet another fire engine sooner or later.

My sixth sense, Maxine's Doggie Radar, had begun to pick up the FR signal. The initials stand for Flight Risk, and you know you're confronted with it when five phone calls a day telling you how much he adores the ground you walk on drop down to one obligatory call, aka booty call, every three or four days. He starts bringing his funky drawers over to your place for you to wash instead of surprising you with a dozen roses delivered to your office because he thinks he has you wrapped around his little finger. He refuses to answer the phone whenever you're over his place. Oh, and doesn't let you make a move for the phone. He'll pull an Emmitt Smith on your behind, run an NFL play on you, jumping over the back of the couch and knocking you out of the way to get to it first. JayQuan was doing all of the above, and I didn't like it one bit.

That's why I decided there was absolutely no way I was missing the new horror movie *Hollow Man*. I'd been waiting for that bad boy to come out for more than a year, hearing tell of all the special effects and watching the HBO documentary about how it was made. I was determined to see it the day it came out in the local theaters no matter what. When JayQuan called with yet another excuse why he couldn't keep our date, I told him to go on about his business and I'd catch him the next day. Frankly, I was thinking it was about time to take his Doberman pinscher behind to the kennel and have him put to sleep. It was time for me to move on, because I had no intention of sitting around waiting for him to dump me. I don't participate in that game—if I can't win, I don't want to play.

I called around to see who was home. I was even more pissed off when I discovered most of my girlfriends had dates that night to go see, what else: *Hollow Man*. A couple of them offered to let me tag along, but being a third wheel was never my thing. I didn't appreciate cock-blockers and didn't have any inclination to become one, not even for a few hours. I grabbed the weekend section out of my *Washington Post* right quick and checked out the show times. There was a show starting in less than thirty minutes a few miles from my apartment. I threw on a spaghetti-strap indigo dress, slid my feet into a pair of black sandals, and ran out the door, taking the three flights of stairs down to the parking lot two at a time.

I got into my car and started warming it up. I call my 1984

Nissan Stanza Tank because it uses a tank of gas to get me to and from work every day. Eventually, I'll get a new ride, but right now making rent is top priority, and my roommate, Angie, ran off with some Rastafarian from the Bronx who told her she reminded him of an ancient Egyptian queen. Now she goes by the name of Empress Heaven d'Honey and works in a reggae club as a topless dancer. Yeah, she's some queen all right.

Tank finally got warmed up, and I took off, jumping the curb to get out into the Friday work traffic before the light changed and fifty-eleven cars came plummeting toward me. I got to the theater in record time, in less than ten minutes, but my face immediately frowned up when I saw the line for tickets. There had to be at least thirty-five people in line, and only one ticket window open. How trifling can you get!

I noticed a brother close to the front of the line who appeared to be alone. He was easy to spot because he was tall, chocolaty, and looked like the word D-I-C-K spelled out. He had on a pair of neatly ironed jeans and a white oxford shirt. I tend to notice fine men, but when I am horny, I notice them even more. I took a quick survey of the people standing to the side and couldn't picture him belonging to any of them, so I decided to be my usual bold self and make a daring move.

I walked right up to him, cut in the line, and intertwined my arm through his. "Hey baby, sorry I'm late," I said seductively and loud enough for everyone to hear.

He stared down at me. Damn, damn, damn! His eyes were a charcoal gray and more mesmerizing than D'Angelo's chest in his *Untitled* music video. He grinned at me, flashing this cinematic smile that made me wonder why people weren't lined up to see him on the silver screen.

"It's no problem," he replied in a voice deep enough to make me give up the panties right then and there.

There is something about a man with a deep voice that makes my kitty-kat purr like the four-legged ones in those Meow Mix cat food commercials. On top of that, he had on some CK cologne, my favorite on a man.

Before I knew it, we were at the front of the line, and the young girl behind the window wanted to know what movie we were going to see. I immediately blurted out, *"Hollow Man."*

Sexy cleared his throat. "Yes, can I have two for *Hollow Man?"* I tried to hand him the ten-dollar bill I had crumpled in my free hand, but he refused it. "It's okay. I've got this one, sweetheart. You can pay next time."

He paid for both tickets and handed me one. I blushed, wondering if there really would be a next time, completely forgetting about JayQuan's shady behind.

Once we got inside the theater, I halfway came to my senses. I tried to get him to take the money once again. "Look, I really appreciate you letting me jump the line, but I don't want to impose. Just keep the entire ten and enjoy the movie."

I started to walk away, getting in the line for the concession stand. I didn't want to be late for the movie, but I knew that particular theater showed about ten minutes of previews. I couldn't sit through any movie without popcorn and a little sumptin' sumptin' to wash it down with. I was digging through my purse for another bill when I felt someone breathing down the nape of my neck. I recognized the cologne and started blushing all over again.

I didn't turn around when he whispered in my ear, "Now, that's not fair. Ditching me before we even get inside and find a seat." He pressed the bill back into my hand. "Please don't insult me again by trying to force this on me."

I giggled but kept my eyes straight ahead. I was afraid to look at him for fear of tonguing him down right there in the lobby. "Are you asking me to be your date?"

He ran the fingertips of his left hand over my bare shoulder, and it felt fantastic. Just that little touch worked wonders. "Only if you're not planning to embarrass me by saying no."

He came closer, and his dick rubbed up against my ass. I'm not sure if it was intentional or whether he was pressed into closer quarters because of the increasingly longer line behind us. The woman in front of us, with five kids all anxious and hyped up about seeing the new Eddie Murphy movie on one of the other screens, was taking forever to order kiddie meals and boxes of candy. I was growing a bit impatient with her, but Sexy's dick stimulating my rear end didn't hurt matters any. It wasn't rock hard, but even in a semi-erect state, it showed a world of promise.

I moved back on it and started gyrating my hips a little. Okay, okay, I was acting like a chickenhead, a slut, a hoochie, but damn, it felt good.

"Sure you can be my date," I answered, turning my neck so I could see him. He gave me that helluva grin again. "By the way, I'm Maxine," I announced.

For five seconds, I had debated about using a fake name but opted against it in case something real came out of what I was about to do. You see, at that point I had already made up my mind that I was going to fuck the brother before I climbed back into Tank that night. Either that, or take him home with me and ride him all night long.

"I'm Orlando." He put his hands around my waist, and we started swaying back and forth, looking like long-term lovers having trouble keeping their hands off each other. "It's a pleasure to meet you, Maxine."

"The pleasure's all mine," I replied as the woman in front of us finally went on her way. The kids all looked happy but she looked stressed the hell out, the same way my sister looks whenever she takes my twin nephews on an outing.

I ordered my popcorn and Coke and insisted on paying for Orlando's Sprite and box of Red Hots since he sprung for my ticket. We gave the usher our tickets and located theater nine. It was packed, leaving us with two options: the front row or the two seats in the back set off by themselves and reserved for the handicapped. It was pitch-black back there, and the only reason we could even make out the seats was because people were still entering. There was no hesitation in my mind that we should sit in the back. I had major plans.

The previews were on as we got settled in. Orlando's long right leg was pressing against my thigh, so I decided to feel it up and see how muscular it was. Just as I suspected, the brother had been hitting somebody's gym with a vengeance. He decided to return the favor and felt my thigh, making me instantly wet.

The opening credits started, and I leaned over to whisper in his ear. "If I get scared, will you protect me?"

I could see his pearly whites, even in the dark. "Certainly. You want to sit on my lap?"

We both laughed. "Not right now, but maybe a little later." I got really bold then and stuck the tip of my tongue in his ear, darting it in and out quickly like swiping a card in an ATM machine. Even his inner ear was delectable, and that did it for me. "There is something I would like to do right about now, though."

He ran his fingers down the center of my breastbone and rubbed one of my nipples through the thin fabric of my dress. It grew hard enough to cut diamonds. If a man can play with my nipples just right, I'm his for the taking. Of course, fucking Orlando had already been predetermined before he went anywhere near my nipple.

"Can I have one of your Red Hots?" I asked him, a lightbulb going off in my head. He took me by the chin and slipped me his tongue, which I gratefully accepted. His tongue was thick and warm, and his kiss was powerful yet passionate. You can always tell a lot about a man from his kisses. If he is rough, he will be rough in bed. If he is selfish, just giving you a little peck and thinking that amounts to foreplay, then he will be selfish in bed. But if he is passionate, then he will give you some toe-curling action in bed.

He handed me the box of candy. "You can have whatever you want, and I mean that literally."

I took the box and started ripping the lid open. "And I'll take you up on your offer, literally."

I put three Red Hots in my mouth, immediately feeling the heat trickle down my throat, and got down on my knees between his legs. Luckily, there were no filled seats for about eight feet in front of us, and the people occupying them were totally caught up in the film, just as I had planned to be. I would just have to catch the special effects later. I was about to make some special effects of my own.

I undid the zipper on his jeans and dug inside for the pot of gold. It wasn't golden, but it was long and sleek, like a Jaguar convertible and just as enticing. I wasted no time licking around the head like it was a cone of Edy's Cookie Dough ice cream. Orlando flinched. Red Hots, Altoids, and mouthwash will do it every time.

After dipping my tongue into his slit, I made my way down the back side of his shaft, distributing kisses all over to let him know how much I wanted to please him. In fact, I looked up into his eyes and told him. "I want to please you."

He was speechless as I grabbed the base of his dick with one hand, caressing his balls through his jeans with the other and started taking him deep, inch by inch, until I had to relax my tonsils to take him all in. I could tell he was trying to keep his moans to a library-voice level. A couple of good ones did escape his lips when he came in my mouth about ten minutes later. The Red Hots weren't completely dissolved, but I could still tell he was sweet. That meant he was eating right, because a man's taste is directly related to his nutritional intake. If you don't believe me, feed a brother a Tex-Mex meal and go down on him. I guarantee you'll come up with refried beans breath.

I sat back down in the seat beside Orlando while he tried to regain some composure, wondering if he planned to return the favor. Indeed, he did! After a five-minute breather, Orlando pulled me up out of the chair and led me to the back wall of the theater, taking his Coke and the box of Red Hots with us. I didn't put up any objections when he lowered the straps of my dress, letting my breasts dangle freely. He took the lid off his cup, took out a piece of ice, put it in his mouth, and started sucking my nipples, first one at a time and then both together, pushing them inward with his strong hands.

I ran my fingers through his silky, black hair, glancing at the scene for a moment and seeing a gorilla appear out of nowhere on a hospital gurney. Mad cool, I thought to myself, but this breast-sucking action is a whole lot better.

Orlando made his way down to my belly button, lifting the bottom of my dress so he could get to it. I had to curtail a laugh because I'm extremely ticklish, and the ice cube in his mouth felt like something out of one of my wet dreams. He started pulling my white cotton panties down over my hips, and I slid out of my sandals so he could get them off easily. I thought he was going for another cube of ice, but he went for the box of Red Hots instead.

"Let me please you," he whispered as he lifted my left leg and placed it on his shoulder, lapping at my pussy lips in a fashion I had never experienced before. He buried his nose and mouth into my center, and I threw my head back in ecstasy, my toes curled up against his back.

"This is so crazy," I said to no one in particular. I was becoming delirious at the fact that I was letting a stranger suck all up on my thing in a crowded movie theater.

Orlando ate me out for a good long time, and I enjoyed every second of it. The brother didn't just have skills. He had skillz with a Z, meaning he worked some magic with his tongue.

I came in his mouth, and before I could take a single restorative breath, he stood up, lifted me against the wall, and invaded my sugary walls with his splendid dick. I wrapped my legs around his back, my arms around his shoulders, and settled in comfortably for the ride. He gave me his tongue again, which was a good thing because it helped to stifle my moans. I could feel his ball sack jiggling up and down against the bottom of my thighs as he picked up speed and caught a rhythm. Someone started screaming on the movie screen, and I couldn't take it any more. I broke our kiss and let out a scream of my own. I don't know for sure if someone heard me and turned around to be nosy. I really didn't care at that point.

One scream led to another, and the sex was so good that I dug my teeth into Orlando's neck and gave him what was sure to turn out to be one big-ass hickey. That must have set off something in him. A moment later, I felt him explode inside me. My own cum was trickling down my inner thighs onto the dark carpet.

Orlando stood there, holding me against the wall for a little while, both of us marveling at the events that had just taken place. All I could think about was taking him home with me, laying him down in my king-size waterbed, and riding him atop the waves for the rest of the weekend.

That's exactly what I did, too. I asked him to come home

with me. We didn't even stay for the rest of the movie. Once you miss the beginning, it's all water under the bridge anyway, and besides, Orlando promised to bring me back to see it the next day. We didn't make it to the theater the next day. We were still going at each other hard at my place.

JayQuan came over unannounced, banging on my door like he owned the joint. I didn't even answer. I told Orlando the truth, that I had been seeing someone but things had long fizzled out, and I needed a man whose wants and desires mirrored my own. That's when we sat down and had a long talk on my balcony over a fruit salad and a bottle of sparkling apple cider, listening to jazz music pump out of the stereo in my living room. As it turned out, Orlando and I have quite a lot in common; everything from our taste in music to clothes, food, and even cultural activities. More than that, I feel like I finally found a man who can stay around for the long haul. Sure, we didn't meet under the most romantic of circumstances, but he has made up for that over and over again during the past six months. Who knows what the future holds? All I know is that a night at the movies turned out to bring me many nights of pleasure, and any way you size that one up, everything comes up roses.

Damn, Sex While You Wash Your Drawers?

I was planning to stay home that night because I was pissed the hell off about my breakup with Trevor. I had to go out, though, and it wasn't like I was going clubbing or any shit like that. I was simply going to the coin laundry to wash some damn drawers. You know how it is when your panty supply gets down to the wire. When you are single, working twelve hours a day and living without the convenience of a washer and dryer up in the crib, you wait till the last minute and take about five baskets of clothes to the 'mat at one time.

That is what I was doing that night—getting my wardrobe straightened out. When I got to the 'mat, there was no one there except this one sistah with the most hardheaded set of twin boys I had ever seen in my life. How she managed to fold clothes and stay calm enough not to beat some ass was beyond me.

She was piling the kids and the laundry baskets of clean clothes into her minivan when he pulled up in a Mazda RX-7. I was sitting there chillin', reading an issue of *Essence* that was about fifty fucking years old I found in the torn-up and ragged collection of mags on the antique table in between the only two pleather chairs in the joint, when he got out of his ride.

My first instinct was, *playa*. Shit, aren't they all? My second instinct was, *foine*. The bruh made my one pair of previously fresh drawers, the ones I was wearing, instantly wet. Made my juices get to flowing. Know what I mean?

He started bringing his clothes in, and he was a typical bachelor. He had his shit in plastic trash bags and had one of those miniature boxes of laundry powder he probably paid too damn much for at the convenience store down the block.

"How you doing?" He gave me a holla while I was sitting there enjoying the view, a Coke, and a smile.

"Fine, and you?"

My southern drawl seemed to be ten times more profound than usual, and that shit only happens when I am horny. Trevor used to always laugh at my ass because I would start talking like a country bumpkin every time he started hitting it from the back.

He divided his clothes like a good little Boy Scout, separating the colors and then tossing them into three different washers.

One of the four dryers my clothes were occupying went off, and I got up to retrieve a rolling cart to move the clothes from the dryer to a laundry table.

He spoke to me again. "So, what's your name?"

I was not even trying to hear it. Foine or not, I was sick-da-hell of men and had sworn off the dick for at least three months. "I don't have a name."

He smirked at me. "Yeah, right!"

"You, bruh-man, are a stranger, and my momma told me never to talk to strangers."

I couldn't help but giggle as I said the shit, because I was sounding more like a four-year-old than a grown-ass woman.

"Hmmm, yeah! You better watch out for me. Late at night. Empty Laundromat. Full moon!" We both laughed.

"Your ass is silly!"

I got my clothes over to the table and started folding them up. I was getting kind of "shamed" when I noticed him watching me separate my bras from my panties and socks.

"Need some help?" He was looking my ass up and down like a bear eyeing a pot of honey. "I don't have shit to do at the moment but wait for my clothes to wash."

"Now why would I want your crusty hands all over my drawers? No telling where those things have been."

He walked closer to me, and my pussy starting throbbing. Why, I have no clue, but my pussy lips were jumping like two castanets. "You are too cute. Tell me your name."

"Hells naw! I am not telling you my name, and you sure as hell better not tell me yours, because I could care less."

"Really?"

He was standing so close to me by that time, I could feel his breath on my neck, and it smelled like peppermint. Fresh breath has always been a turn-on to me. That au naturel shit has to go.

"Yes, really."

I started folding my shit faster because my white lace panties were getting soaked, and I knew pussy juice would start trickling down the inside of my legs any second if I didn't get the foine-ass nucca the hell away from me.

I don't know what the telling signs were, but he knew I wanted his ass. He decided to go for it, and men who are sexually aggressive make my toes curl. I hate the nuccas who look dumbfounded when you tell them to pop a tit in their mouth or suck on your pussy. Some men can't deal with uninhibited sistahs.

He was not fronting though, and my ass cheeks started throbbing when he brushed his dick up against me. He was about five inches taller than me, so his dick was pressing up against the small of my back. Felt damn good, too. Of course, I was not about to tell him that.

"What the hell do you think you are doing?"

"Helping you with your laundry."

"Bullshit!"

He reached around me, with one arm on each side, and started folding up my panties. I froze. "You know, you forgot a pair?"

"Huh?" I was lost like a virgin in a whorehouse.

"You forgot to wash a pair of your panties."

"Bruh, you trippin'. How you know my panty count and shit?" I turned my head toward him and looked up at him.

"You forgot to wash the pair you have on. Let me help you take them off."

He strategically moved his hands from the laundry table to my breasts and started palming them bad boys. Perfect fit, I might add. Like a hand to a glove. Then came the tricky part. I stood there debating whether I should stay on my dick starvation diet and push his hands away or give in to my desires and enjoy the ride.

I looked out onto the street in front of the Laundromat, and there was not a soul in sight. There we were, exposed because the entire front of the place was glass. At that moment, something popped into my head. I decided it was time to stop "freaming" and start "freaking." For those of you who don't know, "freaming" is dreaming of doing freaky shit your ass would never have the nerve to do while you are awake. I pondered over it and decided it was time to get jiggy with it.

I looked at him. He looked at me. I whispered, "Fuck the bullshit!" and it was on. We started tonguing the hell out each other, and he had a thick tongue. Just the way I like them, especially when the tongue is licking my other pair of lips.

I caressed the back of his neck with one hand and his juicy ass with the other as we kissed. His kisses reminded me of the first time I ever kissed a boy back in junior high school. They were passionate and yet a bit rushed.

He turned me around slowly by my hips as our tongues continued to intertwine. Then he started caressing my nipples, which were now very erect and protruding through the sheer material of my spaghetti-strap sundress. That was the moment I knew I was going to fuck that man every which way from Sunday, public place or not.

He reached underneath my dress, and I gratefully spread my legs so he could get two fingers into the elastic of my black lace panties and into the sanctuary of my wet, pulsating pussy.

His fingers felt like they were performing a sensual dance on my clit, and my juices started accumulating.

"Let's take these off." I didn't argue with his suggestion and even helped him along. After they were completely off, he lifted them up to his mouth and sucked my pussy juice off the crotch. Damn, I was just *too* through.

With my panties still in his mouth, he picked me up and sat my ass on top of one of the washing machines that was on the rinse cycle. It was there that he fucked my ass royally.

He ripped his dick out of his pants so fast that I didn't even see him unfasten them. Then he took a condom out of his pocket, ripped it open with his teeth and snatched it out the package. I wanted to laugh because he was trying to seem intimidating, and the shit was not even working.

"You think you can handle all this dick?"

I glanced down at it. It was *huge*, but I wasn't about to give him the satisfaction of letting him know I was truly impressed. "It is rather large, but I've seen *and had* bigger dicks than that inside me."

He winced at my comment and jimmied the condom onto his dick. It barely fit, and I began to get a bit nervous. "Well, you may have had bigger dicks, but you've never had any man fuck you as hard as I'm about to fuck you right now."

"Humph, promises, promises."

He rammed his dick in me and ran his thick tongue up my neck. "How's this for promises?"

"It's a start," I barely managed to say—his dick inside me took my breath away.

The vibrations from the machine added to the experience, because it felt like someone was fondling my ass at the same time.

He went fast at first and then slowed down, gazing in my eyes and planting small kisses on my chin. "Admit it," he said about three minutes into the act.

"Admit what?"

"That this is some good-ass dick." I didn't say a word, so he started going in and out so fast that my inner thighs started trembling. "Now admit it."

I still would not say the words he wanted, so he took his dick out, pulled me down off the machine, and turned me around. My stomach hit the cold surface of the machine, and he kneeled down, spread my ass cheeks open, and started licking the crease of my ass.

"Ooh, you're so nasty!" I exclaimed, loving every second of it.

"You're right." He slapped me hard on the ass. "Now admit you haven't had a man like me before."

I smirked and then lied. "I've had plenty."

He stood back up and then stuck the tip of his dick on my anus. "You talk a bunch of shit. I wonder what you'll say if I stick this all in you."

"I'll say the same thing I just said. That I've had plenty."

"Then get ready to say it," he stated with disdain before sticking it all in me at once.

"Oh, shit!" I yelled out in pleasure.

He pumped his dick around in my ass until he came a few minutes later.

"So what do you have to say now?" he asked as he deflated inside of me.

I gulped before answering, "Okay, I admit it. You have some good-ass dick."

We both broke out in laughter and fell to the floor just as the washer went off.

I never saw the bruh again. Although, it wouldn't have been such a bad thing. It just wasn't in the cards, but at least for one night I actually did something totally off the chain. I was telling my best friend about it the following weekend, and once I finished relating the story, she looked at me in amazement and exclaimed, "Damn, girl! Sex while you wash your drawers? You're my damn shero!"

Full-Time Assistant, Part-Time Freak

I have always been an avid believer in self-confidence. My mother taught me at an early age that African-American women need a great deal of self-confidence to endure all the bullshit that will be thrown at us throughout our lives—bullshit from employers who think we are beneath them. Bullshit from men who think we need them to the point where we are willing to accept just about anything for the privilege of having a man. A shared man. A shared dick. Bullshit in general.

Self-confidence is a necessity, but arrogance is something different altogether. Larabee Blue is arrogant. Arrogant and fake. Unfortunately, she is also my boss. Larabee is an actress. A well-known actress. In fact, she gets highly insulted whenever someone calls her a "star." She wants to be addressed as a "superstar" or not at all. Absolutely ridiculous!

I put up with Larabee for a few reasons. Being her assistant pays extremely well and it beats the hell out of waiting tables until my big break comes along. Then there are the fringe benefits: getting to cruise around in stretch limos day and night, getting to wear designer clothing, and getting to meet influential people. Hollywood is all about networking. Who you know is more important than what you know. I am convinced that one of these days I will come across someone who will recognize my special qualities and give me an opportunity to prove myself.

I have had a few roles. Nothing major. I played a barmaid in *Roughnecks,* one of those rapper-produced high-budget, low-level-of-intelligence flicks. I also played a drug addict who overdosed in the emergency room on *Central Hospital*. That was a great show until it bit the dust after the first season, like the majority of television dramas featuring African Americans in lead roles. The role that garnered me the most recognition was playing a bank robber on *True Crime Experiences.* While that show is strictly comprised of reenactments, people were staring at me on the streets for at least three months after the episode aired. One erratic, half-senile woman actually flagged down a squad car to turn me in. She just knew she was making a citizen's arrest. It took me more than an hour to convince them that I had just been acting and did not have outstanding warrants looming over my head.

The sad part about all of this is that I know I can act. I was born to act. I realize a lot of people say that very thing, but I am for real. I came out of the womb acting and never stopped. Larabee, on the flip side, does not know the first thing about real acting. She has simply slept her way to the top. Even with all the horrid reviews her films get, the studio execs still hook her up with incredible roles just to see her turn them into sideshow performances. They do not care if she fucks up as long as she fucks them.

I know I should not be talking about her like this. After all, she does butter my toast. I cannot help it, though. She is rude, she is selfish, and she is self-centered. Case in point: Hewitt, her boyfriend. Larabee and Hewitt first started dating in high school, back when she was still Constance Sherman from Grand Rapids, Michigan. People called her Piggy in junior high and high school because she had a predilection for Krispy Kreme doughnuts and McDonald's french fries. Even back then, in her pre Larabee Blue days, Hewitt fell in love with her when other boys would not give her the time of day. I have heard this story a hundred times from her. How he would take long walks with her and tell her that she was beautiful. How he would make her paper roses and rub her feet after she had practically passed out from walking around the school track in an effort to drop the weight. How he would call her on the phone late at night so he could listen to her breathe as he fell asleep.

With all of that being said, you would think that Larabee treats him like royalty. Not! She treats him like something off the bottom of her shoe. Damn shame, too, because he is such a sweetheart. Even to this day, he treats her like a princess. I guess that is why I fell in love with him.

There, I said it. I, Tanley Justine Meade, am hopelessly in love with Hewitt Michael Banks. Larabee does not deserve to drink his bathwater. Yet and still, I know that he loves her, he has always loved her, and he will always love her. I am not living in a fantasy world where I envision him leaving her for me. That will never happen, but I did spend one night in heaven. I did spend one night in his arms.

"Tanley, have you seen that red dress I bought on Rodeo Drive last week?" Larabee was running around her bedroom, which was larger than most people's apartments, throwing things into a suitcase, when I came in. "I want to take it with me."

"Don't you think it will be too cold in the mountains for that?" I asked her, recalling the dress that covered up less than 20 percent of her body.

She stopped in her tracks and gave me a perplexed look. "The mountains?"

"Yes, the mountains. You're packing for Denver, right?"

"Denver?"

"Yes, Denver," I repeated. "You're meeting Hewitt at the ski lodge in Denver to celebrate his birthday. Remember?"

Larabee plopped down on her bed and threw her hands dramatically in the air. Even that was sorry acting. "Oh, shit!"

My sentiments exactly. Her stupid ass had once again forgotten something important. That much was obvious.

"Tanley, why didn't you remind me?" she stated accusingly.

I tried to hide my disdain, turned away from her, and walked over to one of the picture windows to gaze out over the ocean.

"Larabee, I wrote it down in your planner. I write everything down in your planner."

"Well, whatever," she lashed out in disgust. "You still could have mentioned it last night or even this morning."

I could not believe she was trying to blame me for her forgetfulness. Then again, I should not have been the least bit surprised, since I get blamed for 99 percent of her mistakes.

I decided to try to be nice about it. "I apologize."

Larabee sighed. "You should apologize. Apology accepted. Now help me find that red dress."

She disappeared into her massive walk-in closet, and I followed her.

"Larabee, like I said, it will be too cold up there for that."

She ignored me and kept sliding hangers from side to side, conducting a search for the dress. Finally, after noticing that I was not attempting to help, she glared at me. "Are you going to help me or not? This is what you get paid for?"

"You're not going to Denver, are you?"

"No, I'm not going to Denver," she replied mockingly. "I have other plans. Major plans. You better go pack, because you're going with me."

"I have this weekend off. Since you had plans for Hewitt's birthday, I made plans of my own, and they can't be canceled."

I was lying. The only plans I had were to take in a movie alone and grab some takeout on my way home to watch *Oz* on HBO.

"Excuse me, Tanley, but you are going with me. I have to fly to New York to meet with Sheridan Rafte from that new studio, and you are not about to mess this up for me."

"How could I possibly mess it up for you? Even if I went, you wouldn't let me say two words in the meeting anyway."

Larabee knew I was right. She is so intimidated by the possibility of someone becoming intrigued by me that she rarely lets me utter a word in her power meetings. She still did not appreciate my comments about it, though.

"I don't know what's up with you, Tanley, but your attitude is unacceptable."

I was definitely being bitchy, but that was because I could not believe that she was going to kick Hewitt to the curb and go to New York instead. Even though biting my tongue would have been more appropriate, I decided to voice my opinion.

"Are you really going to let Hewitt sit up in Denver waiting on you? You promised him that you would spend his birthday with him. This is his big one, remember? He's turning thirty."

"I know how old he's turning!" Larabee stormed at me. "He's my man, and we're the same damn age!" She glanced into her full-length dressing mirror and frowned, fingering the skin around her eyes like she was looking for wrinkles. "I can't believe I'll be thirty in three months."

I can't believe it either, I thought. She was acting more like a fifteen-year-old.

"You're right."

"Excuse me?" I asked in disbelief. I had never heard those words escape her lips.

"I said, you're right. I can't do that to Hewitt. Poor baby. He'll be devastated if he ends up there all alone."

I grinned with delight. "So you want me to start repacking your bag with some warmer clothes."

"Actually, I want you to go pack your bag with warm clothes."

"Come again?"

"I can't miss out on the opportunity in New York. This could be it for me. My Oscar-winning role. The script is out of this world, and all the big names are competing for it. I have first dibs, the first audition, and I am not giving that up for anything."

"Or anyone, apparently," I stated sarcastically.

Larabee came so close to me that I could feel her breath on my face.

"I know you think I treat Hewitt badly, Tanley."

She stood there like she was waiting for me to disagree with her. I did not say a single word. I just leered at her.

"I'm going to make this up to him. I swear I will, but I can't go to Denver tonight. I just can't."

"I understand," I lied.

"I need a favor." She placed her hands on my shoulders, and it took every ounce of self-control for me not to push her off me. "Could you please go to Denver and give Hewitt my present?"

"Sure."

I did not hesitate. The movie, takeout, and yes, even *Oz*, could wait. I would just have to catch the rerun.

Larabee released me and giggled. "I can always count on you."

"That you can," I agreed. "That you can. I better go pack."

"Great! We can just have my ticket switched over to you."

"That shouldn't be a problem." I was halfway out the closet door when I realized something. "So where is the gift for Hewitt?"

Larabee giggled again. She was getting on my damn nerves.

"I don't have it yet. I need you to stop someplace on the way and pick him up something."

I rolled my eyes. I did not care if she caught that move or not.

"What do you want me to get him?" I asked.

She got lost in thought for a few seconds. "I know! How about a bomb-ass watch? Men love watches. Especially ones that cost a grip."

That was the lamest idea I had ever heard. Even I knew that Hewitt wears a watch that his grandfather bequeathed to him and would never trade it for the world. Damn shame that she did not think of that.

"I'll take care of it, Larabee."

"Great! Just put it on my credit at Saks or wherever."

I could not take another second of her. When I got to my room down the hall, less than a quarter of the size of hers, I slammed the door. "Selfish bitch!"

My plane landed in Denver at eight. Hewitt had flown in that morning and checked in to the lodge. During the flight, it dawned on me that I did not have a room reservation, and the possibility existed that I would have to search for a place to stay or fly back that same night. After I dropped off his gift, my job would be complete.

The cabdriver practically drove me insane on the way to the lodge—a raunchy old white man that wanted to take a walk on the wild side and bed a sister. I wished him well in his pursuit of one who would lower her standards enough to go there with him, but assured him that I was not the one. He was still trying hard, so I went there. I told him that if my yeast infection was not causing me so much pain, we could make a run for it right there. He lost interest suddenly, cranked up his country music station, and clamped his mouth shut. Thank goodness!

When I asked for Hewitt Banks at the registration desk, the sister behind the counter lit up like a Christmas tree.

"He's been expecting you! *Gurl,* you are lucky! That man is fine!"

I was about to explain to her that Hewitt was not my man, but then I decided that basking in her compliment felt kind of nice, so I said, "Thank you."

Besides, she was speaking the truth and nothing but the truth. Hewitt is fine. He is about six-two, with a sprinter's body and the smoothest sepia skin. I know at least half a dozen women personally who would kill for his eyelashes, and another three or four who would kill for his charcoal eyes.

Those eyes were the first thing that met me when he answered the door to Suite 518. The quick alteration in them from joy to disappointment spoke volumes.

"Tanley, what are you doing here?" Hewitt asked, feigning a smile. He took a step out into the hall and looked both ways. "Where's Larabee? Is she on her way up?" Before I could answer, he rattled on. "Ah, she's probably down in the lobby being bombarded by fans wanting autographs. The price of being a star."

"Superstar," I corrected him. "She prefers to be called a superstar."

We both laughed.

"Can I come in, Hewitt?" I inquired, realizing that he was blocking the doorway.

"Sure, my mistake." He moved aside and then followed me

in, leaving the door ajar for a lover who was halfway across the country, more worried about getting a movie role.

I turned to face him. He looked incredible in a patterned wool sweater and denim jeans.

"Happy thirtieth birthday, Hewitt!"

"Thank you."

He came forward and gave me a hug. I seized the opportunity and gave him a kiss on the cheek. He blushed.

I decided to get the bad news over with. "Hewitt, Larabee isn't coming."

He sat down in the nearest chair and buried his head in his hands. How could Larabee be such a fool?

I sat on the arm of the chair and gently rubbed his back, forming a lie in my mind. Then I decided that he deserved the truth. He needed to know how disrespectful and self-centered Larabee truly is.

"Where is she?"

"She went to New York to audition for a movie."

I could feel his entire body tense up. "She couldn't miss one fucking audition? She makes five million a movie. Today's my birthday. My special day, and where the hell is she? Off trying to make a lousy buck."

I could not debate his point. He was absolutely right. "Well, apparently she is convinced that this will be her Oscar-winning performance," I said snidely, knowing good and damn well that hovercrafts would take the place of automobiles first. I unzipped my duffel bag, pulled out a box, and handed it to him. "Larabee apologizes for not having time to wrap it."

He popped the box open with fury and removed the velvet case inside. He opened it and saw the expensive watch that I had purchased as Larabee had instructed.

"She thinks that a watch will make up for this?" He got up

and started pacing the floor. "I just don't understand her. Where does she get off trying to buy me?"

I agreed but did not comment. I just let him get all of his anger out.

"Larabee knew I made these plans months ago, and she promised to be here. How many times does a person turn thirty?"

"Once," I answered. I walked up behind him and touched his shoulder. "I really am sorry, Hewitt. I know how you must feel, and while I realize that I am a sorry substitution, I am glad that I could be here to wish you a happy birthday."

He turned to look at me, and I could tell that he was fighting back tears.

"You're always so sweet, Tanley." He put his arms around my waist, and it felt so comfortable, so natural. "I do appreciate you coming up here. You probably had plans, and Larabee made you break them."

I had no business saying it, but I did anyway. "Hewitt, there is no place I would rather be." I cradled his face in my hands and gazed deeply into his eyes. "Happy birthday, Hewitt."

Things must have seemed a little too natural to me, because a second later, I was offering him my tongue. He shocked me by accepting it. Our kiss was brief but powerful, and I am not sure which one of us broke it first, but he was the first to voice an apology.

"I'm sorry, Tanley. I shouldn't have done that."

"I kissed you, Hewitt."

"I know, but I kissed you back."

I pulled away and sat back down. "It's okay. We just got caught up in the moment."

He eyed me seductively. At least, his eyes were turning me on, intentional or not. "For what it's worth, I enjoyed it."

I blushed. "Me, too."

We both laughed.

"Hewitt, can you call the front desk and see if they have any vacancies? I really hate to head back tonight, and I'm not altogether sure there are any more flights leaving out."

He sat down beside me and took my hand. "Forget about the vacancies, and forget about planes. Today is my thirtieth birthday, and I intend to celebrate it, with or without Larabee. She isn't going to ruin this for me."

I caressed his hand gently. "So what are you saying?"

"I'm saying that I have an entire evening planned, and I would be eternally grateful if you would spend it with me."

I decided to get bold. "Does that include the sex you had planned?"

He grinned. "What makes you think I had sex planned?"

"A romantic ski lodge. A birthday celebration. A man and a woman. Common sense."

Hewitt fell out laughing. "Well, maybe I had a little sex planned."

He looked slightly uncomfortable, so I decided to let him off the hook. "I was just joking about the sex, but I am starving. Was there a meal somewhere in your plans?"

"Yes, there is a meal, but the night skiing was going to come first."

Was he for real?

"Night skiing?" Now it was my turn to be uncomfortable. "I have never been skiing before."

He stood and yanked me up off the sofa. "Now is as good a time as any to learn."

"At night? When I can't see the trees I am about to plummet into headfirst?" I asked jokingly.

"I won't let you run into a tree. I promise." He put his hand around my waist, and his touch aroused me. "And I always keep my promises, unlike Ms. Larabee."

I was really hoping he would stop saying her name. That did not arouse me.

Twenty minutes later, I was in the bathroom of the suite, squeezing my ass into the ski suit Hewitt had brought up with him for Larabee. She and I are about the same size, but I have ass for days and she has a pancake one. She keeps saying that she is going to get injections. I cannot picture getting silicon injected into any part of my body, but I would not put anything past her.

I glanced at myself in the mirror. "Okay, Tanley. You can do this. You get to spend time with Hewitt, *alone*. That is the most important thing."

When I came out of the bathroom, he was waiting for me, looking sexy as hell in a red suit that matched the one I was wearing.

"Tanley, I don't think you can fit Larabee's ski boots, so we'll rent some."

"That's fine," I told him. "Are you sure this isn't dangerous?"

"Life is about taking risks." He held out his hand to me. "Come get risky with me."

I would have preferred to stay in the suite and get frisky with him, but risky would just have to suffice, so I took his hand.

Somehow we managed to make it to the top of one of the slopes. When we got on the ski lift, I started screaming and almost fell off. People were laughing their heads off at me. Hewitt calmed me down, and I held onto him for dear life the rest of the way up. Even though it was freezing outside, I could feel the warmth of his body through his suit. I could only imagine how warm he would be inside me. My mind was truly in the gutter.

We skied for an hour and a half. Much to my surprise, I had the time of my life. It was so much fun, and I knew from the first time I glided down a hill, even though I fell on my ass twice, that I was hooked.

Hewitt said that he wanted to show me his "special place." It turned out to be a cave on the side of the mountain with icicles hanging from the rocky interior. It was completely deserted.

"How did you find this place?" I inquired, completely in awe of its beauty. "This looks like something out of a movie."

"So do you."

"Excuse me?"

"You look like something out of a movie." He knocked my ski cap gently with his glove. "Any new roles coming your way?"

Now that was something I really did not care to discuss. However, I was flattered that he was even interested.

"No, not really. I went to a couple of auditions last month, but nothing really panned out. Larabee keeps me so busy that I have a hard time making a lot of the auditions."

He looked angry. "Just tell Larabee that you have to take the time off! She should be able to understand that. She wasn't born a star."

I waved my finger in his face. "Superstar."

He chuckled. "Yeah, whatever."

"Hewitt, can I ask you a question?"

"Certainly."

"Before we kissed tonight, had you ever thought about me?"

"Yes," he replied quickly.

"Really?"

"Tanley, you are an extremely attractive sister. I wouldn't be human if I could spend so much time around you and not ponder the possibilities."

"What type of possibilities?"

"You know. Just wondering what you are like sexually. What it would feel like to hold you."

I have never considered myself to be a backstabber, but after hearing those words flow out of Hewitt's lips, I could not help myself. I moved closer to him and got lost in his eyes.

"You know, Hewitt, I always told myself that if the opportunity ever arose to be alone with you, to be intimate with you, that I would not hesitate. Not even for a second."

I expected him to tell me to get a grip on reality and start professing his love for Larabee. He did not.

He asked, "So what are you saying? Exactly?"

"I'm saying that I want to be with you tonight. Just for tonight. No one ever has to know." I removed my right glove and started caressing his dick. "I have often wondered about you, too. Today is your birthday, and it's almost over, so what do you say? Let's make tonight special."

If there was any hesitation in his eyes, I did not see it. Hewitt drew me into his arms and started tonguing the hell out of me. I gratefully reciprocated. It was freezing in the cave, but it instantly heated up as our passion grew. No man had ever kissed me with such conviction, and my mind wandered to Larabee for a brief second. What a fool!

Hewitt unzipped my ski jacket and slowly pressed it over my shoulders, removing it and tossing it on the frozen ground. He palmed my breasts, broke the kiss, and pulled the edge of my turtleneck down so he could suck on my neck. I was in heaven.

I maintained my pace, stroking his dick though his ski pants in rhythm. I winced in pleasure when he bit on my neck gently, undoubtedly leaving a mark that I would cherish until it disappeared a few days later. I pulled away for a second so I could gaze in his eyes; they were so mesmerizing.

"Are you sure about this, Hewitt?" I asked, touching his cheek.

Hewitt took my hand and kissed my fingertips. "I've never been surer."

"What about Larabee?"

He sighed. "Larabee and I have been together for a long time. That's common knowledge, but over time, she's changed. She used to be this sweet, compassionate woman full of life and aspirations. While she still has aspirations, none of them seem to include me anymore. All she cares about is her career. She and I had major plans, but somewhere along the way, she forgot about them."

He was so sincere, and all I could manage to say was, "I understand."

"A man like me has needs also," he continued. "Sure, it's great being known as Larabee's man most of the time. Every man in the free world is mad jealous, but they don't see the flip side of what it's like to date a star."

I waved my finger in his face and grinned.

He chuckled. "I mean, superstar," he said, correcting his mistake. "But, on the real tip, I have needs, and Larabee just isn't fulfilling them right now. Not from where I'm standing."

"I don't want to cause any friction."

He unzipped my ski overalls. "Well, I want to cause some friction. If you get my drift."

I bit my bottom lip. "Oh, yeah, I get your drift."

As far as I was concerned, we had discussed the issue at hand and both made an informed decision to continue with our little escapade. Like they say, one man's garbage is another man's treasure. Larabee didn't appreciate Hewitt, but I adored and appreciated everything about him. For that reason alone, I wanted to give him something special that he would never forget.

Don't get me wrong. I was freezing my ass off in that cave, but I ended up in my birthday suit, ready to give Hewitt his birthday present. We made a pallet on the icy ground out of our suits and jackets and made beautiful love.

The way Hewitt sucked on my nipples gave me an orgasm,

and that was rather scary, because that had never happened to me before. Normally, I'm lucky if a man can even make me cum with his dick, but Hewitt worked his magic.

After pushing my breasts together and partaking of them both at the same time, Hewitt licked a trail down the center of my stomach and landed it between my legs, which were eagerly spread and waiting. He traced the outside of my pussy lips and then the inside of them. I felt myself cumming all over again. Damn, I was going from a nonorgasmic sister to a multiorgasmic one in less than an hour.

He flicked his tongue at my hardened clit, which made me moan with delight. I massaged the back of his head to encourage him to proceed. Damn, did he! The brother deserved a medal, plaque, or some sort of recognition for being so profound at eating coochie.

Once I came for the third time, I screamed out, "I want you now!"

Hewitt didn't hesitate with giving me the dick. He was holding about seven inches of pure almond joy. I felt his dick enter my walls and push up toward my belly button.

"Umm, it's so damn good," he whispered in my ear. "I've waited so long for this."

I gazed into his eyes. "Have you really?"

"Yes, I have. It was just an awkward situation."

I snickered. It was still an awkward situation, but it was all good. Here I was, fucking my boss's boyfriend after she asked me to deliver a present to him. Well, he did get her present, and now he was getting mine.

He lifted my legs and placed them on his shoulders so he could go deeper. I grabbed onto his ass to aid him in his efforts. I wanted as much of him in me as I could possibly get. Even with him working his mojo on me, it wasn't enough so . . .

. . . I lowered my legs and flipped him over on his back. He shivered and let out a small scream when his back hit the ice beside our little pallet.

"Want to move over?" I asked.

He looked at me and then grinned. "No, actually, now that the initial shock is over, I'm kinda feeling this."

I picked up a small chunk of ice off the ground and rubbed it over his nipples. "Are you feeling this?"

"Aw, yes!"

My knees were so frozen that I could barely feel them as I tightened my pussy on his dick. "Are you feeling that?"

"Umm, hmm. It feels fantastic. Are you about to take a little ride, Tanley?"

"No," I replied. "I'm about to take a big ride."

I grabbed onto his neck with my free hand and continued to rub the ice all over his chest with the other one. He reached for a piece of ice and started rubbing it all over my ass. That only enticed me more as I gripped his dick inside me and moved up and down with a vengeance. He rubbed the ice up and down my spine and then over my breasts. I could feel my cum trickling down onto him, and then I felt him explode inside me.

After our bodies stopped shaking from the unified satisfaction, we tumbled back onto the pallet in laughter. We were totally spent, and it showed. We lay there for a good thirty minutes, buck-naked in the cave. Somehow, we managed to put our clothes back on with frozen fingers and make our way back down to the lodge.

There, we made love for the rest of the night in the Jacuzzi. We went from the cold conditions of the cave to the steam of the Jacuzzi. How therapeutic!

The next day Hewitt started guilt-tripping. I attempted to reassure him, letting him know that I had no intention of revealing our indiscretions to Larabee. After all that shit he talked the night before about her mistreating him, I knew he still loved her and would try to make it work.

Now, a year later, he is still trying to make it work, and she is still treating him like something on the bottom of one of her two-hundred-dollar shoes. She didn't even get the part that she gave up his birthday to audition for, much less win an Oscar for it. In fact, her career has started to go downhill—no one stays on top of their game forever. New young fresh meat comes along, and those women are just as willing to give up the ass to get parts. Studio executives get antsy for something different, and suddenly women who are on top end up as has-beens.

As for me, I'm still her assistant, but not for long. I auditioned for a part last week and got a callback. It is a rather major role, and if it comes through, I will have enough to live comfortably for a few years. Even if I don't get it, I have had enough. It is time to move on. I can't stand to see Hewitt following behind Larabee like a lovesick puppy. Every now and then I catch him staring at me. I know that he remembers our night, and in another world, in another lifetime, he would have been mine. But we are in this world, in this lifetime, and I can't wait around for him to get a wake-up call.

I have my eye on this young brother, a fellow thespian, who I met waiting tables at a local jazz club. If I don't get the role, maybe I'll get a job there and see what kind of magic he and I might work up in the kitchen after hours. You never know!

Gettin' Buck Wild

There is something to be said for being freaky. Sure, you run certain risks by throwing it all out there and putting your ass on the line. However, life is short, and as they always say, "This isn't a dress rehearsal." That's why I made a life-altering decision to get buck wild.

"Buck wild" is a term that goes back a ways. I'm not quite sure when I heard someone say it for the first time, but it was definitely sometime during my youth. Since I'm thirty-five now, it was probably in the early eighties when my friend Keisha yelled it out at a party.

It was a house party. Not many people have house parties these days, since people have become violent or drug addicts or both. The average person won't just allow people to fall up in their crib to get their groove on. It simply isn't safe. But back then house parties were the end-all and be-all. If someone popular was having one and you missed it for any reason (baby-sitting siblings, doing a term paper, sick as all hell), people talked junk about you the following Monday morning at school.

Anyway, we were at this dude Aaron's house up in the Palisades. His place was slamming, too. About 75 percent of the house was completely glass, and they had this indoor pool that was hittin'. The pool made the party ten times better than a normal party because it meant that sistahs could show what they were workin' with in brand-spanking-new bikinis.

My shit was tight. I had on this red number that my mother bought me after I begged and pleaded for damn near an hour. She was always such a stickler for money. Daddy made a grip. No, make that a grip and a half, but Mommy always pretended like we were dirt poor and digging in trash cans for dinner. Amazingly, she always came up with some cash when she spotted an expensive-ass outfit she wanted.

The DJ was mixing his ass off that night at Aaron's. Back then, Michael Jackson was still the shit, and Prince's ass was still making sistahs give up the drawers with a quickness in parked cars. What sistah wouldn't get horny if a dude started singing "Do Me Baby" into her ear?

I must admit that sexy-ass music would make me give up some sex faster than just about any other thing a brotha could possibly throw at me back then. Candles and back rubs were one thing, but slow music, aka "fucking music," would make me want to spread 'em.

It was during such a song that night that Keisha yelled out, "Everybody, let's get buck wild!"

All the lights suddenly went out, and people started getting their freak on with whomever. I had the host in my arms at the moment, and Aaron was all that and a bag of chips. He had this rock-hard body, a six-pack stomach, and the prettiest eyes I'd ever seen on a man. He and I had been cool together but never really hung together outside of school. Still, with the music going, with the bomb-ass party in the bomb-ass house, I was feeling him something hard. And yes, something was hard. His big-ass dick was like a brick. I felt it rubbing up against my coochie, and instant thoughts of fucking flew through my head.

"Essence, you're so soft, Boo," Aaron stated seductively over the music. "Damn, I've never felt anything this soft."

"Word?" I asked him, even though I knew it was true. I used more buffing soap, skin moisturizers, and body oil than any other sistah on the planet, hands down. I knew my shit was on.

"Word."

I couldn't really see what everyone else was doing, but I heard a lot of splashing going on over in the pool, and there were a shitload of moans. Somebody was straight-up fucking up in that piece. I was determined to be next.

"Aaron, why don't you show me your bedroom?" I suggested.

"What do you need to see my bedroom for?"

Was he silly or what? "I want to see your bedroom because I want to fuck." I decided to come on out with it. "You do know what fucking is, don't you?"

He laughed. "Oh, I know what fucking is. I know how to fuck a girl so hard that she sends my mother flowers the next day for giving birth to such a stud."

I laughed. "You're a nut!"

"Seriously though, bedrooms are for sleeping. Let's do something different."

"Something like what?"

He let go of me and disappeared in the darkness. I felt stupid just standing there. A minute later the lights were back on, and boy, what a sight! At least a dozen people were all over the room on chairs, on the floor, or in the pool screwing. I spotted Keisha over in the corner on her knees with a dick in her mouth.

Aaron reappeared and took a position in the middle of the floor before making an announcement. "Hold up, peeps! Every weekend we hang out and do whatever. Tonight let's make it different. Instead of everyone doing their own thing separately, let's do like those white folks in the porn flicks and have an orgy."

Everyone grew silent. Everyone stopped fucking. Everyone was speechless.

Aaron scanned the room for me. "Come here, Essence."

Maybe I was just feeling daring that night or had lost my common sense, but I went over to him and took his hand.

"Essence and I are going to start it out, and then the rest of you just join in."

"Aaron, are you on something?" I asked, totally serious. "I never agreed to this."

"I know, but take a walk on the wild side. Let's get buck wild!"

That was it. The beginning of my "habit." Aaron and I fucked right there in front of everyone, and gradually they all joined in—this time with the lights on. Before I knew it, I had fucked at least eight boys and two girls. The next day I was so ashamed. The day after that I decided that I wanted to do it again, and I did. Again and again. Aaron's parents were out of town a lot, so most of the time we had the orgies at his place, especially since it was the most slamming house in the vicinity anyway.

Now that I'm all grown up, my "habit" continues. I love having sex in the open. I love having sex with numerous partners. I love having sex, *period*.

Last weekend, I had the ultimate experience. I let twenty-nine men run a train on me and starred in my first porno flick. By the tenth man, my pussy felt like it was on fire because the rubber from the condoms I made them wear was irritating me. I kept going, though. I had a goal, and I was determined to meet it. After five hours, I did, and the film will be out on DVD next month.

Keisha and I are still hanging tough. In about a month, we are going down to the islands to Sex Me Down Village and getting buck wild. I hear the shit is off the hook, and I can hardly wait. Of course, I hope my husband doesn't find out.

Yes, you heard me right. I'm married, and so is Keisha, but hey, our husbands are not laying the pipe the way we need it to be laid, so we handle our business in other ways. Besides, even if my husband Steve, who I love dearly, was fucking me right, I know he would never do it in public, and I need that from time to time. I'm not concerned about him seeing the porno because he doesn't watch them. Some of his raunchy friends might, but they would never recognize me because I was wearing a wig and a mask.

I often do disguises, and it works like a charm. Case in point, one time I fucked one of my husband's closest friends, and he had no idea it was me. Chad was hanging out in this hip-hop club. I'm not too big on that type of music, but those clubs are wonderful for picking up young bucks who are young, dumb, and full of cum. The kind that don't ask you silly questions like "Are you married?" or "Can I see you again?" They recognize a one-night stand for what it is.

Anyway, Chad was getting his drink on and acting like the nasty whore that he is. I've never liked him because I always felt he might eventually be a negative influence on Steve. Now, I can cheat, but if I ever catch Steve cheating, hell hath no fury and all that jazz.

I was wearing tinted glasses and a sandy blond wig that night. He was drunk as shit and probably wouldn't have recognized me without the disguise. I don't know what made me do it, other than the dangerous possibility of getting busted. I studied Chad for about twenty minutes until I could ascertain that he was definitely alone. Then I walked up behind him and whispered in his ear. "Wanna fuck?" I asked in an island accent that I had polished over the years.

He turned around and drank me in with his eyes. The skintight black dress I had on was bangin'.

"Don't I know you?"

"No, but you can get to know me."

"I'm not used to giving up the dick on demand to women I meet in clubs. Especially ones that don't say hello first."

I smirked at him, knowing good and well he was a male whore and would fuck just about anything on two legs. "Your loss then, baby. I'll just go find me a *real* man who can give me some *real* dick. I don't have time for silly little games."

I started to walk away, but he grabbed my elbow. "Silly little games, huh?" He gripped my ass. "I've got your silly little games. If you don't watch out, you won't be able to walk tomorrow."

I faced him and pouted, then rubbed my thumb over my nipple. "Promises, promises."

Chad took my hand and headed for the exit. "Come with me, with your fine self."

We went outside and headed for the parking lot. It was late summer, and the heat was excruciating, which is why I didn't have on much of anything. The wig and the glasses were making me sweat, though.

I had no idea why I was out there with Chad. After all, I hated him.

"Where are we going?" I asked, still utilizing the accent.

"To my car. I'm going to teach you a very valuable lesson."

"Which is?"

"Never talk shit to strangers."

If I didn't know better, the tone in his voice would have made him come off as a potential serial killer. Chad has too good of a job and too much to lose for all that. We got to his ride, a 2002 Boxster, and he unlocked the doors.

"I know you don't think we're fucking in this little thing."

"What's wrong? You scared?"

"No, I'm not scared. Just not about to be so confined."

"Well, we can go to a cheap motel then."

"Cheap?"

He glared at me. "Hey, look. I'm not trying to fall in love, so I don't need to lavish you with jack shit. There won't be any fancy hotels, expensive champagne, or flowers on this ride, honey. So are you down for this or not?"

I started to take off my disguise and cuss his ass out. I decided to exact my revenge in another way instead.

I bent over the hood and jacked up my skirt. "Just hit it from the back right here, baby."

He swung his neck from side to side, surveying the parking lot. "Right here in the open?"

"Yeah. What's wrong? Are you *scared?*"

"Hell, no, I'm not afraid of a damn thing, including dying."

"Then prove it. Make good on all that shit you were talking in the club." I reached into my handbag and pulled out a condom. I handed it over my shoulder to him. "No cover, no lover."

He pulled my red silk panties down, and I stepped out of them. "I'll show you, you bitch!"

I couldn't believe he went there. Yes, I was going to fuck him and then fuck him over. A lightbulb went off in my head as he put on the condom. Part of me felt guilty for even thinking such nasty thoughts. Then I laughed as he shoved his dick in me from behind.

"What's so damn funny, bitch?"

"You," I replied, still laughing. Chad wasn't holding much,

and I wanted to make that point known, so I asked, "Is your dick in yet?"

"Oh, you think you're funny!" he lashed out at me, trying to position himself to get deeper. "You know good and damn well my dick is in you. You'll feel it in your throat in a minute."

"I seriously doubt that," I stated, talking mad shit and then yawning. "I must admit this is quite the disappointment, so can you just hurry it up so I can go back to the club and find me a *real* man with some *real* dick."

"I'll give you a real man with some real dick." Chad lost his breath while he tried to ram his dick higher into me. Both of us knew that wasn't even a slight possibility because the front of his thighs were already slapping up against the back of mine.

This continued for a few minutes. He almost freaked when a group of sisters exiting the club spotted us in the parking lot and started pointing and talking trash. I was used to public sex, and that was the single arousing factor of the entire episode.

They went on about their business, got into two separate cars, and pulled out. Chad went back to work. At least, he thought he was working it. I yawned again.

"Oh, you're trying to say I'm boring you?" he asked with disdain. "You know you love this."

His ego was too much for me. What I was about to do was risky, but I said what the hell, reached inside my handbag once again, but not for a condom, and glanced over my shoulder to see if Chad was looking down at me. His eyes were glued to my ass. Good.

I reached between my legs with my free hand and started caressing his balls. I wanted the exact position in my mind. Then I reached between them with my other hand.

"I'm coming!" Chad yelled out. "I'm about to bust this nut all up in you."

"And I'm about to bust your nuts," I said as I zapped his balls with my stun gun.

His immediate reaction was shock. He looked like a deer caught in headlights. Then he let out the loudest wail I'd ever heard. I mean, it was a sight to see and hear. He fell down to the ground, grasping onto his balls, and his eyes rolled up into the back of his head.

I could only laugh. I picked up my panties off the ground and then kicked him in the dick. "That'll teach you to call women bitches!"

I located my car, jumped in, and headed home. I took the wig and glasses off and hid them under my seat, their usual spot. When I arrived, Steve was watching the late-night news and reading the *Evening Post*.

"Where you been, honey?"

"I was just out with Keisha. We went to happy hour."

He glanced at his watch. It was after midnight. "Must've been a long happy hour."

"Well, we got to talking, and before we knew it, time had slipped away. You know how that goes."

"Absolutely."

I went over to the recliner where he was seated and kissed him on the forehead. "I'm going to grab a shower. It's been a long day."

"Nice dress. You didn't wear that to work today, did you?"

I hesitated. I had forgotten to change back into my suit. "No, I actually bought this after work. They were having a sale, and I thought it was cute. Do you like it?"

He slapped me on the ass. "I love it."

I winked at him. "And I love you."

After my shower, I couldn't wait to call Keisha and tell her what had happened. She laughed so hard that I thought she would choke.

Chad called Steve the next morning, crying on the phone like a bitch. I listened in on the extension, and it was hilarious. I know I was wrong for what I did, but hey, when you get buck wild, anything is likely to happen. So men, you better come prepared or don't come at all, because buck-wild honies like the kid take no prisoners.

Back to the Dick

       Wendy and I had been together for seven years. That's a long-ass time. I loved her; I really did. But there was something missing. I needed *the dick*. Now I know it seems like I was a bit confused, and that is a serious understatement. For more than a decade, I had lived the life of a lesbian. There had been half a dozen women in my life before I met Wendy. When I spotted her in one of the clubs I frequented, it was lust at first sight. We barely made it back to my place that night before we were all over each other.

       The sex between Wendy and I was slamming. I couldn't ask for a woman to give me anything more. She was passionate, attentive, and could go at it for hours. But there were times when I found myself masturbating and thinking about the men from long ago who had worked some magic of their own in the bedroom with me.

       The one I fantasized about the most was Henry. I called him "Oh Henry" because that was what I used to always yell out in bed when he hit the spot and made me cream all over myself, him, and the sheets. Henry was a great lover, but he left a lot to be desired in other departments. Namely, Henry was flat-out dumb. I mean, the Negro could barely add two plus two. It wasn't that I needed a man who was highly intelligent, but it was hard not being able to discuss normal day-to-day situations with a man. Sex is only one part of a great relationship, and I needed something to stimulate my mind when the fucking was done.

While Henry had to get "canceled" from my life, sometimes when Wendy was eating my pussy, there he would be like a ghost from the past. Wendy was livid one night when I called out Henry's name in the heat of the moment. She wasted no time laying into me.

"What the fuck did you just say?" she asked vehemently.

"Huh?" was my typical reply when I didn't want to answer someone.

"You heard me, Meridith! Don't play dumb! You just called out some mutha fucka's name in our bed!"

"Damn, my bad." I sat up and tried to console her by rubbing her shoulders.

She pushed my hand off. "Don't even! I can't believe your ass!"

That was the end of the conversation and the sex. Wendy got up and stormed out the bedroom, opting to camp out on the sofa for the rest of the night. I lay in the bed and wondered what the hell I was doing. I was a lesbian, pure and simple, right? Not! The bottom line was that after all those years, I was feenin' for some dick.

I know some people will find that hard to believe. That all of a sudden I would go from being a pussy connoisseur to a rehabilitated dick fiend. I found it hard to believe myself, but before I knew it, I was trolling the streets for a man who I felt should be the one to reacclimatize me to the world of heterosexual sex.

I was sitting in a diner, seeking shelter from a torrential rain, when I spotted him getting out of a tattered Ford across the busy street. He was of medium height, with a goatee and eyes that seemed to light up the dreary sky. He struggled to get an umbrella open—a lost cause, because he was soaked from the second he got out of the car.

I saw his mouth forming curse words as he slammed the car door and made a mad dash for the entryway of a small apartment building. I forked some of my meatloaf into my mouth and waited, contemplating my next move or if there was even to be one.

"Wendy's going to kill me," I whispered aloud to myself.

More and more people piled into the diner looking for refuge, and I knew it was just a matter of time before someone would be stressing me about giving up the table for four I was occupying alone.

My waitress came over and asked, "Would you like anything else?"

"No, I'm cool. I'll just take the check."

She cleared my plate from the table and pulled my tab out of her apron pocket.

I took a twenty from my purse and dropped it on the table.

The waitress picked it up and said, "Be right back."

"That's okay. Keep the change."

I vacated the table and made my way through the crowded entrance to the door. I had a pocket-size umbrella in my purse and opened it before I went outside. The rain was still coming down hard, but the sun had started to break through the clouds. I debated about waiting it out in the alcove or trying to make it to my car without getting drenched.

That's when I saw a light go on in an apartment across the street. I glanced up to the third-floor window and saw him—the brother who had run inside. He sat down by the bay window and looked outside. Yes, he was definitely fine. His skin looked like cinnamon, and I wondered if it were just as sweet. He had dimples, a feature I couldn't recall seeing on someone since high school.

We looked about the same age. I had just turned thirty-six, and I think that was a part of my problem with homosexuality. My biological clock was ticking, and while I had lost total interest in sexing men down for more than a decade, I did love the thought of having a child one day. The mere thought that my body was capable of such a feat was intriguing.

So there I was, staring at him staring out the window. Suddenly his eyes lowered and latched onto mine. He grinned, and I stood there nervous as all hell. Somehow I managed to slightly wave at him. He waved back.

So now what, Meridith? I thought to myself. What I was contemplating was crazy. I didn't know that man from Adam, but he was sitting there looking all good, and I started fantasizing about what would happen if I dared to actually go up there and knock on his door. That was risky at best. He could have been married, shacking up, or hell, even gay. After all, I was supposed to be gay my damn self. But I wanted some dick, and I wanted it bad.

We stared at each other for a good five minutes before he motioned for me to come up. He stood up and started rubbing his crotch. Hmm, he was a straight-up freak. I guess he figured that he might as well try it and see what happened. That clarified one thing for me; he damn sure wasn't strictly dickly.

An elderly man came out of the diner and practically knocked me down. He apologized, but his accidental shove left me in the street getting wet. I thought about Wendy again for a second; all the things she had given me, and all the things that she never could. I thought about what the repercussions for my actions would be. Maybe I'll tell Wendy, and maybe I won't, I thought. That would depend on how good a time I had after making the choice to climb those steps across the street. There was only one way to find out.

A few minutes later I was standing outside his door. He opened it before I could even knock.

"I'm Gillian!" he announced with much pride while extending his hand.

"Meridith," I responded, proffering my own. "I know you must think this is crazy. My coming up here to your place out of the blue."

He moved aside so I could come in. "No, not at all. I'm glad you did. There's nothing like being at home bored when the world is full of such excitement."

"True." I giggled as I went inside. His place was modest and turned out to be an efficiency. He had a plaid living room set and a simple dinette group. The hightlight of the place was his bed; it was king-size, with a black laquer headboard, and he had mirrors strategically placed on the ceiling. "Nice place."

"So, Meridith, would you like something to drink?" He went over to the small fridge and took out a beer. "I have beer, wine coolers, and apple juice."

"Actually, I'll take a wine cooler, if that's cool."

"It's all good."

He handed me the bottle and then sat down on the bed. He obviously wasn't going to try to play games by sitting on the sofa. He wanted to fuck, and he wanted me to know it.

I downed the entire wine cooler in three swigs.

Gillian laughed. "Damn, baby, you might be able to drink me under the table."

I wiped my mouth with the back of my hand. "I seriously doubt that. I'm not a heavy drinker. I'm just trying to loosen up a little."

He patted the bed. "Come sit beside me and I'll loosen you up a hell of a lot."

I laughed nervously. "Sounds interesting."

"Look, Meridith. We both know why you came up here. At least, I think we do."

"Yeah, I guess we do."

He came over to retrieve me from the center of the floor and led me to his bed. He pushed my coat off my shoulders and feasted his eyes on the tight red blouse I had on with a black miniskirt. "Meridith, you are some kind of fine."

"Thank you for the compliment." He attempted to kiss me on the lips, but I resisted. "Umm, Gillian, there's something I need to explain to you first."

He started caressing my left nipple. "Baby, there's nothing you need to explain to me. Just take off your clothes and show big daddy what you're working with. I'm going to make you feel so good."

I didn't push his hand off my breast because it felt great and I could feel myself getting aroused. My panties were getting damp, and that is when I knew that I really did want to experience a man again.

"What I'm trying to say is that I haven't been with a man in a long time."

"So, that's cool. I run into sisters like you all the time that take on that celibacy thing for a minute. Going without sex is all right for a little bit because it only makes you appreciate it more when you get it."

"That hasn't exactly been my case. I never stopped having sex. I just stopped having sex with men."

"Ahh," he whispered, getting my drift. "You've been sexing down the sisters?"

"Just one in particular, but yes, I haven't been with a man for more than ten years. I'm a lesbian."

He smirked at me. "Well, if you're a lesbian, why'd you come up here? You knew the deal."

"I, um, don't know why I came up here," I lied.

He got up from the bed, strutted across the room, and opened the door. "In that case, maybe you should just get out. I'm not going to beat around the bush. I'm way too old for bull-shit. When I saw you standing down there looking all sexy and staring up at me, I thought you were down for fucking, but obvi-ously you're just fucking confused."

"You don't have to get nasty," I said as I got up. "You don't un-derstand what I'm trying to say."

"Then just say it or bounce."

I was beginning to have regrets about coming on to this man. I mean, who did this fool think he was? He was fine and all, but he wasn't exactly living in a mansion and cruising around in a sports car. Not that I'm materialistic, but the brother had a lot of nerve trying to dismiss me like that.

I lashed out at him. "Listen, Gillian, you're not all that, but the fact of the matter is that I did come up here to fuck you. I wanted you to be my first piece of dick after a long-ass drought, but I can see now that you're not worthy of this pussy."

"Worthy of your pussy?" He smacked his lips and rolled his eyes. "Meridith, I don't even know you, but you need to get some help. Unless your pussy is lined with gold, it's just like every other pussy on the planet. Shit, pussy is pussy!"

I don't know what it was about his last statement, but it made me want to prove a point. I grabbed him by the shirt col-lar, pushed him clear across the room and onto the bed. "What if

I said my pussy is lined with gold?" I asked, biting his bottom lip and climbing on top of him. "What if I demanded that you taste it and find out?"

He gripped my waist and pulled my pussy up onto his dick, rubbing himself against me through our clothing. "Then I guess I'd just have to taste it and find out."

We started rolling around on the bed like children wrestling in a sandbox. I don't even remember the clothes coming off, but every stitch of them did and we ended up in the sixty-nine position going for the glory. Gillian could eat a mean pussy, and it was wild experiencing his strength as he grabbed onto my ass, insisting that I hold it just at the right angle for him to get his eat on.

I tried to swallow his dick whole. It had been *too* long since I'd sucked a dick, and I'd forgotten how much I really adored sucking them. I held his dick by the base and waxed it, only taking it out long enough to swallow my saliva and catch my breath. Gillian latched onto my clit with his teeth and pulled it down gently. I exploded with my first orgasm and felt it trickling down the inside of my thighs. He lapped it all up with his tongue and then went back to his entrée.

As slamming as the oral sex was, I couldn't wait to have him inside me any longer. I stood up by the window, placed my palms on the glass, and demanded, "Give it to me!"

Gillian got up from the bed and stood behind me. "Umm, I'm going to give it to you, Meridith!" He lowered himself just enough to place the head of his dick on my pussy and tried to put it all in with one push, but it wasn't going down like that. "Damn, you're so tight, baby."

"I told you it's been a while since I swung this way." I reached my right hand down between my legs and tried to assist him in his effort. "My pussy's precious. Treat it as such."

He ran his tongue over my ear and sucked on my neck while he eased it in gently. Once he got it in, he moaned. "Shit, you're like a virgin."

The rain had eased up into a drizzle as we stood in the window fucking each other's brains out. There was no longer a need for words. We just relished the experience. Gillian placed kisses all up and down my back as he fucked me slowly for a moment and then started pumping hard. He would switch from fast to slow, and it was off the hizzy.

I looked down at the diner across the street and saw the same waitress that had waited on me earlier. A young couple was walking arm in arm around the corner when the man froze in place. He could see us, and he pointed us out to his lover, who threw her hand over her mouth in shock. What effect did it have on me? It turned me on and carried me even deeper into the throes of passion.

Gillian dug his fingers into my ass and screamed out, "I'm cumming!"

I screamed out, "Me, too!" and that's exactly what we both did.

I stayed with Gillian the rest of the night; sleeping, fucking, sleeping, and then fucking again. The guilt flooded in, but I couldn't stop. I *needed* the dick, and more importantly, I *wanted* it. I wasn't sure what I would tell Wendy once I returned home, but I knew that things would have to change.

I ended up coming clean and getting tossed out on my ass within an hour. That was a door that needed to close. Now, three years later, I'm dating both men and women. If I had to choose between one or the other, I would have to choose men. I adore women, but I need men. I came back to the dick, and what a beautiful world it can be.

Till Death Do Us Part or Not

I had no business there, but I couldn't possibly stay away. Matthew was the love of my life, and he was about to exchange wedding vows with someone else. There was no one to blame other than myself. I was the one who had cheated on him while he was away at medical school. I was the one who ended up pregnant by someone else, and I was the one who ended up getting into a marriage of convenience just so I would have a last name for my son.

Vincent had been a wonderful husband to me, always treated me with the utmost respect. I just couldn't seem to get Matthew out of my mind, so I finally came clean and asked to end the marriage. But I was too late, because when I went to beg Matthew to take me back, he turned me down and my heart broke. When I heard he was getting married, the news devastated me. Seven long years had passed, and there was no reason for him not to move on. He had an established medical practice as a cardiologist at Memorial Hospital, and he deserved someone to love him. I only wish that someone could have been me.

I begged one of our childhood friends, Paula, to take me to the wedding on her invitation. After I practically threatened suicide, she agreed to take me with her. When he took his place at the altar with the minister and his best man, I wanted to rush into his arms and plead with him not to do it. How foolish that would have been of me, and how destructive it would have been to his relationship.

I endured the wedding ceremony, clenching my fists at the part where the minister asked if there were any objections. I cried when he repeated his vows and when the soloist sang "Ribbon in the Sky." Most people were crying tears of joy, while mine were full of anguish and despair.

Matthew didn't notice me during the ceremony, but when it was time for the wedding party to receive the guests, he spotted me. I was in the back of the line of guests waiting to wish congratulations and best wishes. Before Paula and I got to the front, I walked away; I could not bear giving well wishes to the woman who had stolen my man. When I turned back, I noticed Matthew was staring at me, and it almost looked as if he wanted to run after me. I knew he still loved me as much as I loved him. It was nothing short of a crime that we lived separate lives.

Paula and I got to the reception, and it was lovely, perfect even, and I was so jealous. I had gotten married at the justice of the peace on a cold, rainy day in September. There was no comparison to the extravagant wedding Matthew had. It should have been me—but this was our fate.

We all dined on the delicious buffet, and the two of them cut the cake. As they were feeding each other cake, I noticed him searching the crowd of people until he found me. We stared at each other, but the gaze was broken when they announced it was time for the first dance.

The two of them embraced and danced slowly to "Adore" by Prince. My ass was done in by that. I couldn't take it anymore. I told Paula I was going to get some fresh air and rushed out the back door of the reception hall into the secluded alleyway.

I started wailing and kicking things around in the alley. I don't know how much time passed. All I know is that I almost fainted when I heard Matthew's voice. "Barbara, are you okay?"

I tried to wipe my tears away with the sleeve of my dress before I turned around to face him. He reached for me and put his hands on my shoulders. I said, not bothering to turn around to look at him, "No, Matthew, I am not all right!"

He swung me around so he could look in my eyes. "Listen to me, Barbara. You know this is not the way I wanted things to end up." He took me into his arms, hugged me, and whispered in my ear, "I waited all this time for you, hoping things would change and we could be together, but it wasn't in the cards."

The tears started flowing again. "I love you, Matthew. I always have, and I guess I will just have to go on being punished forever for a mistake I made when I was young and foolish."

He kissed me on the cheek and then on my forehead. He took his thumb and wiped away my tears. Then he looked me in the eyes again. "I love you, too, Barbara."

I pulled away from him. "This is crazy. You just got married a couple of hours ago."

He put his hands in his pockets and kicked an empty tin can like a little boy getting into mischief. "Yes, I did, and this is crazy, but . . ."

"But?"

"We have made enough mistakes, and maybe it is time to rectify them before we waste another seven years." I bit my bottom lip to make sure I was not imagining the whole thing. "Maybe it is time to make things right."

"How do you suppose we do that?"

"Barbara, when I asked Natalie to marry me, I had no idea you were in the middle of a divorce. In fact, I just found out less than a week ago that you were single again."

Could it be a glimmer of hope? "So, why did you still marry her if you found out?"

"Trying to be a man. Trying to do the right thing. But if my heart belongs to you, and it most definitely does, am I doing the right thing by entering into this marriage?"

I threw my hands up in the air in dismay. "Only you can answer that, Matthew."

"No, I think we have to answer it together, Barbara. You tell me what you want. I have to hear the words."

I looked at him in his tuxedo, and he was sexier than ever. I wanted to make love to him so bad, but it was his wedding day. He was promised to another. I know that there is a right and a wrong way to do a thing, and I know the right thing to do now would have been to walk away. Matthew asked me what I wanted, though, and I could not tell a lie.

There were no words to express what I was feeling, so I decided to show him instead. I pushed his back up against the brick building and starting French kissing him and caressing his dick at the same time. His dick was big, long, and thick just like I remembered it, and I couldn't wait to deep-throat it just like I used to back in the good old days.

He pulled away for a moment, as if the guilt were killing him, and then he whispered, "I want to make love to you, Barbara."

"I want to make love to you, too, but we can't do it right here."

He looked around for a moment and then took me by the hand, leading me toward the entrance of the alley. "Come with me, baby."

I had no idea where he was taking me until we got to the front of the reception hall and he headed straight toward the limousine he and his new bride had arrived in from the church. The chauffeur, who was standing there wiping a few smudge marks off the hood with an oil cloth, was startled to see us getting in the back of the car. He was even more shocked when Matthew told him to get in and drive us around.

After the chauffeur got in, he looked at us through the rearview mirror and asked, "Where do you want to go?"

"Just drive around." Matthew pushed the button to raise the tinted screen separating the driver's section from the rear and then turned on the Quiet Storm radio show.

We tore into each other, and clothes came off. Reality began to sink in, and I asked him, "Matthew, what about all the people at the reception? They are going to kill us!"

For some reason I got the impression he didn't give a shit, and then he confirmed it. "Barbara, I don't give a shit what they think. This is about me and you, and we've waited way too long to be together."

With that said, I figured he was the one who should be concerned. Since he wasn't, I decided to go for mine. I got down on the carpeted floor of the limo and pulled him by the neck, forcing him to join me. We both fell back when the driver ran over a huge pothole and started laughing when I hit my head against the built-in bar and a champagne flute landed right smack on my left breast, enclosing my nipple like it was waiting for me to fill it up with breast milk.

Matthew stopped laughing as his eyes lingered on my breasts, and I caressed the nape of his neck, hoping he would do that thing he does all too well. Many nights, I had lain awake in the bed beside Vincent, fantasizing about the way Matthew used to suckle on my breasts for what seemed like an eternity. Within seconds, the memories were replaced with the actual thing as he partook of my nipples once more.

After he started working on my nipples real good, let me just say, the shit was on. I licked every inch of him I could get at in the back of the limo, and he did the same. It was good. I noticed the glass that separated us from the driver easing down. He thought his ass was slick. At first, I was going to cold bust his ass and curse him out, but then the idea of his looking started to excite me a little.

He shifted in his seat a little, and I could have sworn I heard his zipper go down. That's when I reached for Matthew's zipper and undid his pants. I pulled his dick out and rubbed my hand up and down the warm shaft. My hand took on a life of its own as I commenced giving him an awesome hand job. I remembered how much he used to love them. I maneuvered my hand around his dick until he was moaning like crazy and his eyes were rolling back in his head.

I could hear the driver moaning as well, and it hit me that his nasty ass was up there in the front seat jacking off. While he was driving, mind you.

After Matthew came in my hand, he told me, "Take off your panties. I need to be inside you. I need to be inside you right now."

I worked my panties over my hips and slid them off. I could see the driver lowering the partition even more. Matthew seemed to be oblivious to his antics, especially after he pushed his dick inside my pussy, threw my legs over his shoulders, and started fucking me like he hadn't had sex in ages. It was all good until . . .

. . . the driver lost control of the limousine, and we heard tires screeching. That was the last thing we heard before the crash, which left us both unconscious.

I'm not sure how much time elapsed between the wreck and when I woke up to a panicking Matthew. "Barbara, wake up! Please, baby, wake up!" he screamed as he shook me like a rag doll. I coughed and grabbed onto him. "Thank goodness you're okay."

"What happened?"

"That bastard was jerking off in the front seat and crashed into a tree."

"Shit!" I sat up and looked around the limo. Glasses and liquor bottles were scattered everywhere. I realized we were in motion. "What the hell is going on? Where are we going?"

"He's taking us to the hospital, trying to save his ass and his job!" Matthew spewed vehemently. "Asshole!"

Common sense kicked in as I grabbed for my clothes. Matthew and I were still naked. "We have to get some clothes on. What if someone sees?"

Matthew started trying to get his clothes on also, realizing I was right. It was too late. We didn't realize the limo was already at the hospital until two paramedics yanked open the door and exposed our asses to the entire hemisphere.

"Oh, shit!" That was all I managed to say as the paramedics quickly removed our bodies from the back of the limo and slammed us on top of gurneys. They covered us up with sheets up to our shoulders, but not before quite a few people got more than an eyeful.

They had us halfway down the hallway to one of the emergency rooms when we were spotted by Clifton, and I knew the shit had hit the fan. Clifton was Matthew's archrival, his main competition for the head of the hematology unit at the hospital, and a jackass beyond question.

"Matthew, is that you?" He came rushing over to the gurneys and started laughing his ass off. "Isn't today supposed to be your wedding day?"

"Shut the hell up, Clifton!" It was obvious Matthew wanted to get up off the gurney and whip his ass, but that would have only made things worse. Imagine him in a brawl with his dick slanging from side to side.

They finally got us in the emergency room, where we both proclaimed to be perfectly fine. I spotted Clifton over in the corner, interrogating the nasty-ass driver and getting an earful. He dashed out of the room in a hurry, more than likely to spread the word—every nurse, doctor, and intern in sight was peeking in and out the room trying to see the madness.

After they concluded that we were both going to live, Matthew told the nurse in attendance to go get our clothes from the back of the limousine. We got dressed and wanted nothing more than to get the hell out of there without any more attention being drawn to us so we hauled ass out into the hallway and . . .

. . . bumped right smack into the bride and half of the wedding party we had left behind at the reception. "Matthew, what the hell is going on here?" Natalie looked pitiful and ashamed, and I didn't blame her. I could only imagine how she must have felt, getting married and then finding out her husband was at the emergency room naked along with his ex-girlfriend. "Clifton called the reception hall and told me this ridiculous story!"

She was obviously waiting and hoping we would both deny it, but it wasn't much use. We were busted, caught in the act, exposed, basically ass-out.

Needless to say, Matthew and Natalie never made it to their honeymoon, because the marriage was quickly annulled. Two months later he and I did go on our honeymoon, though. We went to Montego Bay and had the time of our lives. Matthew left Memorial Hospital and went into private practice. Clifton got to be the head of the cardiology department, and I got my man. All in all, as embarrassing as the whole situation was, it was well worth the aggravation and then some.

The Santa Claus

"Absolutely not! I won't do it!" Those were the words I spewed at my boss, aka Broomhilda, when she asked me to throw on a ridiculous outfit and pretend to be Mrs. Santa Claus for the benefit of a bunch of spoiled brats.

"Charissa, there's no one else that can do it," she replied, glaring at me with her beady eyes. "Everyone else is already tied up for the holiday season, and besides, this is a part of your job."

"How do you figure?" Was she for real? "I'm the assistant manager of Hollyville Mall. Not Mrs. Santa Claus."

"Remember when you dressed up as the Easter Bunny last spring?"

"How could I forget? It was one of the most demeaning experiences in my entire life."

She rolled her eyes at me, the heffa. "Well, you didn't complain back then."

"I'll be perfectly honest with you," I replied with disdain. "Back then I was trying to impress you and the rest of the upper management. Now that I realize that raises and promotions are few and far between, Christmas bonuses are always crappy gift certificates, and flexible hours really means double shifts, I'm not as enthusiastic as I once was."

She threw a garment bag over the desk at me and headed for the door of the mall office. "You start tomorrow. Two P.M. sharp."

"Shit! Shit! Shit!" I screamed out to no one in particular, since I was completely alone, opening and slamming my desk drawer each time the expletive left my mouth.

I was so sick of my job that I didn't know what to do. I'd procrastinated about putting my résumé in someplace else for months, and the holiday season was the worst time to look for a good job. Sure, seasonal cheap wage jobs were plentiful, but I had bills to pay, and I just couldn't leave until I had something else lined up.

I went home that night about ten, after staying to close up the mall as always. Every muscle in my body was sore—not because I had been working out, but because I hadn't. Stress was seeping through my pores, and my head was freakin' killing me. I wrapped an ice pack in a washcloth, climbed into bed without even bothering to eat dinner, and fell asleep to a Luther Vandross CD.

The next morning, my head was hurting twice as bad as it was before I fell asleep. I debated about calling in sick, and it would have been legitimate. However, Broomhilda would have assumed that I was just "trying" her, as she always put it.

I didn't move an inch until noon, not even to answer the phone that was ringing off the hook. No doubt it was just the usual suspects: my bank calling to harass me about a bill that I'd already paid, the local firefighters selling the same basket of summer sausage, cheese cubes, and crackers they sell every year as a fund-raiser, and my ex-boyfriend Kelly calling to beg me to take him back. Not a chance.

Kelly's cool, but he's not for me. Mainly because he gives new meaning to the word *sweating*. Kelly, I'm going to the store to buy a new teakettle. Wait, Charissa. I'll go with you. Kelly, I'm going to fill up my car. Wait, Charissa. I'll go with you. Kelly, I'm going to the Laundromat to wash my funky drawers. Wait, Charissa. I'll go with you.

That was the life I led for three years, and that was two years, eleven months, and twenty-nine days too long. He just couldn't get it through his thick head that we were over.

I dreaded putting on the silly-ass outfit and going to work, but I had no options. I put on the red dress, white bib apron, white tights, black patent-leather granny shoes, and gray wig. When I glanced in the mirror, I couldn't hold back my laughter. I was a clone of my grandmother—but she has more style.

Hollyville Mall was packed, even though it is by far the most rinky-dink mall within the city limits. Still, people thrive on old familiar places, and they get that at Hollyville, which has been open for more than thirty years. It hit me when I was getting out of my car in the employee parking lot that Broomhilda had never mentioned who she'd bamboozled into being Santa Claus himself. I prayed that it wasn't Cleavest, one of the sales assistants who swore up and down that he was the finest thing on two legs. Whoever told him that nonsense lied to him because he was straight-up ugly, and for someone who worked in a mall, his taste in clothing was sad.

I went into the south entrance of the mall and slowly made my way to the makeshift stage in the middle, where a tiny house, about ten by fifteen feet, was located. That was Santa's crib. I approached from the rear and couldn't see who was seated in Santa's chair, but I knew that someone was, because more than ten kids and their doting parents were lined up to take pictures.

Gerald, the midget who usually works over at the Orange Julius, was dressed as an elf and taking the pictures. He even had on elf shoes with little bells on the tips of the toes. How cute! When I saw Gerald grinning from ear to ear, I couldn't help but think that I had been doing a ghettoized rendition of Scrooge. After all, it was Christmastime. Time to celebrate. Time to be thankful.

When I was still about twenty yards away, I waved at Gerald. "Hey, Gerald! Having fun?"

"Hey, Charissa! I'm having a ball!" He lowered the camera while the next kid climbed onto the stage to climb on Santa's lap. "You look great!"

"Thanks, Gerald! So do you!"

By that time, I was close enough to hear a deep, masculine voice asking the child what he wanted for Christmas. Damn! That definitely wasn't Cleavest! Cleavest had a high-pitched, irritating voice. So who the hell was it then?

His name turned out to be Felix. Simply put, Felix was fine as all hell, and I forgot all about my gripes and grievances pertaining to portraying Mrs. Santa Claus. Hell, I wanted to marry the man for real, even if that meant moving my ass to the North Pole.

Felix was tall—damn near gigantic, once I saw him stand up. He had to be at least six-eight. He was light-skinned, with hazel eyes, high cheekbones, and a fantastic smile.

Felix and I hit it off well, and Gerald's antics made the time pass quickly. There must have been at least three hundred kids who made their way through the line to ask for Christmas presents. I felt sorry for the parents, because some of those little suckers had lists as long as my arm.

During the fifteen-minute break granted to us by Broomhilda, Felix and I got to know each other a little. He'd just moved to town and was doing the Santa gig until he could find a real job. He'd been offered a job at the mall in the security department, and while he wasn't really feeling it, he was going to give it a try.

That kind of made my day, because if I had to deal with the bullshit, looking at him was definitely an added bonus. My interests still dictated that I get the hell out of Dodge, though. Enough was enough.

The mall finally closed, thank goodness. I was worn out, and my poor feet were killing me. Gerald had taken off an hour before, and all the merchants were busying themselves counting out registers and locking up. I was ready to make a beeline for the exit when Felix suddenly grabbed me and pulled me down on his lap. I didn't know whether to resist or give him a lap dance. The reasonable me thought it was a bit too forward, but my freaky side was aroused in a major way.

"So what do you want for Christmas?" Felix asked with a grin.

"I don't know," I replied bashfully.

"Oh, come on. Everyone wants something for Christmas."

Since he was so insistent, I decided to come clean. "Between me and you, I'd like a new job."

"Not happy here?"

"Not at all."

He patted my thigh and said, "Please don't go. I just got here."

Our eyes made contact, and there was a spark. "Well, maybe you can persuade me to stay."

"Maybe I can."

That was how it all began. The flirting.

We went back and forth with the flirting for three days. The lust was apparent, but neither one of us initiated contact outside of the workplace. It was inappropriate to date a coworker. Then again, I didn't give a shit about my job, so getting fired wasn't exactly a concern.

Felix and I ate lunch together every day. This was after I schooled Broomhilda about that fifteen-minute shit and reminded her that there are federal regulations that guarantee employees a lunch hour. She didn't like or appreciate my abrasiveness, but that was too damn bad.

I finally came to terms with the fact that I wanted Felix to fuck the living daylights out of me. Hell, it had been a while since I had some dick, and it was nothing short of insane to be around a fine-ass man day in and day out and not try to tap that ass. I know that statement is usually attributed to men, but women have needs also.

"Felix, what are you doing after work?" I asked once the last youngster had trotted off smiling, thinking he was getting all the shit on his list for real.

"Just going on home, I suppose," he replied.

"Oh." I contemplated asking him over but had a last-second concern. What if he rejected me? I would be totally embarrassed, and we still had to work together.

"Did you have something in mind?" he prodded. "I'm up for whatever."

Hmm, maybe we could do a little sumptin' sumptin' after all, I thought to myself.

"Would you like to come over for a little while?"

"Your place?"

"Yes, my place." I laughed. "It would be awfully trifling of me to invite you over someone else's place."

He chuckled. "That it would be. I'd love to come over."

"Cool."

We arrived at my place, and I could have screamed. My next-door neighbor's dog had pooted all over my doorstep again. I was going to do something about that damn mutt if it meant doing some hard time.

Felix thought it was funny, though, and told me to calm down when I started shouting at the top of my lungs toward the other house.

"Calm down, Charissa. It's just a damn dog."

"Yeah, but I'm willing to bet that bastard next door brings his dog over here on purpose to do that."

"Why on earth would anyone do something so nasty?"

"Because we have this little feud going over parking space. He doesn't want people parking in front of his house, and my friends often do. He doesn't own the damn curb. No one does."

We went inside, and I poured us some glasses of wine. I wanted to get a bit tipsy, because when I'm tipsy, I can get freaky without guilt-tripping over what my parents told me good girls never do when I was younger. Don't let me get straight-up drunk, because I will blow a fool's back out.

Needless to say, by glass four I was tore up from the floor up and getting aggressive. Not to mention kinky.

"Want to listen to some music, Felix?" I asked, already flipping through CDs.

"Sure, what you got?"

"I have just about everything. Music is my love, and I have a great collection. I keep a limited amount out here and the majority in my bedroom. As much as I love my peeps, things can walk up out of here like crazy if I'm not careful."

"I know how that is. People think you have so much of something that you won't miss anything if it's gone."

"Exactly."

"Have anything slow?"

"Sure, but if I put on something slow, you have to dance with me. Deal?"

"Deal."

I put on some Stevie Wonder, and it was on. Somewhere between "Ribbon in the Sky" and "Overjoyed," we started feeling each other down. His height was a bit of a challenge because his dick was in my chest, but it felt different to be damn near titty-fucked with my clothes on.

"Wait here," I told him, pulling away and heading toward my bedroom.

I rumbled through my drawers, looking for something I'd always wanted to try out. When I found it, I yelled out into the living room and instructed Felix to turn off all the lights.

"All of them?" he yelled back.

"Yes, make it completely dark."

I could hear him chuckling. "Okay, if you insist."

I stripped down to my underwear. Why waste time? I broke open the package, cut the lights in my bedroom, and opened the door. It was pitch-black, with the exception of the dim lighting on my CD player.

I inched my way toward the sofa, shook up the item in my hand, and then snapped it. Instantly, a neon green light appeared from the glow stick I was holding.

"Now this could get interesting," Felix said from the couch. "A half-naked glowing woman. This must be my lucky night."

"If you only knew," I said seductively. "This is your lucky night and mine, too. Now sit back, relax, and enjoy the show."

I didn't know I had it in me. That night I found out that I was one hell of a dancer. I put on a strip show that would make any pro envious. In fact, Felix asked me if I had ever been a stripper and smirked when I denied it. Since he was impressed, I knew that I could always fall back on the profession if Broomhilda and

I ever got into the knock-down, drag-out fight I had been itching for over time.

As I danced to the music, I rubbed the glow stick all over my body, giving Felix glimpses of my white lacy thong and bra. I worked my way over to him, turned around, and bent down slightly until I was grinding my ass on his dick in the dark. I placed the glow stick behind me and rubbed it up and down my crack to entice him even further.

He grabbed my hips and whispered, "Damn, baby," in my ear.

I got down on my knees and started undoing his pants. His dick had gotten rock hard, and I couldn't wait another second to get my hands on it.

"Hold this for me, will you?" I asked, handing him the glow stick.

"Certainly."

Felix held it over my head while I retrieved my prize. In the neon lighting, it looked like a shiny, golden, thick stick.

"Umm, can I taste it?"

"Be my guest."

I licked the head first and was immediately hooked. While I've never been big on sucking dick, something about this man made me want to indulge. I wanted him to know that it wasn't a tradition, so I told him, "I don't normally do this. Especially not during the first sexual encounter. So you better appreciate this."

"Trust me, I do appreciate it," he responded, pushing gently on the back of my head.

I placed warm, soft kisses all over his dick, teasing him until he started moaning loudly. Then I took the head into my mouth and held it there, squeezing and releasing it to a rhythm with my lips. I reached down and caressed his balls gently while I used my other hand to rub his shaft up and down.

I let go of him and sat down beside him on the couch.

"What's wrong, Charissa?"

"Nothing." I took his dick and my hand and rubbed my thumb over the head, spreading my saliva around. "I just want you to stand up and dick-feed me so I can get to it at a better angle."

He laughed. "Dick-feed you? That's an interesting way to put it."

"Well, that's basically what it is. Right?"

"I guess."

He complied with my wishes and stood up, holding the glow stick beside him so I could see what I was working with.

I relaxed my throat and pulled as much of his dick in as I could in one motion. I held it there for about fifteen seconds until he flinched, and then I started moving my head back and forth as I gripped the bottom of his dick to hold it steady.

I'm not quite sure how long I sucked him off, but it was for a long-ass time. Stevie went off, and the next CD in the changer came on. I was a bit perturbed because it was a gospel CD, and I had never imagined getting busy to religious music. However, I was "occupied" and wasn't about to disrupt my flow to get up and change the music.

Felix came in my mouth three times, but the fourth time, I let him come all over my breasts. Something about that shit just turns me on. The fact that he seemed to have no issues rising to the occasion time after time was even better.

"I want to fuck you now," he announced after his fourth nut.

I didn't respond. I just got up and walked toward my bedroom. He grabbed for me in the dark.

"No, come here."

"What?" I asked giddily.

"Just come here."

Felix swept me off my feet, and I straddled my legs around

his waist. It felt strange to be so high up in the air. Normally, when a man picks me up, I am barely a few inches more elevated than I am standing up.

He stood in the doorway to my dining room and slid his dick up into my pulsating pussy. I grabbed hold of the doorframe and tried my best to lay a whipping on his ass. The dick was so good that I wanted to scream. He filled me up entirely and then some.

He ran his fingers up and down my spine with one hand and palmed an ass cheek with the other, digging those fingers into my skin. "That's it! Work it, momma!"

"Umm, work it out on me, daddy!"

We both chuckled at the corniness of our dialogue.

I couldn't hold onto the frame any longer and almost toppled when I let go. Felix carried me over to the table, let me down, and then bent me over. The cool wood on my chest and stomach excited me as he entered me from the rear. He was so tall that my feet were dangling a foot above the floor, so I hooked my heels around the back of his thighs and jiggled my pussy up and down on his dick. It was the shit!

We fucked and sucked all night long, and the only light was the damn glow stick. The things that man could do with his mouth and dick were incredible. I was ready for any and everything after that. To prove my point, I showed up at work the next morning and showed out.

I located Broomhilda going off on Gerald, the midget elf and my buddy since we'd been chilling with each other at the Santa Claus booth.

"You little runt," she was spewing at him. "I've told you twenty times that you're not getting a penny for overtime."

"But how can you expect me to work such long hours and not get paid for it?" he protested. "I have mouths to feed."

"Isn't your wife a Lilliputian, too? Aren't your kids Lilliputians? That means you have *little* mouths to feed." She laughed, even though Gerald was visibly hurt. "Now get back to work. You're on my time."

"Hey, Broomhilda!" I yelled out angrily.

She turned and looked at me. "Who the hell are you calling Broomhilda?"

"Who the hell am I looking at?"

"How dare you? You're fired!"

It was my turn to laugh. "You can't fire me, because I quit! I was trying to hang in here for a while, hoping things would get better or that you'd get some inoperable disease and drop dead, but I see that's not going to happen."

I went over and placed my hand on Gerald's shoulder. I spotted Felix coming toward us from the corner of my eye. He had stopped off at his place to get a fresh set of clothing. He had his Santa suit in a garment bag looped over his shoulder.

"Gerald, are you okay?" I asked compassionately.

"Yeah, I'm okay." He said it convincingly, but I knew he was lying. "I just can't keep working overtime for no money."

"Then don't. In fact, I'm going above this bitch's head and calling the parent company to lodge a formal complaint."

"Who the hell are you calling a bitch?"

I leered at her and replied, "You, *bitch!*"

"What's going on here?" Felix asked when he got closer.

"Nothing," we all replied in unison.

"Doesn't seem like nothing."

Broomhilda and I just glared at each other for a moment. Then the shit was on. Even if I ended up in jail for a night or two, it was worth it when I saw the expression on her face after I punched her dead in the nose.

She screamed and attacked, and before I knew it, we were tussling on the floor. Gerald jumped on the witch's back and started trying to choke her while Felix tried to pull me off her. Customers started arriving as security unlocked the doors. It was a Saturday morning, so an immediate crowd gathered around us.

The two security guards on duty didn't flinch. They were probably glad to see her taking a beatdown. Felix finally managed to get me loose, but not before I landed a swift kick smack dab in her pussy. She buckled over in pain as Gerald continued trying to choke her. Luckily for her, his hands were too tiny to get a good enough grip.

Felix pulled me into the management office and slammed the door. "Are you crazy? You could go to jail?"

"So what?" I responded, hyped up with adrenaline. "She deserved it."

I lifted one of the mini-blinds so I could see out of the glass door. Gerald and Broomhilda were still at it, while little kids guffawed and their parents looked on in disbelief. No one made a move to stop it, though. Free entertainment is free entertainment.

I locked the door and turned to Felix. "You know, I got fired." I yanked his garment bag from him and tossed it on the floor. "You know what that means?"

He grinned. "That you'll be looking for a new job." He smirked. "I guess I will be also. Even though the Santa gig is almost over, I'm not trying to be around here in any capacity."

"Good. Then you don't mind indulging in a little risky behavior with me."

"What kind of risky behavior?" he asked, already knowing the deal.

I slid out of my dress. "For starters, how about fucking me right here on Broomhilda's desk while Gerald is beating the shit out of her."

We both fell out laughing.

I went over to her desk and motioned him over with my index finger.

Felix came over, flipped me around, and bent me over. "Assume the position."

As he yanked my panties off, I replied, "Position assumed."

Funny How Things Change

If you are like most people, you have regrets. I know I do. I have tons of them. If I had a dollar for every single thing I would have, could have, and should have done, I would be sitting on top of the world like Brandy and Mase.

Throughout college and the years it took to establish my medical practice, there was one thing I regretted the most; not hooking up with Jerome Stinson in high school. I know it sounds foolish, pining for someone for more than a decade. Fifteen years, to be exact.

The funny part is that I could have had him *easily*. Back then, I was the most popular girl in school. Voted most likely to succeed, homecoming queen, captain of the cheerleading squad; you know the one. Boys were literally falling at my feet, begging me for dates. Jerome was no exception. He was just against the rules.

What rules, you ask? I'll tell you what rules. The unwritten rules of popularity. Rule number one: never associate with, rather less date, geeks. While Jerome was student body president, he was still a big-time geek—high-water pants, vinyl pocket protectors, thick eyeglasses. The only reason he won the election in the first place was because all the *popular* people were standing in line that morning trying to get tickets for Prince and The Time.

Back to the rules. Rule number two: never associate with people riding the poverty line. Jerome was on the free lunch program, and you could tell his clothes came from thrift stores or even worse, Kmart.

Yes, I was shallow back then, *real shallow,* but it just couldn't be helped. I was a victim of my environment. All of my friends were shallow and stupid is as stupid does.

Rule number three: never date a boy without a car. Correction: never date a boy without a sports car. Jerome did have a car, but it was a hoopty. When he used to pull up in the school parking lot, people covered their mouths or ran for cover before his exhaust fumes knocked them the hell out. To this day, I have no idea what kind of car he had. It was just plain ole ugly. Three or four different colors of paint. Mismatched tires. A vinyl convertible top that looked like Freddy Kruger had done a slash job on it with his steel nails in *Nightmare on Elm Street, Part CXII.* Did they make enough of those bad boys or what?

Speaking of slasher films, it was during a showing of *Halloween II* that I realized Jerome wasn't half as bad as I originally assumed. I was there with Kyle Johnson, every girl's fantasy and my nightmare. Let's just say that Kyle talked a good game but didn't practice what he preached. He was always trying to *edumacate* the brothers. The fool couldn't even pronounce the word right, rather less actually do it. Nevertheless, he considered himself a man's man, and I was his prize trophy.

Kyle had it all—a candy-apple-red Corvette, a walk-in closet full of designer clothes, and he lived in the finest neighborhood in town. He was my ideal mate, socially speaking.

I simply could not stand his stepmother, though. She had "gold digger" embedded in her forehead. All the expensive clothing in the world couldn't make up for the fact that she was nothing but a tacky bimbo underneath all the silk and makeup.

I always had my suspicions that she was trying to hook up with Kyle behind his father's back, which was just plain old skank. That's not all too surprising, if all of the rumors about her were true.

I heard it from a very reliable source, my own mother, who heard it from her hairdresser, who heard it from her baby's daddy's cousin, that Kyle's stepmother used to be a stripper, a rump shaker, a paid hoochie momma. They say she's a legend at all the booty clubs on Light Street. Her stage name was Lickem Low. Without her makeup, she looked like she'd been licking on an ugly stick.

Anyway, Kyle and I were there at the movies that night along with my best friend Darlene and her flavor-of-the-month, Richard. I'm not going to call Darlene a whore, so let's just say she loved her some sex, and variety was extremely important to her.

We were sitting all the way in the back, which I always hated because I'm nearsighted. Kyle always insisted we sit in the rear so we could make out, and that night was no exception. Kyle was tipsy from a six-pack of beer he split with Richard earlier that evening, and his hands were all over me. He was roughly palming my breasts, and that was bad enough. When he tried to push my panties aside and finger me, I couldn't take it one more second.

I told Kyle I had to go to the bathroom but took it a step further. I lied and told him I had to take a dump, hoping the mere thought of it would make him keep his fingers to himself once I got back. Truth be known, I didn't have to go to the bathroom at all.

Instead, I went out into the lobby so I could check out posters of upcoming flicks. I've always had a thing for movie posters, and over the years, I've accumulated quite a collection of posters from black exploitation films. After killing about ten minutes, which I deemed an appropriate time limit to be away taking a dump, I decided to grab a pack of Twizzlers from the concession stand. Darlene swore up and down that a Twizzler a day curbed your appetite. Personally, I think she read that in one of the numerous women's magazines she subscribed to and bought into the idea so much that her psyche actually believed it. I decided what the hell and purchased a pack.

I was on my way back in when I bumped into Jerome. Now Jerome had appeared many ways to me over the years, but he had never appeared fine. Not until that very second. There was something different about him. He had a fresh haircut, his clothes were neatly ironed and fitting every curve of his body just right, and he flashed this wonderful set of teeth at me.

"Hello, Salina, you look very nice tonight," he said, throwing me a nice compliment.

"Thanks. So do you."

He lowered his eyes to the floor. He was so shy. "Thanks. Are you here with someone?"

I rolled my eyes and smacked me lips. "Unfortunately, I'm here with Kyle."

"Why is that unfortunate? I thought you two were extremely tight."

"No, not really." I opened my Twizzlers and took a bite. "Kyle and I are having some problems right about now, but it's all good."

"Well, have a good evening," Jerome said, moving from my path so I could get back inside.

"You, too."

That was the extent of our conversation that night, but it was the beginning of my long-ass wait to hook up with him again. Like I said earlier, I went through college and medical school, and I was still wondering what Jerome was like in the sack. It was insane, but I could not get that man out of my mind.

I often asked about him, but I had to do it in a slick manner. For all I knew, he was still considered a nerd and might have been collecting garbage or something. Most people didn't even remember him, and the few that did could only tell me that he had moved away.

Ironically, I was nowhere near our hometown when I ran into Jerome again. I was in Honolulu, Hawaii, of all places. I had decided to take advantage of some frequent-flyer miles and a reduced rate at a hotel. The season was easing into fall, and I had not had a vacation in more than two years, since I was determined to become the top cardiologist in Cleveland.

I took the trip along with one of my old roommates from college. Fiona was a teacher in New Jersey and needed a break before school started up and she had to once again deal with the madness that a roomful of eight-year-olds could create.

We arrived on a Thursday night, checked in to our lovely hotel, and then explored the beach in the moonlight. It was okay, but it would have been romantic if there had been some men with us. Fiona and I had a lot in common, including being recently divorced. Her marriage had lasted a good eight years, while mine lasted a good eight months.

I married Harris on a whim, a bad whim, and lived to quickly regret it. He was nothing I had imagined, and I guess the same stood true in regards to his expectations of me. I was overly ambitious, and he had no ambitions at all. He liked to lie around the house on the weekends doing absolutely nothing, and I loved to hang out in museums and check out the latest movies.

I am a popcorn fanatic, and the movie theater nearest to my home was one of the few that still popped it fresh.

Anyway, Harris and I came to an agreement to just part ways because neither one of us had time to waste. Fiona's man had cheated on her in a major way. She was bitter and didn't give a damn who knew it. In fact, when she suggested the trip, she told me straight up that she was going over there to find a man to fuck. She meant business, because she found her some dick action the very first night we got there, and I barely laid eyes on her for the rest of the trip.

It was the third day of our adventure when I ran into Jerome. He was coming out of a local marketplace with a stack of island shirts over his shoulder.

"Oh, my God! Is that you, Jerome?" I asked in disbelief.

He looked just as stunned as he tried to place me. "Salina, wow, is it really you?"

"In the flesh."

He eyed the lime green bikini I had on and commented, "Nice flesh."

I couldn't help but blush. "I can't believe I ran into you after all these years. I've been asking around about you."

He seemed really shocked then. "Really? You were looking for me or something?"

He's fine as shit, I thought to myself. "Yes, kind of. I was just wondering what happened to you. I haven't seen you since high school."

"Actually, I've been here in Hawaii since high school."

"Here in Hawaii?"

"Yes. It was always a dream of mine to come here. I came for a visit, and I stayed."

"That's major." I licked my lips without even thinking about it. It's a habit of mine when I get horny. "So what do you do here?"

He pointed behind him to the market. "Believe it or not, I run a stand here in the market. It will never make me rich, but it pays the bills."

"Well, making bills is all that really matters."

"What do you do?"

"I'm a cardiologist in Cleveland."

He laughed. "I guess you don't have any problems making your bills."

"No, just making time to enjoy life. Unless you're enjoying the ride, what's it all for?"

"This much is true."

Jerome and I stood there grinning at each other for a good two minutes in silence after that. I think we were both at a loss for words. Then he approached what was obviously on his mind.

"So, Salina, are you here with someone? Your husband, per-haps?"

"I'm no longer married, but I am here with someone." He looked utterly disappointed until I added, "My friend Fiona is with me, but she's locked away in her hotel room with a man she just met two days ago."

"Aw, I see." He sighed in relief. "She's making the most of her vacation, huh?"

"I guess so. Are you single?"

"Absolutely," he replied, grinning from ear to ear. "Well, since you're going solo right now, how about I show you around the island?"

I blushed, thinking it was about damn time he asked. "That would be great. I need to go back to the hotel and freshen up, but I can meet you back here in about an hour."

"Sounds good."

*   *   *

I rushed back to the hotel, but it really seemed like I was floating on air. I had a date with Jerome; a date that was years in the making. I had no idea where we were going, but I was determined to make it the best date of my life.

When I got back to the market, he was closing up shop, and what a cute little shop it was. He had island clothing, shot glasses, leis, dolls, and just about anything else a tourist could possibly want to get their hands on during a visit.

"Jerome, this place is really nice." I sat down in a straw chair and waited for him to finish securing everything for the night. "What made you decide to stay here?"

"The peacefulness. When we were growing up, I didn't have many friends, but you know that already. My parents and I were never close, so it wasn't like I was leaving anything of importance behind." He took my hand and pulled me up. "Ready?"

"Yes. Where are we going?"

"To a special place."

"A special place?"

"Yes, I want everything about tonight to be special."

I blushed as we walked along the beach. Jerome suddenly stopped and pulled me into him. "Salina, can I be honest with you about something?"

I gazed into his eyes. "Sure, you can tell me whatever you like."

"I used to be so in love with you in high school. You were the end-all and be-all to me, but you never gave me the time of day. Except for once."

I knew what he was talking about but played dumb. "Once?"

"That night at the movies when we bumped into each other. For a brief moment, I felt close to you, and then you were gone. You probably don't even remember."

"Yes, I do remember," I blurted out. "I felt something for that brief moment also, and I've felt it ever since."

Jerome kissed me, and it was all that I had imagined it would be over the years. He was gentle yet strong, and he handled me tenderly in his arms. We made out on the beach for a little while and started walking again. We ended up at a luau, and it was much fun.

I wasn't too crazy about the roasting pig. It didn't look appetizing at all, and it reminded me of the pig pickings my grandparents used to have in North Carolina. I did learn how to hula dance as Jerome looked on and tried to suppress his laughter. Those Hawaiian chicks were cut, and I felt inferior as they worked their hips in the straw skirts.

I had several drinks, and I'm not even sure what the names of any of them were. I know I had quite a mixture. I was so tore up that Jerome had to give me a piggyback ride all the way back to my room, which was really more of a bungalow. Housekeeping had left a fresh plate of fruit on the nightstand, their equivalent of mints on the pillow. The bungalow had an ocean view, and he opened the wicker doors so we could see the waves from the bed. Yes, the bed.

The time had finally arrived, and there we were, lying side by side and speaking our desires with our eyes. It was completely quiet except for the waves crashing against the shore, and the cool breeze was so relaxing that I had to fight sleep. There was no way I wanted to doze off and miss out on the opportunity of a lifetime.

Jerome reached for me and teased my nipple between his thumb and forefinger. I sucked in a deep breath and then exhaled loudly.

"Jerome, it's funny how things change." I placed my hand on his chest so I could feel his heartbeat. "At first, I had the same opinion of you as everyone else. Mostly because it was the cool way of thinking. But I realized that you were special that night at the theater. There was just something about you that made me want to be with you."

"Well, I'm glad that we're here together now. Here in Hawaii where there are no outsiders involved in our business."

I climbed on top of him and slid my tongue in his mouth, holding it there so I could remember the feeling always. I could feel him growing hard underneath me as I placed my knees beside his thighs and started grinding my pussy onto his dick. "Umm, you feel so good, Jerome."

Jerome was all into it, but suddenly he held back a little. "Salina, what is it we're doing here?"

I laughed. "I *think* we're about to have sex. That's what you want, right?"

"I want to do what pleases you."

I began to unbutton his shirt and kissed him on the neck before whispering in his ear, "Then we're *definitely* about to have sex."

I climbed off him just long enough to stand up and pull my dress over my head. I was braless because of the heat, but I had on white cotton panties. I slid them down over my hips and let them hit the floor.

Jerome stood up, and I helped him to disrobe. Then I pulled back the bedspread and lay on the sheets. He picked up the plate of fruit and placed it beside me.

"Sweets for the sweet," he said, taking a piece of pineapple and placing it between his teeth. He leaned over and swiped it across my breasts and down the center of my stomach to my navel, swishing it around inside.

I couldn't help but laugh. "Stop! That tickles!"

He took the pineapple from his mouth. "Sorry. I just wanted to lick the juices off you."

Watching those words leave his lips changed everything. "In that case, go for what you know."

He put it back in his mouth and went lower, brushing my pussy hair with the tip and then spread my thighs so he could work the pineapple up and down the insides of them.

Jerome completed his task and then seductively ate the piece of pineapple. I didn't miss a chew. I craved for him to work his mouth like that on me. He leaned over me and began to lick the pineapple juice from every inch of my body it had landed. I was never a moaner, but the way he meticulously licked me in long, slow strokes had me making all kinds of noises.

He made it down to my pussy and kissed me there. I exploded from the second his tongue landed on my pussy. "Damn, Salina," he said as he licked his hidden treasure. "You like that, huh?"

"I love it," I said, pressing his head between my thighs, urging him to explore me further.

He spread my pussy lips with his fingers and buried his tongue deep inside me. I sucked my index finger and then rubbed it across my nipples, elevating my hips to meet his efforts.

"I want to taste you, Jerome. Play fair."

Jerome didn't stop eating me, yet he managed to turn around on the bed and place his dick within target range. I circled the head with my tongue at first, relishing the fact that I was finally with him after so many years. Normally, when you fantasize about sex, it is never as good as the dream. This was better than anything I had ever imagined.

I took Jerome in my mouth an inch at a time until I was working all of him in and out with a rhythm. He tasted sweet, even without the pineapple. I sucked on him until he came and then asked him, "Fuck me, please."

He got off me and gazed into my eyes. "I don't want to fuck you, Salina. I want to make love."

He picked me up and carried me out onto the balcony, placing my ass on the rail. I wrapped my legs around his waist as he entered me. It was there that Jerome took all of me and I took all of him.

We made love throughout the night and woke up to Fiona banging on the door the next morning. Even though I had been concerned about her, the timing was all bad, and I secretly cursed her for showing up then. When I opened the door, she immediately thought I had been whoring around with some stranger, much like her. I explained that I had known Jerome in high school and that we were kindling a flame that should have been ignited long before.

Fiona was elated for us, even though her Mr. Right had skipped out on her for an island beauty. She made herself a ghost for the rest of the trip anyway, so that Jerome and I could continue to get reacquainted.

Now I have a private practice in Hawaii. It was never in my game plan, but love is stronger than ambition. It's funny how things change, but I'm damn sure glad they do. So for all you ladies out there who won't give a brother the time of day because of opinions and peer pressure, you might want to take a second look.

Do You Really Want to Touch It?

"Keisha, I need to run out for a few minutes!" Rapheal exclaimed, almost tackling me like a linebacker for the 49ers before the tip of my acrylic nail could make contact with his doorbell.

I glanced down at my watch. It was ten minutes to three. "Rapheal, I thought you said the shoot was at three?" I asked, smacking my lips.

"It is at three. It was, rather." I watched him toss a leather portfolio in the passenger seat of his gray Porsche convertible. "I have an emergency," he added as he ran around to the driver's side, swung the door open, and hopped in. "A corporate client is demanding to see these proofs right away, or I might lose the business."

"So what am I supposed to do?" I asked sarcastically, throwing a hand on my hip and working my head from side to side. I was disgusted and not even trying to fake the funk. It had taken me almost two hours to get up to his loft in Del Mar, it was hot as hell outside, and I had to drive my roommate's hoopty because my own rinky-dink piece of shit was in the shop getting a new tailpipe.

Rapheal flashed me one of his cinematic smiles while he revved up the engine. Fine or not, I was pissed, and his good looks weren't going to work magic on me that day. "The other girl is already up in the loft. You two keep each other company until I get back."

"Keep each other company doing what?" I inquired.

"Whatever!" he hollered and then pulled off, almost side-swiping a delivery van that was headed in the opposite direction.

"SHIT!" I couldn't believe Rapheal's skank ass. It was bad enough I let him talk me into doing this low-paying photo spread in the first place, but he had the audacity to leave me hanging like that after all I went through to get there. I stomped up the steps to his loft, changing my mind back and forth fifty-eleven times on the way up. I started to just turn around, get back in the hoopty, and take my ass home. Then again, low pay or not, I needed the exposure.

It had been two years since I left Boise, Idaho, for California to pursue my dream of becoming a model/actress. Instead, all I had become was a cocktail waitress/exotic dancer. If something didn't break for me soon, I was going to have to head back to Idaho and take up where I left off; stuffing russet potatoes into cellophane bags at dirty old Mr. Wilson's factory. He was such a pervert. Always trying to feel up some damn body.

Then there were my parents—in particular, my mother, who swore if I walked out of her house, I better not ever come back. My sister called me two weeks after I left and told me that I no longer had a bedroom. My mother turned it into a sewing room and donated all of my belongings to the church flea market. No, I was going to wait for Rapheal and do the shoot. No way was I groveling back to Idaho.

Once I got to the top of the steps, I almost fell back down them when I caught a glimpse of the other model. She was sitting on Rapheal's black leather sectional drinking a glass of wine and flipping through a photo album. She looked so exotic— long, flowing reddish brown wavy hair, smooth caramel skin, deep-set sienna eyes, and full, luscious lips. I figured she must have been from Paris or maybe an island in the Caribbean and had a flamboyant name like Genevieve or Dominique or something like that.

She spotted me and gave me a warm smile. Before I could even say hello, I just had to know, "Where are you from? Paris or Rome or some place like that?"

"Chile, please!" she exclaimed in the most countrified accent I have ever heard. "I'm from Lexington, Kentucky!"

I couldn't help but fall out laughing. She reminded me of the people I used to watch Saturday mornings on *Hee Haw*. How could someone who looked so spectacular be such a country bumpkin?

She shut the book and got up off the couch so she could meet me halfway across the loft to shake my hand. She had on this revealing spaghetti-strap sheath, making me look extremely underdressed in my jean shorts and my "I Wasn't Born a Bitch. Men Made Me This Way!" T-shirt.

"I'm Betty," she announced. So much for Genevieve or Dominique. "And you are?"

"Keisha," I replied, feeling a little more at ease, even though I was alone with a stranger. I had met some very, how shall I put it, freaky people during my short stint as a model/actress/cocktail waitress/exotic dancer. Betty seemed like she was cool peeps, though, so I decided to keep it real. "So, how 'bout that Rapheal bastard bouncing on us like that?"

"Rapheal's a trip. I don't even know why I deal with him," Betty stated with disdain.

"That makes two of us," I concurred.

I dropped my duffel bag on the carpet, plopped down on the couch, and threw my feet up on his marble coffee table. Etiquette went out the damn window. "Do you even know what this shoot is about? He didn't tell me much when he called me the other day. Just that he wanted me to get here on time or else."

"I'm not sure. I think it's for one of those nudie magazines. *Black Asses* or something."

"Say what!" I exclaimed, sitting up on the edge of my seat less than five seconds after I had gotten perfectly situated. "You mean we're supposed to be taking coochie pics?"

"Coochie pics." Betty chuckled. "That's cute. I'll have to remember that one."

"So are we?"

"Are we what?"

"Taking coochie pics?" I reiterated.

"Oh, come on!" she squealed, throwing her hands on her hips and walking over to the wet bar to pour me a glass of wine I never even asked for. "Don't tell me you've never posed nude before! Aren't you a stripper just like me? Rapheal said you were."

"Yeah, I'm a stripper. I dance down at the Black Rose."

"Oh," she sighed, handing me the wine and looking down her aquiline nose at me. "That's a trashy joint. I danced there for a couple of weeks when I first hit Cali."

She made me feel like something off the bottom of her shoe. I knew it was trashy. She didn't even have to rub the shit in. "So where do you dance now?"

"Chile, I'm at Paradise," she boasted in her country accent. "Those men up in that joint tip big-time."

"So I hear," I mumbled. "I auditioned at Paradise once. They threw me and my itty-bitty titties right back out the door."

Betty made no comment. There was none to make. Anyone could see that her 40DDDs put my 34Bs to shame, even a man who was blind in one eye and couldn't see a damn thing out the other one. My breasts looked like thumbtacks compared to hers.

She must have known I felt shamed, because she finally said, "I wouldn't sweat that. Look at you. You're gorgeous!"

She sat down so close beside me that her knee was rubbing up against my thigh. "You never answered my question."

"What question?" It had honestly slipped my mind somewhere between our skin making contact and her rubbing her index finger around the tip of her wineglass like she was fingering a nipple.

"Have you ever posed for nude pics before?"

"Not really," I hesitated, not sure whether the naked pics my two cousins and I took one Fourth of July behind my grandparents' barn would qualify. "I have no problem being naked though," I added, trying to save some face. "That's obvious. Otherwise, I wouldn't be dancing."

"True. So why are you acting so nervous, then?"

"I'm not nervous. It's just that dancing in a club and posing in magazines are two different things. Out here in California, I don't have to worry about being recognized. Nobody in my family ever leaves Idaho, but what if my daddy spots my ass up in a magazine? I would never be able to live that shit down!"

"Oh, does your daddy jack off to skin mags?"

The mere thought of that made me want to hurl. Then I realized that my daddy would never get off on nudie magazines. Hell, I remember eavesdropping through the paper-thin bedroom walls and hearing my mother practically beg him for a little nookie nookie. "No, my daddy doesn't, but I'm not too sure about some of his friends and a couple of my uncles on my mother's side."

"I hear you." Betty took her red high-heeled pumps off, and I noticed her toenails were painted the same color as mine. At least we had something in common. "Well, my daddy did see me when I did the cover of this boobs mag."

I was shocked. My mouth fell wide open. "You're kidding? I would have died. What did he say to you?"

Betty grinned at me. "All he did was call me up and tell me that he didn't know I had gotten a boob job. He wanted to know the name of my doctor so he could make an appointment for my mother."

We both fell out laughing. I don't know when I finished the entire glass of wine, but my glass was empty, and I was feeling a little buzz.

"You mean you have fake tits?" I exclaimed.

"Yeah," she replied, looking down her own dress at the top of her mounds. "Everybody's doing it these days. You should get some."

"Naw, I don't think so," I said, shaking my head. I was curious though, so I asked, "Can you still feel anything? I mean, when men are sucking on them?"

"Sure, I can feel it when men suck on them." She reached out and started caressing my hand. "Of course, I get even more stimulation when a woman sucks on them."

Oh, shit, she was coming on to me! I jumped off the couch and went to the wet bar to get some more wine. Hell, I needed the entire bottle. Not because she was coming on to me—it happened all the time down at the club. A lot of the dancers went both ways. I guess seeing other women shake their booty in front of you day and night can do that. I had never been attracted to any of them, though. I admired some of their beauty but was never attracted. Not until Betty, and that was making me sweat.

Before I could turn around to head back to the couch with

the wine, I felt her right hand reach around my waist and land on my belly button. "You've never been with a woman before, have you?"

"No," I quickly replied, taking a huge amount of wine in my mouth and swallowing hard. "I get the impression you have been, though."

"Just my roommate, Dominique. She's a model, too." Betty starting sucking on my earlobe, and I could feel my love coming down in my panties. I had to hold in a giggle. I knew there had to be a Dominique in there somewhere. "She and I have done it a few times."

Fleeting thoughts of my own roommate, Shontai, rushed through my head. I couldn't even picture doing such a thing. What would I say to her? "Hey, Shontai, want to go get a manicure, do some grocery shopping, and then come back to the crib and suck on each other's coochie-coos?" Now picture that for a Saturday afternoon!

"You never answered my question," Betty cooed in my ear, letting her other hand explore my ass cheeks.

"Damn, you sure have a lot of questions!" I polished off my second glass of wine and then started drinking straight out of the bottle.

"And you sure know how to avoid them," she came back at me with sarcasm.

After that, we both got quiet. I was wondering if I actually had the guts to experiment with another woman, and I have no clue what she was wondering. All I know is it was so quiet in there, you could have heard a mouse pissing on a cotton ball.

She took the bottle out of my hand and set it back down on the wet bar. Then she grabbed my hand and started pulling me toward the middle of the floor. "Let's dance."

"I don't hear any music," I said, stating the obvious.

She let go of my hand, went over to Rapheal's bookshelf system, and started flipping through his CD collection. A couple of minutes later, some smooth reggae started emitting from the speakers, ricocheting off the high ceiling and falling onto my ears. I was so used to dancing, I couldn't help but get into the groove, and the alcohol didn't hurt.

I started swaying my hips to the music, and Betty joined me, putting her arms around my waist and drawing me in to her until our legs were intertwining as we bent our knees up and down to the music. Our pelvises met and rubbed against each other. So that's what they mean by "bumpin' coochies."

She was tall, probably close to five-ten. Even in my three-inch heels, we were looking each other dead in the eye, and what mesmerizing eyes she had.

Then she just blurted it out. "I love itty-bitty titties."

I didn't reply. I just drew back a few inches, just far enough so that I could pull my T-shirt up and off. I wanted to find out just how much she loved them. It didn't take long to find out.

She seductively started rubbing my nipples in between her thumbs and forefingers. My nipples were hard enough to cut diamonds. She knelt down so she could suck one of them into her mouth and tickle it with the tip of her tongue. I shut my eyes and ran my fingers through her long, wavy hair while she partook of my pearl.

By the time the first song ended, I was lying on the couch, and Betty was pulling my jean shorts off with her teeth. She expertly repeated the task with my white satin panties. I massaged my own breasts while she started in on my clit, licking it up and down and then spreading my pussy lips open with her fingers so she could get to it better.

She was gentle with my pussy. Much more than any man had been. She moaned and oohed and aahed, telling me how sweet I tasted. All I could do was stare at the designer moldings on the ceiling and try to prevent my body from having spasms. Yes, her oral sex was that damn good!

In fact, it was so impetuous that I let her devour me for close to an hour. Rapheal still hadn't reared his inconsiderate head, and frankly, I didn't care if he ever did at that point in time.

Betty knew how to work magic with her fingers, too. Every time one of her acrylic nails would slide in and out of me, locating and causing friction against my G spot, my pussy walls would shudder and try to clamp onto her fingers like a vise—the same way I would contract my pussy muscles on a man's dick. And every time I climaxed, my curiosity grew tenfold, imagining what it would be like to return the favor to her.

Whenever I asked one of my lovers what my pussy tasted like, he would reply, "like chicken," or "like peaches," or some other corny line. I never actually believed that, but suddenly I had a craving to find out for myself.

I finally worked up some chutzpah and went for it. "When do I get a turn?"

Betty suckled on my clit one last time, gently nibbling on it with her teeth, and then raised her head from between my legs. I could see my juices smothering her lips and trickling down out the sides of her mouth. That was such a massive turn-on.

"Do you really want to touch it?" she asked me.

I hesitated for a brief moment and replied, "I want to do more than that!"

That was all she wrote. We retired to Rapheal's bedroom like we lived there. It was like a scene from an old, romantic black-and-white movie, walking off into the bedroom to finish the feelings. The only difference was, we both had innies instead of outies. And what a nice, delicious, scrumptious innie Betty had.

I helped her out of her dress and then sucked her breasts. It was such a strange and wicked feeling, but I loved it from jump street; having my mouth bursting at the seams with the meat of another woman.

Then I went down on her, ate her, found her G spot, and maneuvered my fingers inside her body until she came all over them. She didn't taste like peaches or chicken exactly, but she did taste good.

So good that we continued our little afternoon escapade in the shower. Steam was rising all over our bodies, and we took turns washing each other's private parts with vanilla bath gel and a huge sponge. Betty told me to prop my right leg up on the side of the tub, and I eagerly complied. There she took me to a height of passion I had never experienced before that day. That's when I knew I had been missing out on something special.

Don't get me wrong! I love dick! There's nothing like deep-throating a big, juicy dick, but eating pussy is running a close second in my book these days.

Rapheal finally showed up around seven and caught us getting freaky in his shower. Neither Betty nor I was willing to stop what we were doing, so we asked him if he wanted to watch.

He shouted, "Now that's what I'm talking about!"

He sat down on the closed toilet seat and took it all in. After a few minutes of watching us suck all over each other, he couldn't take it, whipped his dick out, and started jacking off.

I always thought Rapheal was fine. Seeing him there with his massive dick in his hand made me want him. So, while Betty was going to town on my pussy, I reached over and started rubbing my right hand up and down his shaft.

I swirled his precum around with my fingertip, and that made me explode. I came on Betty's tongue and then climbed out of the shower so I could climb onto Rapheal's dick. Betty followed me and I took turns between tonguing Rapheal and sucking on Betty's titties while I rode up and down on his dick.

We ended up staying in that bathroom for another three to four hours, doing things to each other that are probably illegal in about thirty-nine states.

We finally got around to taking the pictures the next morning. They came out awesome, too, because we ended up taking them on his balcony with the sun coming up in the background.

As for me being shy about taking nude pictures—let's just say I let all my inhibitions go that night, and they damn sure are not coming back. In fact, I'm doing the cover of two skin mags next month, and Betty and I are toying with the idea of doing some pornos together. I think it's a great idea. I get to suck on all that good, juicy pussy and get paid, too. What more can a sistah ask for?

Off Da Damn
Hook

The Headhunter

Let me tell you straight up that my situation will seem crazy to the average person. But, for me, sex is an incredible way to make a living. The simple version of the story is that I make money, a *whole lot* of money, doing what most women have been doing for free since the beginning of time. I have sex for money. No, I don't mean that I'm a hooker. Hell, no. I don't stand on anyone's corner waiting for Lawd knows who to stop his car and offer to take me to an alley for some quick, cheesy sex. Nope, not me. In fact, while I sleep with only men, 100 percent of my income comes from women. *Successful women.*

It's like this. A lot of women these days are extremely busy building their careers, making their dreams come true, etc. They don't have the time or the patience to hang out in nightclubs, churches, or wherever else, trying to find a decent man. That's where I come in. I locate and "test out" brothas for sistahs that want to get to the crème de la crème without all the hassle of trial and error.

I have an ad that I run in the local weekly paper. I haven't changed a word of my ad for the past five years, because it works like a charm. Like they always say, "If it ain't broke, don't fix it." My ad reads:

Looking for a good man?
Let Vixen Headhunters, Inc.
Find the perfect man for you
Whether you like them big and tall
Or short and small
We will locate your perfect mate
Call 301-555-HEAD
For a confidential interview

Vixen Headhunters is my brainchild. I started out running this gig alone, but now I have six full-time employees. My name is Gypsy, and hell no, that's not my real name, but it is the name I go by. In case the law ever comes sniffing around, I am not about to have my real name mixed up in jack shit. In fact, that is a requirement for all of my employees. They can't give out their real names to people because in the end, that's only asking for trouble—especially if one of the brothas we "test out" becomes overly infatuated with the sex or even worse, pussy-whipped. None of us want to be bothered with that bullshit. Our work is all about the benjamins. Dick is dick. There is nothing special about any one in particular.

Now there have been a few men who stood out from the rest. Not because of their actual dicks but because of their other amenities. For instance, there was this chick named Linda, a stockbroker from a rich background that had afforded her a lot of financial opportunities, but not a single freaky one. She wanted to meet a man who was successful enough for her to take home to her parents. She was desperate enough to look over the fact that she was butt-ass ugly, though heavily endowed.

This was a tough assignment for the team, because none of us are even close to butt-ass ugly. We're all fine as shit. But Linda was paying me a grip, so I told the other girls I would handle it. I went to see an image consultant—not to look better, but rather to look worse. I asked Harold, a transsexual—who looked more like a woman than half the women I'd seen—to transform me into something hideous. I wanted him to make me look fucked da hell up, and that's exactly what he did.

He put some kind of gook on my long, ebony hair that made it mat up something crazy. Then he removed my fake nails and trimmed my real ones down so low that they looked like I had been biting them daily since childhood. He gave me these drops that made my eyes turn red and some fake teeth that protruded about an inch from my regular ones, giving an entire new meaning to being bucktoothed. He also gave me this pencil to use to make these nasty-ass blackheads all over my face.

Then came the hardest part of all: wearing off-the-rack clothing. That was the most traumatic experience of my entire life. I can't understand how sistahs can play themselves by stepping out the house in any outfit that costs less than three bills. I'm designer all the way. I mean, come on, we only live once.

I made sure that no one I knew saw me walking into a department store, one of those ones where you can purchase everything from laundry detergent to screwdrivers to toilet tissue to *clothing*. Cheap-ass clothing. I found this little cotton dress that wasn't even twenty bucks and a pair of ten-dollar shoes. Yuck!

I tested the waters that night at this club where all the big ballers supposedly hung out. Not! It was a teeny-bopper club, and none of the men in there could have been making more than thirty grand a year, unless they were slanging dope. Linda wouldn't be able to present a drug dealer to the family, so they were out. A lot of the men and women snickered at me, and I don't blame them. I did look busted. However, there was this one chick gritting on me that I almost had to set straight. I started to tell her that I pull down more ends in one night than she probably made in a damn year.

I tried again the next night but scoped out a jazz club instead. Now we were talking. Most of the men in there were coupled off, but there were a few lingering around the bar who were obviously flowing alone. One in particular stood out from the rest; he looked like money, and he was fine.

I made my way over to the bar and asked if the seat next to him was taken. He assured me that it wasn't, and I sat down. It was time to go to work. His name was Kincaid, he'd never been married, wasn't seriously involved, and made about half a million a year. Yes, he would do.

Kincaid did seem a bit apprehensive about talking to me at first, but after a while, I guess he figured that any attention from a woman was better than none. I told him my name was Sheila, not that I consider Sheilas to be busted, because I know a few fly-ass chicks with the name—it was just the luck of the draw and the first name that came to mind. We chatted throughout the evening, and then I came on with it. He was obviously qualified in the basic departments and had not cringed at my face, so the only thing left to find out was if he could fuck.

The club had last call and people were getting up to beat the bum rush to the door. I leaned in to him, caressed his wrists, and asked, "So, you want to go someplace and do me?"

"Do you?" he asked with a raised brow, playing dumb.

"Yes, do me. You know, fuck me. Cum inside me. Hit it from

the front and the back. Make my toes curl. All that." I flicked my tongue over his outer ear. "I bet I can make your toes curl."

He grinned and searched the room, probably to see if anyone was looking at my ugly ass pressed all up on him. "I don't believe I've ever had my toes curl."

"Then you've been missing out."

He took my hand and got up. "Where do you want to go?"

I did not hesitate. "Your place."

Going to his place was a must. I had to make sure his ass was not lying about his financials. More importantly, I needed to assure that his ass was indeed single in every sense of the word. Men tend to have various definitions of single, and I wanted to find out if Kincaid's was the right one.

We went back to his place, and it was exquisite. He had mad taste. It was actually a town house, but shit, the thing had to run about eight hundred grand, and the property in that particular neighborhood was appreciating with lightning speed.

As soon as we got inside, I started taking off my clothes. His chin almost dropped to the floor. While I looked busted in the face and had skanky hair, there was nothing I could possibly do to mask my bomb-ass body. He was impressed.

"Um, would you like something to drink, Sheila?" he asked after composing himself.

"Yes, I want some dick milk." I went over to him and stood before him naked. "So take off your clothes."

"You don't want to talk first?"

"We talked at the club. I want to fuck."

Kincaid took his time undressing, and it was all I could do not to yawn. Once I finally saw what he was working with, I was a little disappointed. He wasn't tiny, but he wasn't a Mandingo either. That wasn't my problem though, because I was getting paid to check out the dick, not marry it.

I pushed him down on the sofa and climbed on it by strad-
dling my feet beside his thighs. I lowered my pussy onto his face
and demanded, "Taste me."

At first, I thought he was going to punk out and push me
away. Most men can't handle aggressive women, but Kincaid
fooled me. He lapped at my pussy like it was a bowl of milk and
then pulled me down harder onto his face. His tongue slipped
inside my pussy walls, and it was nice and warm and thick.

I put my knees up on the back of the sofa so I could balance
myself better. I moved my pussy back and forth on his tongue
and palmed my breasts with my hands. Kincaid grabbed a handful of ass with each hand and started nibbling on my clit.

I sat on his face for a good thirty minutes and came to the
conclusion that Kincaid was definitely a prize catch. This was before I had actually experienced the dick. Any man that could eat
pussy like that was worth coming home to every night. There are
some men who do it just to satisfy the woman, and then there
are those who do it because they love the way it tastes. Kincaid
undoubtedly loved it.

Once I climbed off his face, I fell back on the sofa in exhaus-
tion. That didn't last long because Kincaid got on his knees between my legs and lifted my ass up until it was elevated to his
dick. He entered me and worked it like a pro. My shoulders and
head were the only things touching the sofa. Everything else was
elevated. This was definitely a new position for me. I was used to
being multiorgasmic, but damn, I came so many times that I lost
count.

Kincaid and I went at it for at least four hours before falling
asleep on the dining room table, another place where he had
made me cum half a dozen times. I crept out of his place before
he woke up, walked down to the corner, and caught a cab back
to the club to get my car.

I reported to the client the next day that I had found the perfect mate for her, and she had a courier bring my final payment over in cash. Cash is always the way to go in this business.

Less than six months later, I saw their wedding announcement in the paper. I couldn't help but yell out, "You go, girl!"

Linda was a lucky sister. I knew that firsthand. There have been a few others like Kincaid, but they are few and far between. Business is booming these days now that the word has really gotten out. I am considering taking on some more girls, but there is such a thing as growing a business too fast, and the more girls, the more the risk that someone will run their mouths and end up getting us all locked up.

For now, I'm going to continue to do this business, because there is nothing like searching for "good head."

Bottom-Line Bitch

I'm a bitch, and that's the bottom line. I wasn't born this way, but people I've crossed paths with throughout my life made me this way. There used to be a time when I would bite my tongue, but then I realized that no one else was biting theirs with me. My mother laid into me just about every day while I was growing up. The truly fucked-up thing was that none of her issues and hang-ups had anything to do with me. I was just the object of her vengeance.

If something went wrong at her job, she would come home and cuss me out. If something went wrong with one of the numerous relationships she became involved in, she would come home and cuss me out. If she got a nail in her tire or a parking ticket, she would come home and—guess what—cuss me out.

My grandfather was just as bad. He would cuss me out because my mother couldn't trap a man into marrying her. He would cuss me out because my real father ran away. He would cuss me out because he was going bald. Everybody felt like they could just run over Beatriz for the hell of it.

I caught on quick, and by my freshman year in high school, I was taking no prisoners. My English teacher tried to play me in front of the room. We had to do book reports on a stupid-ass book—a so-called classic—that no one felt like reading. I took a shortcut and watched the movie. Back then, I had no idea that movies are often *way* different than the book. So my report had a ton of inconsistencies, which Mr. Richards took much pride in pointing out. When I revealed the fact that I had spotted him more than a dozen times coming out of the gay club down the street from my house, he didn't have shit else to say. The rumor spread so fast through the school that the fool was forced to resign in shame less than a month later. That taught him not to fuck with me.

People still try to play me. Just the other day, I was headed into the supermarket. I grabbed the first spot I saw, which happened to be one of those reserved for expectant women or those with small infants. I got out of my car, and some ninety-nine-year-old skeezer asked me if I had noticed the sign. I looked at her like she was crazy.

"Yes, I noticed the sign," I responded in disgust. "And?"

"And are you preg-a-nant?"

Now there I was minding my own damn business, and she had to go there. She was loading her groceries in the car and about to roll out, so it wasn't like I was preventing her old ass from getting a space.

"Yes, I'm pregnant," I lied, trying to squash the shit before I had to put my foot up her ass.

She placed her hands on her hips and leered at me. "Well, you don't look preg-a-nant."

That did it! "First of all, you need to learn how to pronounce the damn word. It's *pregnant,* not *preg-a-nant!* Secondly, unless you've been crawling around in my uterus, you don't know whether I'm fucking pregnant or not! This is 2002! You have a lot of damn nerve getting into grown folks' business. That kind of shit can get you shot these days."

She scanned the parking lot real quick, probably wondering who would save her if I did indeed whip out a gun. She started making a dash to get the remaining groceries in her car.

"That's right!" I yelled out, continuing to badger her. "You better get the fuck out of here! You better be glad I don't have any powder in my purse because I'd put some in my palm and pimp-slap your ass!"

With that, I walked away and went inside to get a dozen buffalo wings from the deli and a small container of salad for dinner.

After I got home and got my grub on, the phone started ringing off the hook. My mother called, asking to borrow a hundred bucks. She wanted to buy sexy lingerie for some new idiot she was trying to trap. I told her to bite me. She never did shit for me but try to break my spirit. And now that I'm an adult and out of her household, I relish paying her back for all her dirt.

No sooner had I slammed the phone down on her than it rang again. This time it was my ex-lover Web trying to make a booty call. Web is a sexy mutha fucka, but he isn't getting any more of this. They call him Web because he has these spiderweb tattoos all over his body. Nothing turns me on more than a roughneck, so I was used to be feeling that shit when we got naked and went for it. Any man who would permanently mark up his body like that is hard, and usually hard men work it out in the bedroom. Plus, Web had me thinking we might really have something together. Well, that shit wasn't true. It turned out that he was dating not one but two of my closest friends on the sly. The sluts. Once I found out, I cut them all off. But Web was still begging. He knew whose sex was on the money. Too bad for him, because my pussy went off limits from the moment I found out he was a cheater. When he asked if he could come over, I said yes, as long as he didn't mind me slicing his dick off once he got there. He called me a crazy bitch and hung up on me. *Good!*

My cousin Rochelle called me next. She was tripping because she wanted to know where she could get some weed. "Do I look like Drugs 'R Us?" I asked. "Because last time I checked, I don't even smoke the shit." Sure, way back in the day I puffed a time or two, but not anymore. Other than greasy food once or twice a week and soda, I don't put *anything* bad in my body. That includes bad dick, which is why I started contemplating about giving Antoine a call.

Antoine wasn't a pretty boy in the traditional sense of the word, but he damn sure had a pretty-ass dick. I met him at a gas station. It was one of those times when I had purchased enough gas to qualify for a discounted car wash. Normally I take a pass, but my car was funky dirty, so I decided to go ahead and pay the three bucks to get the works.

I pulled my car over to the car wash entrance and waited my turn. There were two vehicles in front of me and one inside the unit with the doors down. I cranked up my Snoop on the radio and rocked my head to the beat. Then I noticed a brother vacuuming out an Escalade across the way. I couldn't make out his face because he had on a Negro League baseball cap, but he was rocking this tank top, and his muscles were cut.

He leaned inside the car and bent over to vacuum something deep inside his truck, and his ass was protruding in my direction. What an ass it was! Shit was so lovely I had to lick my lips.

I didn't realize that my turn had arrived until some whore behind me started laying on her horn. I rolled down my window and yelled out, "Shut the fuck up!"

I could see her eyes rolling from afar but didn't give a damn as I pulled in. I couldn't get ole boy's body out my mind and started willing the wash cycle to hurry up and finish. I didn't want him to pull off without getting a chance to holler at him.

When the exit door finally opened, I sped out of there so fast that I almost hit the right side of the building. I grinned when I saw that he was still working on his ride. I pulled over to him, rolled down the window, and tooted my horn. He glanced at me, and I waved him over.

"Yeah?" he asked once he was right up on me.

"I was wondering if you could give me some directions," I replied, trying to sound seductive.

"Where are you trying to get to?"

"Your bedroom."

He looked dumbfounded for a second, and then he started blushing. "Let me get this straight. You want directions to my bedroom?"

"Yes, I hear it's a place worth checking out."

He chuckled. "And who told you that? Do I know you?"

"No, but you can get to know me. You can get to know me today."

He took a step back and eyed me suspiciously. "Naw, things like this just don't happen."

"Things like what?"

"Fine-ass women coming up to me at gas stations talking about letting me tap that ass."

"Well, it's happening today."

"Are you for real?"

I rolled my eyes. He was beginning to irritate me, but my pussy had started thumping, and it needed to be fed. "For real."

"For real, for real?"

"Look, my name is Beatriz, and I'm telling you straight up that I'm horny. I saw you while I was waiting in line for the car wash, and you were looking all good and shit, so I decided to come see what was up. But if you can't hang with a freak like me, let me know now so I can go on about my business and find someone who is down."

"No, no, I'm down," he stated anxiously. His voice wasn't the only thing that was anxious either because I could see his dick harden underneath his royal blue basketball shorts. "My name's Antoine. What did you say your name was again?"

"Beatriz." We stared each other down in lust for a few seconds before I asked, "Do you live near here, Antoine? More importantly, do you live alone, or are you married or shacked up or some shit like that?"

"Honestly?"

"I wouldn't have asked if I didn't want you to answer."

He looked down at the ground. "I'm engaged."

"Aw, how sweet." I bit my bottom lip and looked at his groin. "Does your fiancé make your dick hard like I just did?"

He seemed embarrassed. "From time to time she does."

"Uh-huh, I bet she's some prissy chick that doesn't even want to sweat her hair out during sex." He smirked, and I knew I had hit the nail on the head. "Surely you're not used to dealing with a bottom-line bitch like me."

"A bottom-line bitch?"

"Yeah, did I stutter?" I asked sarcastically.

"Why would you call yourself a bitch?"

"Because that's what I am, and I'm damn proud of it." I put my car in park and hopped out. "Listen, are you down for this or not, because a sistah could be getting her nails done or something."

I checked out my nails, and I did need a fill-in. I peeped his, and they were neatly clipped and clean; a definite must when it comes to men I fuck—any man with dirty nails generally has dirty balls, and that shit just ain't kosher.

He hesitated before saying, "It's just that—"

"That what?"

"I've never cheated on her before."

"I can dig that. I had a man cheat on me, and I dumped his ass, so she would probably do the same to you."

He laughed nervously. "I'm sure she'd do the same thing to me."

I moved closer and rubbed my pussy up against his dick, since we were about the same height. "Danger can be very sexy. I'm not trying to fall in love. I'm just trying to fuck."

"And you want to go to my house?"

"Yeah, I do."

"Why can't we go to yours?"

There was no way I was taking a strange brotha to my house. What if he got pussy-whipped and started stalking me?

"There's no danger at my place, Antoine. The possibility of getting caught is such a turn-on." I flicked the tip of my tongue across his cheek. "Wouldn't you agree?"

It took about ten more minutes to convince Antoine to play the game. Five minutes after that I was parking beside him in the two-car garage of a brand-spanking-new three-level home. The shit was off the chain. He led me inside. The ceilings on the entry level had to be at least fifteen feet tall. The main living area was airy and encased by picture windows with the back facing a thicket of woods. The house had oak hardwood floors, leather furniture, and a black kitchen with a marble counter.

I went into the kitchen and jumped up on the countertop. "This looks like a good spot to fuck."

"In the kitchen?" Antoine asked in amazement. "I thought you wanted to see my bedroom?"

"I do and I will." I glanced at the digital clock on the microwave. It was two-thirty. "So what time does Miss Prissy get home from work?"

"She's really not even like that. She's a great woman."

"If she's so great, why am I here?" I demanded to know.

Antoine shrugged his shoulders. "I guess because this is an adventure."

I clamped my ankles around his waist and pulled him to me. "It's not an adventure yet but it will be."

After putting my arms around his neck, I slipped my tongue into his wet mouth. His tongue was kind of rough but he knew how to kiss well. I took his cap off and noticed that he was a lot better looking than I thought. He still wasn't pretty though.

He had brown, curly hair and dark eyes, which complemented his even darker skin. I pulled my baby tee over my head and revealed my braless upper body. Antoine wasted not a second plopping a titty into his mouth and trying to devour it whole.

"Mmm, that's it, baby," I whispered in his ear. "Milk this bitch!"

The house was silent with the exception of Antoine's sucking noises. I kicked off my sandals and hooked one toe of each foot into the waistline of his shorts, using them to pull them down. Then I repeated the move to get his drawers off.

I pushed him off my titty. "What do you have good in your fridge?"

Antoine appeared stunned by my question. "You're hungry?"

I giggled and pushed him farther away so I could get down from the counter. "No, silly. I want to see what you have to enhance the experience for us." I opened the fridge door and spotted what I was searching for. "Aw, hot sauce!"

I took the bottle out and turned around with it in my hand. The expression on Antoine's face was worth a mint.

"What the hell are you going to do with hot sauce?"

I approached him and got down on my knees. "For starters, I plan to lick it off your dick."

Like most brothas, he tried to guard his dick with his hand at the mere mention of something foreign being placed on it. Antoine was getting off easy, and I let him know.

"Relax," I said, putting pressure on his hand and moving it aside. "You're getting off easy. Usually I love to play around with candle wax."

Antoine shook his head. "Now that shit is out."

"Whatever. We'll save that for next time."

"Let's make something perfectly clear, Beatriz. There's not going to be a next time."

I smirked at him. "If you say so. I must warn you, though. If the sex is on point, I'm going to want some more, but I'm still not trying to fall in love. You can marry Miss Prissy but this beautiful-ass dick of yours might end up belonging to me."

I drew all that dick into my mouth, and Antoine started trembling something fierce. It made a sistah wonder if he'd ever been given head before.

"You are so damn nasty," he managed to get out between moans.

I released his dick from my cheek grip for a second to reply. "Bottom-line bitches are always nasty. We get straight to the point."

After taking the cap off the hot sauce, I poured a few drops along Antoine's shaft and spread it around with my tongue. He winced, but after the initial reaction, that shit couldn't help but feel good. I lifted his dick up and splattered a few more drops on the underside before putting some on my tongue and sucking his balls gently.

"Oh, shit!" he screamed out in ecstasy. "I can't take it."

Antoine tried to push me off, but by that time I was on a mission. For the next thirty minutes, I sucked, licked, and devoured his dick. He came four times, and even his cum was scrumptious.

Then we took it to the master bedroom, and it was also off the chain. The room was decorated in animal prints and had the biggest bed I'd ever seen. It was in that bed that Antoine attempted to break my back for the next two hours. Either that Negro had popped some Viagra on the sly or he hadn't had any *real* pussy for a long-ass time. We fucked in the missionary position followed by the doggy-style, followed by the scissors, and ended the marathon with me on top riding him for dear life.

After he exploded inside me for the umpteenth time, we were both covered in sweat, and so were the sheets.

I leaned down and kissed him on the nose. "Baby, you've got some good-ass dick."

"And you have some good-ass pussy."

The hot sauce had made the trek to the bedroom with us, and I sprinkled some on my left nipple. Antoine took it in hungrily. The hot sauce penetrating my skin with the assistance of his warm tongue sent me into a frenzy. I wanted to go for another round, but then it suddenly hit me when I glanced at the alarm clock beside the bed.

"You never told me what time Miss Prissy gets home."

Antoine sat up and grabbed the clock. "Oh, shit! It's after five! She'll be home any second!"

He pushed me off him and started grabbing for something to put on. The only problem was that all my shit was still down in the middle of the kitchen floor, along with his. He ran down the steps two at a time, but I took my little sweet time.

"Hurry up!" he lashed out at me.

"Hold up!" I stopped midway down the steps in all my glory,

where anyone that walked up to the front door could see me through the glass panes on the sides. "Don't you dare try to talk down to me after you just fucked me for hours!"

He reached the bottom and turned to face me, flailing his arms in the air. "Okay, look, Beatriz. I'm sorry if I yelled at you, but I really need you to help me out here."

I descended the rest of the steps and jumped into his arms, locking my legs behind his back. "I just helped you out."

"That you did, but now I need you to get dressed and get out of here before she gets home."

He carried me into the kitchen and sat me on the counter. Then he got dressed with the speed of lightning. Again I took my time, but I did get my clothes on and follow Antoine to the garage, where he rushed me into my car and pressed the button to raise the door.

I rolled down my window and informed him, "I'm not leaving without some digits."

"I can't give you my number," Antoine stated with disdain. "This was a one-shot deal."

I rolled my eyes. "Fine, I'll just drop by tomorrow around the same time, then. Either you can give me the number, or I'll just roll through."

"Shit!" Antoine started feeling imaginary pockets for a pen and paper. I got them out of my glove compartment and handed them to him. He started scribbling. "I'll give you my cell number, but please don't call it late at night."

He thrust the paper at me, and I tossed it on the passenger seat before starting me engine.

"Can I just ask you one thing before I leave?"

"Please, Beatriz. Cut a brotha a break. Just call me later."

He was darting his eyes back and forth from me to the road.

"I just want to know if you had fun."

He couldn't help but blush. I know my pussy was on point. "Yeah, I had fun."

"Cool."

I backed out of the driveway and started down the road. A sistah in a red Corvette passed me and I could see her pulling into the same spot I had just pulled out of through my rearview mirror.

"Hmph, Miss Prissy!"

I didn't see Antoine again. I was halfway bullshitting him about the number. I just wanted to see if he would cave in and give me one. Sitting in my apartment with nothing to do one day, I recalled our adventure. I put slippers on and went out to my car to search for the number. I finally found it among a bunch of miscellaneous junk beneath my seat.

Once I was back inside, I didn't hesitate to call. His sexy ass answered on the third ring.

"Hello."

"Hello, Antoine. You know who this is?"

"No, I can't say that I do."

I picked up a candle from my coffee table and wondered what reaction Antoine would have to candle wax all over his dick.

"Baby, this is your lucky day. It's your bottom-line bitch!"

Cum for Me Boo

Oh, how I love cum.
I love it in the springtime and the fall.
Oh, how I love cum.
I love it best of all.

First, the facts, and trust me, I know my shit well. Years of research and hands-on experience have schooled this sistah.

Here is the lowdown:

Semen: A fluid that activates and protects the sperm after it has left the penis during ejaculation.

It only takes about a dozen muscles to smile, but more than a hundred to cum. Each tablespoon of cum only has about seven calories. One good ejaculation can knock up more than half the women on the face of the earth. A man will cum thousands of times during his life span, and about a third of those times will be from masturbation. Dicks have about ten times more blood in them when they are hard than when they are soft. A shitload of men masturbate on a daily basis, no matter what. Some men can get hard again instantly, and some can't get it up again for weeks. Most men get hard-ons around the clock. Dicks are extremely durable, so ride the hell out of them, ladies, 'cause you can't break them.

> **Contents of semen:** Ascorbic acid, blood-group antigens, calcium, cholesterol, chotine, citric acid, creatine, DNA, fructose glutathione, hyaluronidase, lactic acid, magnesium, nitrogen, phosphorus, potassium, purine, pyrimidine, pyruvic acid, sodium, sorbitol, spermadine, spermine, urea, uric acid, vitamin B-12, and zinc.

And they have the nerve to say, "Milk does a body good!"

In case, you haven't figured it out by now, I have a weakness for cum. To be even more specific, a man's cum. I love everything about it, especially the taste. A man can never cum too much for me, and I can't understand why any woman would not love to gulp it down. The concept of not swallowing is beyond me.

Sperm is a delicacy, especially when the man eats, drinks, and even smells certain things. The smells of pumpkin pie, lavender, licorice, and doughnuts increase blood flow to a dick. Alkaline-based foods such as meat and fish produce a buttery or fishy taste, while dairy products make a brother taste foul. Asparagus creates the foulest taste of all, so for goodness sake, never let your man eat asparagus. You following me?

Acidic fruits and alcohol make cum taste sweet. Yummy, yummy, yummy, I got cum in my tummy! Chemically processed liquors make cum have an acidy taste, and so on and so on.

Now that you know about my weakness for cum, let me tell

you about my "cum daddies," as I affectionately call them. I have two of them at present, Brandon and Travis. They are both good lovers, but that is not why I am with them. I fuck them both because I just love the way they cum.

Take Brandon, for example. He is a junior in college, a few years too young for me emotionally, but hell, I am not trying to walk down the aisle with him or no ridiculous shit like that. That'll never happen.

I met him in the college bookstore. I am working on my doctorate in the graduate program and was looking for a textbook I needed when I spotted him in the next aisle. He had that look about him—the look an experienced sistah, such as me, can spot right away. The look telling me he could fuck his ass off. I targeted my mark, and as always, I hit the bull's-eye and picked his ass up right then and there. The next night I invited him over to my place and tore his dick the fuck up.

I seduced him with little effort and had him sucking my toes within fifteen minutes after he hit the door. Young brothers are so pussy-controlled. You offer them some coochie, they are going to hit it whether you are eight or eighty, blind, crippled, or crazy. Like Run DMC said, "It's like that and that's the way it is."

Brandon is one fine mutha fucka, though, and if he was a few years older, I might just marry his ass. Nothing wrong with an old ball and chain when it looks as good as him. He is five-ten, 185 pounds, medium complexion with light eyes. He has a nice build from working out four times a week. More like seven or eight times, if you include the three or four times he works out with me.

Our first night of sex was interesting, to say the least. I tied him to a dining room chair with his ankles bound and his hands tied behind his back with electrical tape and even covered his mouth with the shit, after taking off my panties and shoving them in his mouth first. Yeah, I am kinky like that. It's not like he couldn't breathe through his nose. So anyway, I rode his dick real good, like a wild horse galloping through the woods, until I could tell he was about to detonate, got off his dick, and extracted the catalytic fluid from him orally.

Let me tell you, I thought the man was going to have a freaking heart attack. When he came, he reminded me of a scene from a movie I had seen once. I can't recall the name, but there was this scene where a couple had been bound and gagged by some masked intruders who later cut their throats and watched them bleed to death, shaking and quivering, until the end finally came. Not the best simile, but that is what Brandon looked like when he came, like a condemned man having a thousand volts galvanized into his system while strapped in an electric chair. Dayum, that shit turned a sistah on, and I came more than he did. And the cum, the cum was nothing short of remarkable. It tasted so dayum savory, like I knew it would. When a man eats a balanced diet and works out the way Brandon does, there was no way I could steer wrong with the cum.

That was our first night, our moment of glory. I was satisfied, and Brandon was pussy-whipped, and it was all good. I untied him, let him get in my bed and rest up some, and then woke his ass up with one hell of a blow job because I was still mad hungry. It has been five months now since we met, and I still have him wrapped around my little finger. Like I said, controlled by the pussy. They say this is a man's world, but all of us women know the real deal. Every man from the flats of Compton to the White House is controlled by the pussy. This is a woman's world. They are just squirrels trying to get a nut. Get it?

Now, let me tell you about my other "cum daddy," Travis. He is older than me, but I still would never marry him because there is a certain idiocy about him and I don't like his ways. I do, however, have a great appreciation of the way he fucks and nothing but love for the way he cums.

Travis and I encountered each other at an art gallery showing one evening. I was there checking out some abstract paintings by a young, up-and-coming black artist. He was doing the same. We started a conversation pertaining to one painting that showed the outline of a black couple. The woman was on her knees, as was the man positioned behind her, and he was eating her ass out.

Travis asked my opinion of it, and after looking back and forth between his refined ass and the painting, I told him the scene portrayed in it made me horny. You see, Travis is a fine-ass man, too, and fine-ass men who have that fuck-you-till-you-beg-for-mercy air about them simply thrill me.

Travis is not as built as Brandon. He is more slender yet very athletic as well. He is a daily runner who follows a strict vegetarian diet, except for when he eats me of course. He is as dark as they come, originally from the West Indies, six-two, 180 pounds, dark bedroom eyes, and a smile that is a bit crooked, and he has a pleasing disposition.

I asked him back to my place for cocktails, and he accepted after buying the eating-ass portrait for me. I have it hanging on the wall over my bed to this very day. We chatted into the wee hours of the morning, exchanging childhood stories and then bringing things up-to-date.

He was about to leave around 3 A.M. Or so he thought—but I wasn't even having it. I told him that instead of heading home, he should stay and suck on some of my pussy. From the look on his face he was not accustomed to sexually uninhibited women like me, but he was dayum sure glad to finally run across one.

I led him to the bedroom, and we got butt-naked and became engrossed with each other's sexual organs, caressing all the good parts. I decided to conduct an experiment on his ass. As a rule of thumb, I generally like to get straight to the fucking as soon as possible, but I decided to tempt fate that night and draw out the process.

I told Travis he couldn't stick his dick in me until we played a game. I went into my bathroom and pulled out the basket of flavored oils I keep in my linen closet. I have quite a variety and proceeded to put a different flavor on various parts of my anatomy before I returned to the bedroom, where Travis anxiously waited for my return.

Then I laid out the rules of the game. He had to lick the different parts of my body and guess what flavor I had on each one. If he were to give a wrong answer, he had to get dressed, carry his sorry ass home, and take a cold shower.

I told him to lick my lips first, and he got that one easy. It was lemon. I told him to lick my neck, and after a moment's hesitation, he figured out it was peach. My tits were next. One was sporting raspberry and the other vanilla. He named both. He lingered a bit on the right tit, though; giving me the feeling he was a breast man. After three months of fucking him, now I know for sure he is a breast man, 'cause he is always reluctant to let my nipples loose once he gets hold of them.

Next came my belly button. He recognized the chocolate taste right off the bat. Then he had to lick my inner thighs. The left one was strawberry and the right blueberry. This is when the game got tricky. I was beginning to think I would be faced with the decision of carrying through with my ultimatum. Would I really make his ass leave, or back down and give the pussy up anyway? Travis pulled it off though, getting both flavors right.

He had one last obstacle to cross to get the gold medal, though. That was figuring out what flavor was on my pussy. I thought it was easy, but his ass didn't know the answer on the first few licks. My patience was growing thin! He kept licking and licking and still didn't have a clue. So I gave him one.

"What is a nickname for pussy?" His ass still didn't know, so I continued, "What word completes this sentence? 'I am gonna bust her (blank)!' "

That was when I knew he was an idiot, so I told him that it was a fruit and had a stem. He finally figured out it was cherry, and the fucking began. The night took a turn for the better then, because Travis fucked my ass royally. He hit it from every direction. I told him to make sure to tell me when he was about to cum, 'cause I wanted to swallow it all. That turned his ass out, and he really started wearing this nana out.

He was fucking me doggy-style when he pulled out and told me he was cumming. I turned around faster than the speed of light and caught that cum like an action hero. It was a speeding bullet, and I was about to catch it between my teeth. Once again, I was right on the money: Travis is the king cum daddy. I swear his cum was like a forty shooting down my throat, tasted like cinnamon rolls. I know that sounds ridiculous, but it's true.

As far as his cum style, Travis gets tens straight across the board for delivery, expression, and creativity. He always comes with such style and grace, like a gazelle prancing through a field of lilies. I am used to men making all kinds of noises and shaking like an earthquake when they come, but not Travis. He just lies there, as if in a trance, with glazed eyes and shallow breathing. His body freezes up like an Eskimo stranded on an iceberg without a coat. It is such a turn-on. I can't get enough of it.

Well, now you know all about my two cum daddies. I don't love them, but I lust them, and that's just as good. Every time they cum for me, I lust after them even more. Cum is scrumptious, nutritional, and great for the complexion. "Cum does a body good!"

Kandi Kan Make U Kream

For a good time, dial
1-900-694-KANDI

     Don't judge this book by its cover . . . cuz I'll look like rated G but do you like XXX! The name is Kandi, and I have more dicks than a mutt has ticks. I am pleased to make your acquaintance. I don't chase after nobody's man; they come to me. I am always just a phone call away, and when a man calls, he gets to play out the wildest fantasy of his dreams.

     There is only one drawback to what I do; I can only do it locally, since I act out live fantasies for my clients. I would much rather be an international lover, but all in good time. I am very particular about the type of men I service. If they are coming at me, they better come correct. If they have problems hanging in the bedroom, they better be taking yohimbe, zinc for men, ginseng, and vitamins plus drinking about a gallon of OJ and a dozen raw eggs on a daily basis.

     I hate it when women step to me with all their self-righteous bullshit. Just out of spite, I will fuck their men. While they are out at the hairdresser or getting their nails done, I will be at their houses teaching their husbands, boyfriends, and baby's daddies the horizontal lambada. Ain't no shame in my game; chile, please. My legs stay open like 7-Eleven.

Basically, what I do is have phone sex with men and discuss their wildest fantasy. Once we play the whole thing out on the phone, I arrange to do it with them in real life as well. I will give you a couple of examples.

Osaze is this Nigerian guy who is happily married with kids. However, like most marriages, his is lacking in only one department; the sexual one. He had a fantasy about doing it in an adult bookstore, so one night I met him at this sleazy one in downtown NYC.

He was all the way in the back of the store flipping through some porno magazines. He spotted me but turned his back, pretending he did not recognize me. Truth be known, he had never actually seen me before, but I was wearing nothing but a black trench coat and some black stiletto heels, as per his instructions. The idea was to make love to a stranger. That was the big turn-on.

I walked up behind him slowly and felt all eyes on me. The various perverts and the clerk at the counter were checking me out because not many women frequent the place. After I got all the way to him, I wasted no time pressing my stomach up against his lower back and reaching around with one hand to caress his dick. I must say I was pleasantly surprised at the size, because you never know. Men say one thing, but some quote numbers in centimeters instead of inches. Osaze was not fronting, though; he had said he was nine inches, and he was at least that.

I kept caressing his dick as I made my way beside him, pretending to be looking at mags as well. He took his hand closest to me and stuck it into the opening in my trench coat so that he could caress my thigh. I opened my legs a little more so he would have no trouble getting his fingers inside my pussy walls when the time came. I unzipped his fly and reached my hand inside his pants. He had no underwear on, so it was just skin against skin, and I loved the way his veins felt as his dick pulsated in my hand.

We never uttered one word to each other as he removed his fingers from my pussy and I, in return, removed my hand from his pants. He took me by the hand and led me over to a booth. A black velvet curtain was the only concealment. The booth was small and cramped, but we both managed to get inside and pull the curtain shut. It was one of those booths where you put a quarter in a slot to see a thirty-second porn movie.

He didn't put a quarter in the slot but elected to unbuckle the belt of my trench coat instead. He pushed it back over my shoulders and completely off, letting it drop to a floor which was covered with dried-up cum.

Osaze looked deep into my eyes as I undid his pants and let them drop down around his ankles. Then he picked me up in the air and placed my back against the concrete-block back wall of the store. The wall felt cold against my skin, but it made me tingle all over. He started sucking on my breasts and tried to get some tongue action, but I pushed his head away from mine. I had made it clear that I never tongue-kiss clients. That is too personal.

I could hear some footsteps of people gathering outside the curtain, wondering what we were doing—as if their stupid asses didn't know. Osaze put me back down on the floor and then turned me around so that my breasts were on the cold wall. Then, as agreed, he didn't fuck in my pussy, but stuck his dick all the way in my ass instead. He could get pussy at home; brotha-man came for the ass.

I had never taken a dick that big up my ass before, and I tried my best to keep my composure. However, once he started pumping his dick in and out faster and faster, I couldn't hold it in any longer and started moaning extremely loud. In fact, my moans ended up drowning out all the other noise in the store. Curiosity got the best of all the men standing on the other side of the curtain, and one of them got bold enough to pull it back. There we were, exposed.

Osaze didn't quit, though; he finished his business, and I never asked him to do otherwise. People watching him fuck me in the ass didn't bother me in the least. In fact, if anything, it increased the pleasure.

He finally finished doing what he had to do and pulled his dick out of me just in time to shoot his hot cum all over my ass cheeks and down the crack. It trickled all the way down onto the floor and joined the rest of the cum spots that were already there. That was the first time I did Osaze, and as far as clients go, he is one of my favorites.

Then there is Wesley, a single brotha who just can't seem to find a woman to satisfy his needs. So he pays me to do it instead. His biggest fantasy was to fuck on the Staten Island Ferry. We decided to do it late at night so that the ferry would be mostly empty and so it would be dark out and hard for others to see.

He wanted to experience fucking a woman with the waves crashing up against the sides of the boat. I met him there, and we did just that. He was waiting for me on the uncovered area on the back of the ferry when I arrived. As he requested, I wore a skimpy sundress with spaghetti straps and no panties. I was freezing my ass off but figured once we got busy, I'd warm up.

When I walked up to him, he already had his pants undone and dick out, only covered up with a sweater. I looked around to see if any of the few other passengers or crew were looking, and then I leaned my head down toward his lap so I could suck his dick.

I went straight for the corona, a ridge on the bottom side of his dick, which is the G spot for men, and when I licked it, he fucking lost it. Then I started deep-throating his dick and humming on it as it hit the back of my throat and my tonsils. He started to say something but refrained. To me, the fun part of a fantasy is the silence, and we had talked enough on the phone. When most people fantasize, they don't picture long, drawn-out conversations, so I try to make them as real to life as possible.

I kept sucking on his dick until my own saliva, mixed with his precum, was trickling out the corners of my mouth. He held the sweater over my head so people would not be able to see if they should walk by. After a good while, he came in my mouth and then told me it was time for me to take a little ride.

I got up and sat on his dick backward so that my back was to his chest. I sat down slowly on his dick until it was all the way up inside my stomach. Wesley is another well-hung individual. As I started riding his dick, he stuck a finger in my ass, and that only made me get more into it. He started slapping me on my ass, and since both his hands were busy, I decided to help myself along. Shit, just because I am getting paid doesn't mean I shouldn't cum also, so I started caressing both my breasts and lowered the straps on my dress.

I pushed each breast up to meet my long tongue and flicked the tip of it across my nipples. That aroused me so much that I started bouncing up and down on his dick like a pogo stick until the poor baby couldn't take it anymore and exploded for the second time.

I do a lot of men a lot of different ways, and I love doing it. So I didn't grow up to be a ballerina or an actress. As far as I am concerned, what I do is even more fulfilling. I give men what they want and what they desire. If you are ever in the NYC area, dial 1-900-694-KANDI, and "Kandi Kan Make U Kream!"

Life Imitates Art

I love movies—always have and always will. I totally lose myself in the characters, become them even. When I was a little girl in Detroit, we lived near a drive-in theater, and I could look out my bedroom window and see the people and images moving around on the big screen. I could never hear the actual words they spoke, but I became quite the expert lip reader.

My mother, who was a single parent, couldn't afford to take me and my three brothers to the movies so we would cook some popcorn on the stove, the old-fashioned kind that comes in a little aluminum pan with foil that expands as the kernels underneath pop, and then have our own little night out at the movies.

My brothers would only watch the movie once or twice and then go play with their action figures or pretend to be cowboys and Indians. I would watch the same movie over and over again for as long as I could keep my eyes open. I would prop myself up on the windowsill in my bedroom with a pillow behind my back and become enthralled with everything from the love scenes to the bang-bang-shoot-'em-up scenes.

The mere thought that people could become larger than life, with millions of people all over the nation, sometimes even the world, watching them at the same time, was amazing. It was pure magic to me. I remember thinking how beautiful all the women were, with their painted fingernails and lips, thick eyelashes, and fancy hairstyles. The way they moved around the screen with such elegance and grace. The handsome men they got to fall head over heels in love with, sinking into their arms, kissing them passionately, caressing them all over their bodies and, in the R-rated movies, even sucking on their breasts. It was electrifying.

By the time I was ten, I was hooked on a dream. I wanted people to someday stand in line to pay their money and watch me on the silver screen. I wanted to capture the hearts of men everywhere and gain the envy of women. I wanted to be larger than life, to have people run up to me, ask for my autograph, and scream out my name. I wanted to travel the world and have people cater to my every wish and obey my every command. I wanted to be a movie star.

Now, fifteen years later, at the age of twenty-five, I am indeed a movie star. Men of all ages and races want to take me to bed, women and teenage girls want to mirror my image, and I am worth millions. I am now in the position to give my mother and brothers everything they ever dreamed of, but unfortunately, I can't.

My mother died from breast cancer when I was nineteen. I was devastated. For two years, I thought of only one thing: suicide. I used to sit in the dark and cry for hours and hours, analyzing the quickest and most painless way to end my own life. Only three things dissuaded me from going through with it: my brothers. I am the oldest, and it is my responsibility to ensure that they make it in this world. We have no grandparents. They all went to heaven a long, long time ago.

When our mother died, I was working in a video store in the daytime because I loved the fringe benefits. I got free movie rentals and the privilege to see videos the day they were released. Once she died, I was rudely awakened to the fact my minimum-wage salary wouldn't even begin to cover the expenses of clothing and feeding the four of us. I couldn't stand the possibility of my brothers becoming wards of the state.

So I did what I had to do and became a stripper. It was cool because it gave me the opportunity to cook breakfast, see my brothers off to school, be there for them when they got home, help them with their homework, and cook their dinner. My brother Paul, fourteen, was old enough to watch the younger ones, Jonathan, ten, and Reggie, eight, when I went to work at night. The entire situation worked out pretty well, but it would have been better if our mother was still there.

I was so-called discovered during one of my performances. A theatrical agent named King James—yes, that is really his name—approached me after the show and told me he wanted to represent me. I thought he was full of shit, of course, and he halfway was. He expected me to fuck him for his representation, and I did. I fucked a lot of men to get where I am; producers, directors, agents, whoever. It's all a game. Bottom line is, when the smoke cleared, I was on top. Most women give it up and never land even one role for all their efforts. I have made six movies so far, and this is only the beginning.

When it comes to acting, I take it very seriously. Since I never had the opportunity to take formal acting lessons, I have learned to improvise. In fact, I developed a fool-proof method for acting my ass off in any role I am challenged with. No matter what the role is, no matter what it calls for, I prepare myself for the task by acting out all the vital scenes for real. Life imitating art, so to speak.

My first role was the easiest; it was as an exotic dancer, so no role-playing needed there. My second role was a bit more trying. I had to play an invalid, so I got in a wheelchair and pretended to be handicapped for a month to portray the role more realistically. I even participated in a wheelchair race to raise money for birth defects, and the publicity was great. It worked, because it was the role that made me a star. I became a household name and got nominated for several awards, even an Oscar. I still say the only reason I didn't win them is because of the melanin in my skin.

Once my third acting role came along, things began to get interesting, to say the least. I landed a role as an escort, so I put on a wig, some colored contacts—a disguise, if you will—and went to an agency and became an escort on the real. It was interesting, word up on that, and I only did it for a few days to get the gist of the role I was portraying. The three men they sent me out with were true freaks, and of course there was no publicity. I am not that fucking crazy.

The first man took me to a boring-ass opera and then wanted to spend the rest of the evening sucking on my toes. He had a serious foot fetish. I couldn't believe his ass paid to suck some toes, but hey, my dog Spot used to lick my toes when I was a little girl, so no skin off my back.

The second fool took me out to a fine restaurant, followed me to the ladies' room when I went to go take a leak, and then ate me out in the bathroom stall. He was all right at it, but I wouldn't nominate him for any pussy-eating awards or anything.

The third man, who was also the reason I quit after three days, was a straight-up freak. He had the agency send me directly to his hotel suite. When I got there, it was cool at first. He was attractive and had a nice seafood dinner ready and waiting for me by candlelight. After dinner, he went in the bedroom and came out in the sitting area of the suite dressed as a drag queen.

He started talking like a woman who sounded like she had a dick stuck in her throat and wanted to play out a lesbian scene with me. I told him to get the fuck off me and left. I called the agency from my cell phone, cussed the owner, Devina, the hell out and quit. She was this old-ass hoochie with tits that rested all the way down on her stomach and a sagging ass to match.

My fourth role was as a blind pianist. Just like all the other roles, I took it seriously, and the publicity was even better than it was in the invalid role. I donned a pair of dark glasses and wore patches on my eyes underneath so I couldn't see. I also took piano lessons and became pretty dayum good with the eighty-eight keys in a couple months, but most of the actual scenes from the movies involving playing were still done with trick photography.

My fifth role was the one that turned out to be downright dangerous—not during filming, but during my quest to portray it in real life. The role was as a member of a female gang. Once again, I put on a wig and some contacts, changed my appearance around a bit, and thought I had it all covered. But I was seriously mistaken.

One night I was hanging out with some of the girls from this gang on the Lower East Side, trying to get them to accept me and jump me in. Yes, I was actually going to go that far to see what it was all about. They told me to come to a party with them at someone's house, and I told them I was down.

We got to this house, and there were drugs and guns and liquor everywhere, along with several male undesirables. One of them, nicknamed Smoke, was fine as shit, and he and I got to drinking together. He convinced me to try some weed, something I had never done, but I figured it was in my best interest to pretend I was experienced with such things.

It must have been laced with something, because I started

freaking out and shit, hallucinating and seeing three of everybody. Smoke carried me into one of the bedrooms, and we
started getting nasty together, kissing and licking and sucking
until we were both undressed. He ripped my wig off, which I
had partly covered up with a bandanna, and told me he knew
who I was all along and that we were going to have a real good
time together.

Before I knew it, he called all the rest of the people in the
room to watch. I was attracted to him big-time and feeling nice,
so I went along with the game plan. I had never fucked someone
in front of a group, and now I was about to fuck this stranger in
front of gang members—gang members who could expose me
at any second to the press and destroy my career. It was pure in-
sanity, but nothing was going to prevent me from fucking Smoke
that night. Not a damn thing.

I got lost in his touch and blocked everyone else from my
mind as he swiftly removed my clothing and then slipped out of
his own. He was cut like an Adonis and hung like a bear. I was
taken off guard when he handcuffed me to the bed but didn't
protest. If I was going to let it all go, I might as well go for the
ultimate experience.

Smoke forced my legs open and told two of his buddies to
hold them open, and they did. I had no idea what he was going to
do to me, but it excited me. He climbed in between my legs on
the bed, grabbed both of my breasts, and sucked on them
roughly one at a time. After several minutes of that, I came with
a vengeance.

I could hear people laughing at me and saying things like,
"Damn, Smoke, you can suck a titty till a sister comes!" and
"Look at this shit! Smoke is doing a movie star! Ain't nobody got
a camcorder up in this bitch?"

He stuck his long, thick dick in me, and I succumbed to the

ecstasy of it all. If I hadn't been drugged up, I would have worked my ass all over his dick, but I could only lie there and enjoy. I had always been an undercover exhibitionist but never had the nerve to actually go there.

Smoke slammed me so hard with his dick that I could feel it in my abdomen. His friends implied that they wanted to take a turn with me, but Smoke made it clear that the shit wasn't happening. He fucked me for a good hour, and I lost count of my orgasms. I'm not sure if it was the dick, the situation, or a combination.

Once he was about to cum, he pulled out and jacked himself off until he came all over my tits. Then I sucked his dick something fierce. He fed it to me while I was still handcuffed to the bed, and tasting my pussy juice on him was the greatest turn-on. There was a moment when I almost gagged, but I relaxed my throat just enough to get it all in.

Smoke and I fucked until sunrise. All of the others eventually cleared out of the room. Half of them were stoned, and the other half just had better shit to do or needed to go someplace and fuck around themselves. That morning, he cooked me breakfast, and I found out a lot about him. He was in a gang, but he was also smart as shit and quite the entrepreneur. People can say what they want about drug dealers, but name another profession where someone can make upward of ten grand a week by word of mouth and zero paid advertising.

Smoke and I got along so well that we started dating officially. In fact, he lives with me now in my mansion, and the newspapers and tabloids are having a field day with the story, but fuck them. This is my world!

Now, I am in the process of making my sixth film. I portray a serial killer. This is the first time I can't act out all the vital scenes in the real. This is the first time life can't imitate art. Or can it?

Out of Control

The first time I saw him, he was sitting across from me at the hotel pool. I couldn't get a great look at him because the sun was beaming down on my head, and I had left my sunglasses back in my room. As much as I dreaded the sun, the thought of having to make the trek back through the massive hotel to the bank of elevators, go up twenty-two floors, and walk down two hallways to get to my room was even more unappealing. That is the one drawback to staying at a luxury hotel. There is such a thing as being *too* damn big.

Anyway, there I was chilling in Atlantic City, the city that never sleeps, or at least *one* of the cities that never sleeps. My fiancé Morris was supposed to be vacationing with me, but he wimped out at the last minute after his mother asked him to take her shopping. Talk about a momma's boy. What kind of man misses out on a weekend full of fun in the sun, gambling, and sex to take his mother to a mall for an afternoon? Only fools deal with such nonsense.

I was seriously thinking about calling off the wedding. I was in love; there was no damn doubt about that. However, love is one thing, and happiness is something totally different. Just because two people love one another does not necessarily mean that they should be together forever, because forever is a long-ass time.

That was what ran through my mind as I eyed the bronze brother lying on a green-and-white striped lounger on the opposite side of the pool. All kinds of naughty thoughts started floating through my head. In the lead was the thought of fucking him right there in the pool in front of everyone. Not that I would ever have the nerve to do something that bold—freakiness has never been a problem for me, but that was a bit much. A sister can always fantasize, though, because what happens in a person's private thoughts carries no risk or judgment.

He jumped up from the lounger and stretched. Uh-huh, that Negro was fine. He was about five-nine, with curly black hair— that naturally curly shit, not the kind you buy in a box. His body looked like it had been carved, and he had very distinctive facial features. Yes, I was definitely in lust, which was not a good thing for an engaged woman to be.

He had on these tight-ass black swim trunks, and I zeroed in on his dick like a missile. The bulge seemed mighty large, and I wondered if the brother knew how to work all of that. He suddenly looked directly at me and smiled. I smiled back as he walked closer to the edge of the pool and jumped in. He disappeared underneath the water, and I lost him in the masses of people enjoying themselves in the pool for a moment. Next thing I knew he was coming up for air less than five feet away from where I was sitting.

"Pretty day!" he called out to me.

"Yes, it is! Kind of hot, though."

He winked at me. "Most people like hot things."

Umm, he was coming on to me. Things were about to get a bit scandalous for real.

I tried to think of a clever reply. "Yes, most people do, but only until they get burned by them."

He pulled himself up out of the water by his arms and came my way. The water glistening on his skin made him look like something out of a health spa commercial. You know, one of those spots where they encourage you to get in shape for summer by joining today at a reduced rate. I got bamboozled into one of those deals and didn't go five times because working out was pushed onto the back burner. The bottom line is that if a person is committed to getting in shape, they will do that no matter where they are. Like the majority of Americans, I had several pieces of exercise equipment collecting dust at home.

"What's your name?" he asked me as he sat down on the lounger beside me.

"Sam."

"Sam? Is that short for Samantha or something?"

"Nope. Actually, it's Sam Jr."

"Sam Jr.?"

"Yes. My dad always wanted a son, and after six daughters, he demanded that the baby had to be named after him or else."

He chuckled. "So you're the baby of the bunch?"

"Unfortunately. Trust me, it is not a pleasant position to land in."

"I can't imagine. I'm an only child."

"And does Mr. Only Child have a name?"

"Sorry, I'm being rude." He offered his hand. "I'm Austin." We shook hands.

"Where are you from, Austin?"

"I'm from San Diego. I'm here for a pharmaceutical convention."

"I'm from Richmond, and I'm here to have one hell of a good time."

"Not a damn thing wrong with that." He reached over and patted my thigh. It felt incredible, too. "Maybe we can have one hell of a good time together."

I blushed. "One never knows."

He started checking out the big-ass rock on my finger. "Whoa! If you're here with your husband, I don't want any drama. I can just move on."

"I'm not married, Austin. I'm engaged." As the words left my lips, something just didn't feel right about them. "My so-called fiancé backed out on this vacation at the last minute, so I'm not really happy with him right now."

Austin grinned and patted my thigh again. "His loss is my gain."

Austin and I ended up having a ball for the rest of the day. After chatting for about two hours by the pool, we went back to our respective rooms to change into casual clothes. I met him down in the casino at the quarter slots because anything more than a dollar at a time was not leaving my possession. Some people can justify spending their entire paychecks on "what-ifs," but not me. I was reared to appreciate and stretch every dollar. I must admit that the gambling was mad fun, though. I won some money, lost it all back, and broke even in the end.

By the time we had rotated from machine to machine for a good four hours, I was also pretty drunk. All those free drinks were a blessing and a curse. They were a blessing for obvious reasons—something free is something free. They were a curse because I tend to lose my senses when I'm drunk.

I guess that's why I didn't object when Austin asked to escort me back to my room to share a private dinner. I was actually hoping that I would *be* his dinner, but he ended up ordering room service anyway.

As we shared a bottle of champagne and dined on porterhouse steaks, roasted garlic potatoes, and string beans, I finally started asking him a few personal questions. I found it difficult to believe that a man as fine as he could be readily available.

"So Austin, is there a Mrs. Austin back in California?"

He snickered and shook his head. "No, but there is an ex–Mrs. Austin someplace in the world."

"Hmm, that makes it sound like you don't know where she is."

"That's because I don't. Katherine had a lot of ambition, and being a wife wasn't in her game plan. She wanted her career more than she wanted me."

"Why couldn't she have both?"

"She could, but not the way she wanted them. She expected me to stand by and not comment on inappropriate things that she was doing."

"Like?"

"Like cheating people, for one." He smirked. "She's a financial adviser, but the only person's finances she's truly concerned about is her own."

"That's a shame, but you know that karma is a bitch, and whatever we do in the darkness always comes out in the light."

"Absolutely." Austin took my hand in his. "Does that include *everything* that we do in the darkness?"

I laughed. "Yes, every single thing."

He got up from the small round table and cut off the single lamp that was on in my room. A few of the bright city lights shone in through the half-drawn curtain. He came over and pulled me up into his arms. Then he gently slid his tongue in my mouth. "Umm, you taste so good, Sam," he whispered.

"You taste good, too."

We kissed for a few moments, getting the feel for each other's passion. Then Austin picked me up and carried me to the bed, laying me down ever so gently. I watched in appreciation as he took his time taking off his clothes and neatly folding every piece as he went along. I couldn't really make out every inch of him, but I could see enough, and he was magnificent.

He lay beside me and suckled on my earlobe. "Now it's your turn, Sam. Show me what you've got."

"You can't really see what I've got in the dark."

"I like a little something left to the imagination at first."

I got up from the bed, and he slapped me playfully on the ass. I let out a fake "ouch" and started undressing. "A little strip music would be ideal, but I guess I'll just try to wing it."

I swayed my hips to imaginary music and slowly unbuttoned my blouse, letting it fall off my shoulders and onto the floor. I bent down to pick it up. "Should I be folding my clothes up also?" I asked jokingly.

Austin licked his lips. "Naw, just go for what you know."

We both giggled.

"Okay, I'll do that," I stated as I reached my hands behind my back and unhooked the clasp of my bra.

After my breasts were free, Austin commented, "Umm, nice and full, just like I love them."

"So you're a breast man?"

"Oh, yes, I love playing with succulent breasts. It's the greatest turn-on to me."

"Well, it turns me on also. I love to have my breasts sucked."

"Then we're going to get along just fine."

I lowered my shorts and stepped out of them. Then I inched my panties off by lowering each side an inch at a time.

Austin reached out his hand to me. "Come here."

I climbed on top of him and began kissing him again, this time more intensely. He grabbed my buttocks tightly and pushed me up against his dick. I didn't hesitate for a second to ease down on top of him until he was completely inside.

"You feel so good, baby," he said as he thrust himself up into me.

I gripped onto his dick like a vise and rode him slowly and methodically. "I don't think I've ever had a dick this good."

I stopped riding him just long enough to get off my knees and place my ankles on his shoulders. I put the soles of my feet against the headboard and started going back and forth on him like I was rowing a canoe. I had seen that shit in a porn video once and had always wanted to try it.

I went faster and faster until I could feel the head of his dick rubbing up against my G spot, and that caused me to go into a frenzy. I dug my fingernails into his chest as I achieved the first of many orgasms I had that night.

Austin told me to turn around, so I changed positions and climbed onto him with my feet still against the headboard, but this time my toes were pointed to the bed. I grabbed onto his ankles, and he held onto mine. I don't think I've ever felt such excitement as I did in that position. It was incredible.

Austin and I fucked and sucked all night. Then the guilt started hitting me like a baseball bat. Morris was too attached to his mother, but did he really deserve a cheating fiancé? I did love him, even if I had issues with him from time to time.

Austin had to head back to California that afternoon, and it was just as well. He asked to exchange numbers, but I declined. I did tell him that I would never forget our special time together, and believe me, I never did.

Six months later

The big day had finally arrived, and I was a nervous wreck. I couldn't believe I was about to become a bona fide wife and eventually a mother. Morris and I had worked a lot of things out, but he was still catering to his mother way too damn much. She and I had a long discussion that almost turned into a catfight, but we finally came to an agreement to disagree. She obviously saw me as some sort of competitor for his affection, and while every man should always love his mother, he also needs to show respect for his wife at all times.

The church was packed, and my daddy was pacing the floor in the vestibule the way he probably paced the hospital hallway when I was born.

"Daddy, you're making things worse," I told him as he turned around for the hundredth time.

"Sam, this is a big day. My baby's getting married, and all I can say is that man better not ever hurt you, or he'll have to deal with me."

I stopped him in his tracks and hugged him. "Morris takes great care of me. Sure, we have our problems, but who doesn't? Everything's going to be fantastic. I promise, Daddy."

"It better be."

All of the bridesmaids and groomsmen had already entered the church, followed by the two flower girls, and it was now our turn.

"You ready, baby?" Daddy asked.

"Absolutely!"

A huge awe came over the invited guests as we entered the door. I had to admit that my dress was slamming. I had it custom made by an up-and-coming African-American designer out of Philly.

Morris was at the altar waiting for me, and I could've sworn

I spotted some tears in his eyes. That's when I knew I was doing the right thing—any man that would cry over my ass deserved my affection for life.

We were halfway down the aisle when something drew my attention to the left. It must have been a gut instinct, because I immediately spotted Austin in the crowd. He had a look of dismay on his face, and I guess I did also. I couldn't imagine why on earth he would be at my wedding, especially since I never even gave him my contact information.

Somehow I managed to make it through the ceremony without fainting, which is what I felt like doing. What if Morris knew him?

At the reception, I found out the real deal. Austin came through the receiving line, and Morris threw his arms around him for dear life.

"Austin! I can't believe you made it, man!"

"I can't believe I'm here either," Austin replied, breaking away from the embrace and staring at me. "You must be the lucky bride."

Morris guffawed. "Of course. Man, you're still crazy. I want you to meet, Sam. Sam, this is Austin, one of my closest friends from childhood. I haven't seen his ass in more than a decade, but our mothers have stayed in contact, so I asked them to make sure he showed up."

"It's very nice to meet you," I said nervously, offering him my hand.

He lifted it to his lips and kissed it. "The pleasure was all mine."

He winked when he said "was" instead of "is," making a subtle reference to our night together.

"So what's up, Austin?" Morris asked. "Where are you living now? What are you doing?"

"I live in San Diego, and I sell pharmaceuticals."

"So you must travel a lot. It must be exciting."

Austin eyed me seductively, and I prayed Morris didn't pick up on it. "Yes, travel is a major part of my job. It can be dismal, but sometimes an exciting opportunity comes along, and that makes it all worthwhile."

I cleared my throat. "Morris, I'm going to go talk to Daddy for a second. I forgot to tell him something."

Before Morris could point out the fact that there were still several people in the line behind Austin, I took off. It was a truly fucked-up situation, and I wanted no part of it. At least, I didn't until . . .

Austin crept into the bridal lounge while I was in there, hiding from all the madness for a few minutes. This was after we'd done all the traditional things such as cutting the cake, the first dance, etc. I just needed a few moments alone to collect my thoughts.

"Can I come in?" I heard him ask from the doorway.

"No," I quickly responded, turning to face him. "That's not a good idea."

"It's probably not a good idea, but I'm coming in anyway." Austin came in and closed the door behind him. "We need to talk."

"There's nothing to talk about," I stated vehemently. "You tricked me."

"I didn't trick you, Sam. I didn't even realize that this was your wedding until you walked down the aisle in that dress."

"How could you not know?" I asked in utter disbelief. "Didn't you get an invitation? How many women do you know named Sam Jr.?"

"I never got an official invite. My mother called me and told me to come just last week, and I didn't make my travel plans until yesterday morning. I didn't know who Morris was marrying. Like he said, we haven't spoken in ages."

I rolled my eyes. He obviously was telling the truth, but that did nothing to improve the situation. "Thanks for coming in here to explain. You can leave now."

Austin reached out and caressed my cheek. "Sam, I—"

I pushed his hand away. "No, don't even think about it."

"Sam, I haven't stopped thinking about you since that night in Atlantic City. I had no idea how to find you. I even tried bribing someone at the hotel into giving me your information, but the brother backed out on me when he thought about jeopardizing his job."

I looked into his eyes. "None of this matters now. I got married today, which means I am off limits *forever.*"

Austin turned toward the door, and I put my back to him. I never heard the door open, though; just the lock clicking. Before I knew it, he had grabbed my waist from behind and pressed me up against the wall. He started caressing my breasts through the lace of my wedding gown and kissing my ear and neck.

"No, we can't do this," I objected, trying to get him off me. "Stop it, Austin."

"You don't really want me to stop," he whispered in my ear. "You want me, too. Admit it."

I didn't respond because I knew he was halfway right. As much as I had tried to convince myself that what happened between us was simply a one-night stand, there was something special about it that could not be denied.

Austin grabbed a handful of my dress and bunched it up until he could get his other hand in between my legs. He pushed my white satin panties to the side, the ones that Morris was supposed to take off when we consummated our marriage, and started finger-fucking me.

I attempted to contain my moans but ended up giving in to them. I could hear the band playing in the reception hall, and it was merely a matter of time before someone came looking for me.

I pulled Austin's hand out of my pussy and faced him, lifting his hand to my mouth and licking my own juices off his fingers. I let the last one linger on my lips as I said, "We have to hurry up if we're going to fuck."

I couldn't believe those words had just left my lips, but they did. Austin pulled my dress up again and went down on his knees. He placed one of my thighs on his shoulder as he ripped my panties off. Then he buried his face in my pussy. I couldn't even see him because of all the material, but I could feel him going to town on me and my pussy juice trickling down my white lace-topped stockings.

"I want you so much, Sam," he said to me from down below.

"Damn, this is so wrong," I screamed out, pushing his tongue deeper onto my clit by palming the back of his head. "But I want this, too. I always have."

Austin ate me out for about five more minutes and then stood up with my leg still elevated. He grabbed hold of my ankle and held it in place so it wouldn't slip off. I helped him undo his belt and zipper with his other hand, and it was a joint effort to get his dick out as fast as possible.

He slid inside my pussy, and I trembled. The dick was too damn good. We tongued each other down as he banged me slowly up against the wall. We were going at it hard when a knock came at the door. We stopped in mid-stroke and held ourselves there.

"Sam, you in there?" we heard Morris ask as he tried the handle. "Some people are leaving, and they wanted to say good-bye."

Austin and I just looked at each other in silence for a few seconds. Then he whispered, "You better answer. He knows you're in here."

I tried to catch my breath and calm down before I yelled out, "I'll be there in a minute! I'm just freshening up!"

I could feel Morris's hesitation before he came back with, "Okay, but hurry up! Why's the door locked anyway?"

I didn't respond. I just listened carefully for his footsteps as he finally walked away. Then we started stroking again until we finished. I went back out to the reception, and Austin left, but not before giving me his numbers.

I know what I did was wrong, but I couldn't help it, and if I had it to do all over again, I would probably do the same thing. Tomorrow is promised to no one, and while I'm one heck of a good wife to Morris, Austin gave me something special on two occasions.

I did consider doing it again, and even called, but a woman answered his home phone. I wondered if it was his ex-wife but came to the conclusion that she could have been anyone. The only thing that mattered was that a woman did answer the phone, which meant he had moved on.

I know the day will come when Austin and Morris hook up again for whatever reason. I just hope I can keep my composure. I figure that as long as he and I are never alone in the same room, nothing will happen. Then again, I might just want it to. Maybe I'm just out of control.

Penitentiary

Prisoner #456912
Name: Dalton Wayne Lewis
Aliases: Dalton William Lewis, Wayne Douglas, Robert
Morgan, Delante Young
Convicted of: Possession of Narcotics with Intent to Distribute
Length of Sentence: Three Years

So he's a convict, big deal. Do you have any idea how much good dick is going to waste in the prison population worldwide? Dalton may not be a superhero, but he is dayum sure a superman. My superman, my dick supply on the inside—that helps the time pass more quickly when I am on the clock and bored to death. Yes, I'm a prison guard, and I guard my favorite dick like the prized possession that it is.

Nobody fucks with Dalton. Nobody! If they even look at him cross-eyed, I make sure it never happens again. No matter what it takes. This hoodrat came in one time trying to start some shit. (I hate playa haters.) I had his ass thrown in solitary for a week, he came out acting like a church mouse. I can't have my baby boo harmed while he is locked up. He is the sunshine of my life. When he gets out, we are getting married the same day.

It is against the rules for a guard to have "relations" with a prisoner, so we keep it on the down-low. Sometimes it is hard for the two of us to creep away so I can knock him off a piece. It's extremely sexually frustrating to be so close to your dick supply you can smell it and still can't get any. It is pure hell.

I fell in lust with Dalton the day he was processed, and now I simply love his ass. The other day I found out that I'm pregnant. I'm so happy about it I could do a jig. The hurting part is maternity leave. The prison makes you go on leave or work in the office as soon as you start showing. I can understand it, though. They don't want to accept responsibility for whatever may happen in the case of a prisoner getting rough with me. Heaven forbid if a full-fledged riot broke out. So, I can dig it.

But being away from my baby for months is gonna kill me. The fact he won't be there for our baby's birth is too much to bear. I knew what I was getting myself into. I just have to maintain. He's only doing three years, half of which is already up, and with time in for good behavior, he could get out even sooner. When he does, I am putting in my resignation, marrying him, and having two or three more of his babies. That's how much I adore my boo.

The first time I saw him, I was sitting at the processing desk where the uniforms, sheets, towels, combs, bars of soap, shampoo, and toothbrushes are handed out, and where the prisoners are assigned a number. It was hot as hell that day. The heat seemed to be coming from both the sky and the ground at the same time. It was the kind of heat my siblings and I used to experiment with as kids by frying eggs on the sidewalk.

The usual stream of gangstas, hoodlums, roughnecks, and

such were being guided past my post. They come from the intake room, where they are strip-searched from their ear canals to the cracks of their asses and inspected for paraphernalia. This dude with an upper gum full of gold teeth walked up to me and made his play. They disgust me when they do that. His ass was so ugmo, he probably couldn't give his dick away with food stamps attached to it in front of a supermarket filled with broke women stressing formula for their babies. Yet he thought I would actually flirt with his stank ass. I do mean stank, too. The brother had that natural aroma thing going on, and it made me want to hurl.

After I issued him all his prison garments and such, I told him to take a hike. I was hot, bitchy, and sexually frustrated because the man I'd been shacking up with for over a year went on tour with his band. It would have been unfair for me to ask him to stay. He was talented on the real. Plus, I didn't love him like that, so I said cool. I had loved men in my past but had never been in love. That is, until Dalton.

He was the next one in line, and when I saw him, my first instinct was to yank him over the countertop and tongue his ass down. I wanted to suck his dick and use his cum as a facial and then a meal. I wanted him to fuck me like a computer with enough RAM to boost my ass up to the moon and back. But his ass was Prisoner #456912, so I figured I was shit out of luck.

Things started looking up when I found out he was assigned to my cell block, though. I was on the day shift when he first came in. I used to spend my days watching him from my post on the top of the fence while he lifted weights, played basketball, and hung out in the yard. Watching him bench-press all that weight made my pussy wet. I wanted him to pick my ass up like that and fuck me up against a wall in midair.

My paragon of manhood is so refined, he is a defiance against nature. Dalton is six-nine, and you know what they say about tall men; they go deep. He is dark-skinned with eyes that look like black pearls in the sunlight and has enough muscles to lend a dozen men some and still be built like hell.

I used to masturbate so long imagining him fucking me that I would almost work myself into dehydration. I lost all interest in the men who were calling to ask me out, preferring to play with myself thinking about a convicted felon.

There was one major snag. Since I was on the day shift, I could never get his ass alone. He and I had brief conversations, but not the kind love affairs are made of. So one day I marched into my supervisor's office and put in a request to work the night shift, deciding that one must make sacrifices in the name of love. After a month, my request was approved, and I started working graveyard duty.

That was only the beginning, though, because I still had to figure out a way to get at the dick. All prisoners are supposed to be on lockdown at night, so it was going to be a bit tricky. But there are not as many guards on duty at night, and there is less activity to monitor.

There are two other guards, Ryan Sanders and Cameron Mays, who work cell block three at night along with me. Both are moderately cute, but I have no interest in them. The only way my plan would work is if I cut some sort of deal with them. I would do something for them, and they would do something for me, like turn the other way when I was doing my thing with my baby.

The prison system is more corrupt than politics. All sorts of shit goes on behind bars. Guards sneak in everything from cigarettes to girlie mags to drugs, as long as they are getting paid. One night I approached Ryan and Cameron and told them straight up how I was feenin' for Dalton's fine ass. I asked them what it would take for it to happen.

If you know anything about men, you can probably guess what they wanted. Yeah, they took turns fucking the shit out of me in a broom closet while the other one kept an eye out. After that, I had a clear path to the man of my wet dreams.

The one good thing about cell block three is each prisoner has an individual cell, a rarity in the system today. It had to be that way since the cells were barely big enough to fit one man in them.

The night after I fucked Ryan and Cameron, I made my move. I waited until about 2 A.M., ensuring most of the prisoners would be in the deep stages of REM. Then I walked the landing, got to his cell, and motioned for Cameron to release the electrical door of his cell.

He was sleeping so peacefully when I entered his cell that I hesitated to even wake him, but I thought it over and decided I wanted the dick more than I wanted him to get his sleep. I used my nightstick and tapped him on the leg; he immediately jumped up. You learn to react fast in prison. For all he knew, I may have been some male prisoner who had paid off a guard to let him in to snatch some ass. That type of shit is common, but highly unlikely in Dalton's case 'cause he is so fucking big.

He was about to start swinging when he realized it was just little ole me. He knew the deal without me having to spell it out for him. In fact, he never even asked my first name until after we got done fucking the first time. He just knew me as Officer Johnson.

I quickly took off my uniform shirt. He sat back down on the bed and started helping me with the buttons. Both of us had been checking the other out for a long time, and pussy is scarce in prison, so you know he was all about it. We managed to get my shirt off with mutual effort, and he pulled my bra straps down and started nursing on them bad boys; shit felt good, too.

I whispered, "That's what I'm talking about! I have been saving all this pussy for you!"

That made him even hotter, and he started unzipping my uniform pants while he still sucked "his" tits. Uh-huh, I said "his" tits. These are Dalton's tits, this is Dalton's pussy, and this is Dalton's ass; simple as that.

He got my pants off with the speed of light and then threw me down on the iron bed. He reached for something off the bookshelf over his bed, and for a second, I thought he might be violent, and I was about to get something I hadn't bargained for.

Instead, his hand returned with a box of cough drops. I was lost, but not for long, 'cause he popped one in his mouth, pushed my legs open—putting one over each shoulder—and started eating me out with the cough drop in his mouth. I don't know how to describe the sensation, but if you've never had your pussy eaten by a man sucking on a medicated cough drop, know that it is a must.

Then he pushed my legs back farther so he could get at my ass and started eating it out also. I didn't think I would have a hard time getting some from him, but dayum, brotha-man was ready to tear some ass up.

I felt like I was doing a public service or something. Like the movie stars back in the day that were flown in by helicopter to battleships in order to keep up the morale of the men who were away from their family and friends for an extended period of time. Well, Dalton was away from his normal day-to-day situation too, so I was just trying to keep him happy.

I told him we had to hurry up because I knew Ryan and Cameron would be worrying that we would all get caught. I started working at his pants to get them off. I knew any man six-nine had to be fucking hung, and I was oh so right. They say the biggest functional dick on record is eleven inches, and I am ready to debate that shit, 'cause Dalton is packing more than that. His dang-a-lang is at least a foot, probably bigger. I know, I've had it all the way up in my stomach too many times to mention.

It is mad thick, too. I nicknamed his dick "Shocker" because it can paralyze a pussy.

When he whipped it out that first time, I wanted to run for the border. I started whispering again, "I can't handle any shit that big!"

He spoke for the first time. "You in here now; you taking all this!"

With that, he rammed it in me, and I was frozen for a good two–three minutes. It was like all of a sudden having a contraction when you never even knew you were pregnant. I regained my composure and started grinding my hips upward onto his dick; not much, but I didn't want to give the impression I am one of those women who just lies there. Never that!

Dalton was tearing "his" pussy up when I heard some footsteps approaching the cell. I tried to push him off me, but he was too heavy and big for me to move him an inch. I was petrified, assuming one of the night supervisors must have somehow caught on to the shit and was about to embarrass my ass big-time. Not to mention getting fired.

Dalton didn't give a shit who was coming, since his only concern was cumming his dayum self. He was knocking the bottom out my pussy when I heard Ryan, who was standing outside the cell door with his back to us, whisper, "Come on, dammit! This is taking too fucking long!"

Dalton was surprised to see that at least one other guard was in on it and probably flattered I would go through so much effort to get some of his "stuff." In fact, if I didn't know better, I would say the idea of that made him cum more so than my pussy. He came so hard, it felt like he shot a gallon of sperm up inside me.

Ryan raised his voice a little when he recognized the noise a man makes when he blows. "Okay, his bitch ass came. Let's go, NOW!"

When he said "NOW" so loud, I started beating on Dalton's shoulders for him to get off before he fell asleep inside me. I hate when men do that foolishness.

He got up, and I started grabbing at my clothes, throwing them on as fast as I could. That's when he asked my first name, and I told him it was Phoebe. I told him, "I'll be coming for that dick again!"

He simply replied, "No problem!"

That was how the love affair of Dalton and Phoebe began. Now, over a year later, with his baby inside me, the quick fuck we had the first time has turned into pure love. We go at each other every chance we get. I no longer fuck other guards to get at him because he is still running his drug business from the inside, and he gives me cash to pay them off.

When he gets out, his ass is all mine, and my ass is already all his. Like I said, he may not be a superhero, but he is dayum sure a superman.

The Dick You Down Crew

They were known as the Dick You Down Crew. Women across the nation spoke of them in whispers and sometimes even in code. Women who had actually experienced them sometimes resorted to speaking about them in tongues. There were three of them: the Wishmaster, the Lickmaster, and the Dickmaster. The Wishmaster was the one who granted your every wish and helped you to live out your every fantasy. The Lickmaster was just that: a master at licking you wherever and whenever it pleased you. The Dickmaster was, aw Lawd, what can I say? He was the master of pleasure, pure and simple.

I saved up for eleven months to acquire their services. Once I hit twenty-nine, it became painfully clear that the man of my dreams was not going to come along. The thought of turning thirty without ever really having an earth-shattering orgasm was too much to bear. So I saved and I saved until I had accumulated the necessary five thousand to hire them for the evening. I know five grand is extravagant, but after all I had heard, I felt it was well worth the investment.

I made the initial contact through their Web site, *www.dickyou downcrew.com,* and received an instant reply from an auto responder. It informed me that my inquiry had been received and that someone would contact me within forty-eight hours. I actually fabricated half the information on the form I was required to fill out. I don't trust the Internet, no matter how secure they claim it to be. I am one of those sisters who prints out the mail-order form instead of ordering online at those e-commerce sites. Sure, I can get things faster if I do the real-time credit-card processing, but I prefer to wait the extra time and play it safe.

I lied about my name. I said it was Chiquita Locksley instead of Laura Connelly—same initials but reversed. I used my free e-mail address instead of my regular one with my real name attached to the end of every message. I had to put down a phone number, so I put in my cell phone. If things got out of hand, changing it was nothing but a thing because less than a dozen people had the number in the first place. Besides, my live-in boyfriend would have had a fit if someone called me from dickyoudowncrew.com and left a message on the voice mail.

I know. I know. I said that the man of my dreams had not come along, and he hadn't. That didn't mean I was determined to go without sex altogether. Puleeze, that was not even an option. I was living with Scott, and most of my girlfriends were crazy jealous—but if they only knew. Sure, Scott was fine, brilliant, successful, and drove a seriously fly car. The convertible Jaguar had always been in my top three for the bomb-ass-car-of-all-time award. That's how he managed to pull me. I was walking down the street during rush hour, and he almost ran my ass over in the crosswalk. My first instinct was to cuss his ass out, but when he got out of the car and I got a look at him, the sun started shining even though it was forty degrees and dismal a moment before.

He was fine. True, that. Six-one, tight body, deep chocolate skin, and a smile that could light up a room. Little did I know that he was seriously lacking in the sex department. The first time we threw down, I wasn't even sure that his dick was in until he started yelling, "I'm cumming!" I wondered how the hell he could be cumming when I hadn't even begun to get my freak on.

It must seem strange that I ended up living with him, huh? Well, to be quite honest, Scott was good at some things, like sucking on my breasts—which happened to be one of the greatest turn-ons to me—and sucking on my toes. Besides, I adored his mother and the rest of his family. His sister and I had become the best of friends over the three years we had been together. Yet and still, I needed something extra in my life. I needed to be fucked six ways from Sunday.

I only made thirty grand a year at my administrative job, but I managed to come up with the five thousand I needed. I asked Scott to cover all the bills for a few months, and he happily obliged. I think it made him feel more like a man, having a woman dependent on him. I realize my methods were shady, but hey, I needed the money before I lost my damn mind for real.

For the next two days, I patiently waited for a phone call. One time my battery went dead on my shitty-ass cell phone. Why do they lie and say that a battery has a long life when they know it sure as hell doesn't? As soon as I had it up and running again, I checked for voice mail messages, and there was a message from this dude named Joe. I didn't feel like being bothered with his ass.

Joe had been my first "creeping" experience during my lackluster relationship with Scott. He talked big game but turned out to be just that; all mouth and no action. I got naked, and he acted like a scared bitch. For a second, I thought the fool might have been a thirty-three-year-old virgin, but he got his act together and did a little sumptin' sumptin'. Still wasn't worth my time, effort, or ribbed condom, though.

I was juggling three paper grocery bags and my briefcase up the stairs to our second-floor apartment when my cell phone rang, exactly forty-eight hours after I had hit the submit button on dickyoudowncrew.com. In my haste to catch the call, I dropped one bag and heard the carton of eggs splatter on the outdoor carpet.

"Hello," I breathed heavily into the phone in disgust.

"Is this Chiquita Locksley?"

What the hell was this? There was a woman on the other end of the line. Surely, she couldn't be the Wishmaster or Lickmaster, and she damn sure couldn't be the Dickmaster unless she was working with a strap-on.

"Who is this?" I demanded to know.

"This is Robin."

"Robin. Hmm, I don't think I know a Robin."

Looking back, I don't know why I was frontin'. The odds of some sister ringing my damn cell phone, having the wrong number, and happening to ask for my recently created alter ego were slim to none.

"Once again, is this Chiquita Locksley?" she asked in a pleasant enough voice. "Did you fill out an information request form on dickyoudowncrew.com?"

"Umm, yes I did." I put the bags down and put my key in the lock, making sure to avoid stepping in the egg yolks that were all over the place. I hesitated for a moment and peeked over the balcony to make sure Scott's Jaguar wasn't in his assigned space. I didn't want to go inside if he was home, because he was the nosiest brother on the planet. "I filled out the form, and I've been waiting for you to call."

"Sorry for the delay, but we get a ton of requests, and some- times the staff gets a bit overwhelmed."

I managed to get myself and the groceries in the house, opt- ing to clean up the mess in front of the door later.

"Hmm, you have that many women asking to get put on, huh?" I asked, wondering if it was such a good idea after all. I mean, damn! How many sisters had these dudes knocked off?

The sister on the other end of the line started laughing. "Well, the men are rather popular. It seems that the word has really gotten out lately."

"So, how much is it?" I already knew the price but decided to ask anyway, in case they were running some specials. In fact, I asked, "Are you running any specials?"

She laughed again. "No, sorry. We just have the flat rate of five thousand a night."

"What exactly constitutes a night, and what services are per- formed for the five thousand?"

I could've sworn I heard a lip smack on the other end of the line. No, she wasn't tripping on me all of a sudden. We were talking about five thousand damn dollars.

"Didn't you read the description of services on the Web site?"

"Yes, I did but it didn't define 'night' to my satisfaction. Are we talking a certain amount of hours, sunset to sunrise, or what?"

"You get eight hours. Additional hours are available upon re- quest, but there is a fee."

"And how much are the extra hours?"

"Five hundred an hour."

"Damn!" I exclaimed into the handset.

"Is there a problem, Chiquita?"

"No, no problem." I collapsed onto the sofa, wondering if I was doing the right thing. After all, five grand could stretch a long way at my favorite mall. Fuck it, I was going for it. "So, when can I get an appointment?"

"Hmm, let me check."

There was a brief silence, and I could hear paper shuffling on her end.

"We have Tuesday, July ninth, available."

"That's a month from now."

"Yes, I know, but it is our only available date. Would you like to be scheduled or not?"

"Yes, yes, I'll take it," I answered excitedly. This was going to be more interesting than I imagined. July 9 was my thirtieth birthday.

"Cool. I need to get some further information from you, like where you would like the gentlemen to meet you. I'll assume you want them to come to your place?"

"No, no, no! They can't come here!" I yelled in a panic. Imagine that. Scott coming home with roses and a birthday cake, only to find me ass out with three men slapping skins.

Robin didn't skip a beat. "What city and state are you in?"

"Chicago, Illinois."

"Not a problem. We have various hotels that we work with throughout the country. We have several there in the Chicago area. I will e-mail you a list, and you can make the appropriate arrangements."

"Hold up. Are you saying that I have to pay for the room?"

"If you want a room, you have to pay for it. The five thousand simply covers the sexual favors and travel expenses."

"Fine," I stated nastily. At least they weren't trying to take me for plane tickets, meals, and all that shit.

"Wonderful. You will have an e-mail within the hour detailing our rules and regulations, a list of local hotels in your area, and payment instructions. All monies must be received at least seven days before your appointment."

"Okay, whatever."

"Thank you for your time, Chiquita."

Just like that, Robin was gone.

July 9 was the strangest day of my life. Scott woke me up with his tongue. Now Scott had licked a lot of things in three years, but he had never licked my pussy. But there he was with his head buried between my legs, going to town on my coochie. I didn't have a lot of experiences to compare that one to, but he seemed to be doing okay with it. He wasn't making my thighs tremble or anything like that, but it was interesting.

"Happy Birthday, baby," he whispered about ten minutes after I'd opened my eyes to his surprise. "Thirty years old. You're about to be over the hill."

"The hill you crossed over four years ago, huh?" I asked jokingly.

"Hey, that was a cheap shot."

Scott tickled me until I was screaming for mercy.

"See, that'll teach you not to make fun of a brother's age," he said after finally letting me go.

"You started it," I childishly replied.

He reached over and retrieved a small black velvet bag from the drawer of the nightstand on his side of the bed.

"Seriously, happy thirtieth, Laura." He handed me the bag. "This is something special for someone special."

I took the bag and just stared at it. What on earth was he up to?

"Laura, open it already." Scott laughed.

I undid the drawstring on the bag and pulled out a black velvet box. At that moment, I knew the thing I had most wanted and dreaded at the same time was about to happen. I tried to think quickly, but instead my mind went completely blank.

Scott took the box from my hand and snapped it open, revealing a two-carat diamond ring. It was stunning.

"So, will you?"

I was speechless. My eyes fluttered from the ring to his face and back again.

"Laura, will you do me the honor of becoming my wife?"

I didn't know what to say, so I said the first thing that made sense. "Can I have some time to think about it?"

The look of disappointment on Scott's face was nothing short of depressing. We sat in silence for a couple of minutes before he asked, "How much time do you need?"

"Just a day or two," I replied hesitantly. "It's just that I wasn't expecting this."

"But what do you have to think about, Laura? We've been together for three years." He set the ring down on the comforter and gently took my hand. "Don't I make you happy?"

"Yes, Scott, you make me happy," I said halfheartedly. "I still just need a little bit of time. Cool?"

"Cool."

Scott got up from the bed, and while he didn't exhibit anger in his movements, I knew he was fired up inside. He had taken the ultimate step to commitment, and I had shot him down.

He got dressed, and as he was leaving, he asked, "Do you want to go out to dinner tonight to celebrate your birthday?"

"Umm, I can't." My lies were about to begin. "I promised my mother that I'd spend tonight with her. Like you said, this is a big day, and she really wanted to do something special for me."

"Kind of like I tried to do this morning," he said.

I ignored his comment. "In fact, we might be out kind of late, so I'll probably just spend the night and head to work from there in the morning."

"Laura, all I can say is, enjoy your birthday, and I guess I'll see you when I see you."

Scott walked out the bedroom, and a few seconds later I heard the front door slam.

Taking the day off from work was a given. My boss was not a happy camper about it, but that was his personal problem because I never, ever work for the man on the day of my creation. I spent the morning being pampered at a day spa. If I could put out five grand to get laid properly, I could splurge on a pedicure, manicure, hairstyle, and massage. By one o'clock, I was walking out of the spa on pillow-soft toes and looking fly as shit.

I lucked out and found a spot in front of my favorite lingerie store. I selected a hot pink satin bra and thong set, even though I didn't anticipate having it on too long.

While I was standing in line to pay, I called my mother from my cell phone to do an intervention. If she happened to call Scott for any reason to discuss making plans for my birthday, my ass was toast. I told her that I would be spending a quiet, romantic evening with Scott. She was disappointed but felt better once I promised her that we would do lunch the following day.

By three, I was ready to check in at the luxurious downtown hotel that I had selected from the list Robin e-mailed to me. It was actually the most expensive, but anything worth doing was worth doing right. The men were not due until eight, and that was cool because the nervousness had set in. What the hell was I doing?

The room had one big-ass bed. I read the card placed on the pillow and couldn't believe the prices of the bedding offered to guests that wished to purchase items in the gift shop. Eight hundred dollars for a down comforter? Only big ballers could roll like that. For one night, I was going to be a big baller. A big baller surrounded by big dicks.

Once I got settled into the room, I realized that I was about to starve, so I trotted down to the hotel restaurant. I was all about splurging that day, but the prices for their food were ridiculous. Thirty-two dollars for a steak, and then you had to pay for the potato and vegetables separately at five bucks a pop. I didn't even think so. I took my ass right down the street to Hooters and threw down on some wings.

Men are hilarious. Every time I go into a Hooters by myself, they look at me like I'm crazy. Shit, good food is good food. Besides, women walking around in tight-ass tops and barely clothed bottoms is no different than a day at the beach. Scott and I had gone there once for lunch, and he was so embarrassed that he was ready to leave before the food arrived. I explained to him that a man looking at tits and ass flashed in his face was perfectly normal, and I would've been more concerned if he wasn't looking at them.

I returned to the room with a full stomach and ran a warm bath with some vanilla sugar bath gel, my favorite. I had been tempted to get a cup of chili with my meal, but the last thing I needed was to be all gassed up when the Dick You Down Crew arrived. Normally I only shower in hotel rooms, but since this particular one was so pricey, I was hoping their cleaning was thorough and on point.

I drew the shades, dimmed the lights, and sank into the tub. I had Jill Scott doing her thing on the CD player/radio beside the bed, and I took a little time to get myself ready for the action later that night. Masturbation has always been a major aspect of my sex life. Without it, I would've gone cuckoo years before. Besides, there's nothing like pussy that has been simmering in juice for a while before a man hits it. It's like comparing a marinated steak to one thrown on the grill straight out of the package.

I cupped my left breast and rubbed my nipple with my thumb while I fingered myself with my right hand. I lost myself in thought as I tried to decide what wish I would request of the Wishmaster that night. There were so many fantasies that I had never lived out. That in itself was a damn shame. Somehow, I would have to narrow it down to just one, and it was a toughie. So I ran the different scenarios through my mind as I mastur- bated, and finally there was one that made me climax like a clap of thunder. Yes, that was the one I would ask for.

I sprayed myself down with body oil after my bath and put on the lingerie, or "lingeree," as they call it in the hood. Before I knew it, I had dozed off. A knock at the door stirred me back awake about an hour later.

"Oh, my gosh!" I exclaimed as I catapulted up off the bed. The reality finally hit, and I asked myself, "What the hell am I doing?"

Scott had proposed to me that morning, and I shot him down. He might not have been perfect, but he loved me. He'd even shown it by going downtown that morning for the first time. I knew that was a big hang-up of his, but he had done it anyway.

Then there was my mother. Why was she popping up in my head when I was about to fuck three men? Because I had lied to her for the first time in years, and I should've been spending my thirtieth birthday with her and my man. Instead, there I was in a ritzy hotel with three men on the other side of that door who had come to smoke my boots.

I inched my way to the door, took a deep breath, and flung it open, expecting to see the Dick You Down Crew. Instead I saw an old-ass man whose eyes were about to pop out his head. I imme- diately ran to the closet to get a white hotel robe to throw on.

"Who the hell are you?" I asked after covering up.

He grinned at me, and I could almost see the nasty thoughts running through his head. "Maintenance. Did you call about a blown out lightbulb?"

"No, no, I didn't call."

He started trying to smooth down his dirty coveralls and smooth back his even dirtier hair. "Maybe I should just come in and check you out. I mean, check it out."

I glared at him with disdain and tried to shut the door. "I didn't call about a bulb, so leave me alone before I call downstairs and report you."

The expression on his face went from lust to fury as he pressed his hand against the door. "All that ain't even necessary. I thought this was the right room. Can't fault me that you answered the door half-naked."

I tried to knock his hand off the door. "Just leave."

"I will as soon as you tell me you ain't calling downstairs. I need this here job. I got eight kids at home."

I was dying to ask him what kind of woman would birth eight of his children, but refrained. I just wanted him to go away. He looked to his left toward the bank of elevators and sucked his teeth. "Damn, what have we got here? Is the Mr. Olympia Competition in town?"

I peeked around the corner and saw them: the three finest brothas I'd ever seen in my entire life, and they were headed my way.

I looked back at Mr. Nasty. "Look, I'm not going to report you, all right. Just leave and enjoy the rest of your day."

The three men stopped right in front of my door, hovering over him because he was blocking their path.

The tallest of the three asked, "Chiquita?"

"Yes," I quickly responded.

Mr. Nasty lifted his clipboard and perused it. "Chiquita? It says here that your name is—" I slapped my hand over his mouth, which he swatted away. "What on earth is wrong with you, girl?" He looked up at the three men and back at me. "Maybe I'm the one that should be reporting something to the front desk. An assumed name. Three men showing up at your door. Are you a hooker?"

"Hell, no, I'm not a hooker!" I yelled in anger. "Now leave before this gets ugly."

One of the other men asked, "Is everything straight here?"

Mr. Nasty moved out of their way. "Everything is everything."

I also moved to the side so they could all enter the room. "Look, I'm not sure which room needs a lightbulb, but it's not this one. Thanks for your effort, though."

I tried to be nice so he would drop the hooker theory, although he wasn't far off base. I just didn't happen to be the hooker. I was the john.

Mr. Nasty moved closer to me, and his foul breath almost did me in. "Listen, after you're done with them, what can I get for fifty dollars?"

I smacked him in the face. "Get the fuck away from my door!"

He rubbed his face and took off down the hall, turning around just long enough to spew the word "bitch."

After closing the door, it hit me that *they* were in the room. The Wishmaster, the Lickmaster, and the Dickmaster. I was alone with the Dick You Down Crew.

I froze and could barely breathe. One of them walked up behind me and started massaging my shoulders. It felt incredible. He leaned over and whispered in my ear, "Relax. Whatever drama just happened, whatever fears you have, whatever brings you pain, all of them are about to disappear, because the Wishmaster is here."

"Damn, the Wishmaster," I whispered before glancing up over my shoulder at him. He was the tallest one, and a tall drink of water he was. Deep chocolate with a bald head and a smile that could make women melt.

He swept me up in his arms and carried me over to the bed to lie me down. The other two, who were equally fine, were standing by the window. They didn't have any luggage, just briefcases. They probably discreetly had rooms booked someplace else where they would relax after knocking me off.

After laying me on the bed, he started rubbing my feet. Thank goodness I had taken the time to get a pedicure—if my toes had been jacked up, I would have been ashamed.

"So, tell me, Chiquita . . .tell *us* what you would like to happen here tonight."

"Um . . . I don't really know," I said. "What do you usually do?"

"Whatever is asked of us." He glanced at his two friends. "Each of us has our own specialties. Of course, I make wishes come true, so what's your wish?"

"I actually gave that a lot of thought before you got here."

"And?"

"I want to know what it feels like to have someone in all three holes at one time."

He grinned, and I could hear the other two chuckling. "That's easy enough. The only question is, can you handle it?"

I was honest. "I don't know but I'd like to try. I've never personally tried it, but I saw it once in a porno film."

"And it turned you on?" he asked.

"Yeah, it did, but my boyfriend would never agree to something like that. In fact, he would probably kill me if I even suggested it."

The Wishmaster lifted one of my feet to his lips and ran his tongue over the underside of my toes. "Well, he's not here tonight, so he doesn't matter."

I started trembling for some reason, probably because of fear. This was really it, and while the thought of having all three holes hit at once was arousing, it was also downright scary.

The shortest of the three, a light-skinned brother with hazel eyes and wavy black hair, came over to the bed and stood over me. He reached down and palmed a breast in each hand. "You need to relax. The Lickmaster is going to loosen you up a bit. How about that?"

I didn't respond. I just allowed him to lower my bra straps, exposing my nipples. He rubbed them between his fingers for a few seconds and then reached below my back to unsnap my bra. He took it completely off and then leaned over me to suckle on my nipples. I could see his dick, his *huge* dick, through the tan slacks he was wearing. It was leveled right above my head.

I knew that an opportunity such as this would never come my way again, so it was time to let go of all my inhibitions. While he continued to work his way back and forth from breast to breast, squeezing tightly the one he didn't have in his mouth, I reached up and undid his belt buckle. I toyed with his zipper until I got it down and pulled his dick out. He teased me with it by lowering it just enough for me to taste it with the tip of my tongue and then lifting it back up out of range.

I have to admit that it made me laugh, because he was making me indulge in some strategic moves to get to the dick. Finally, I just grabbed it and started milking him like a leech. Apparently I must have been on the money, because he moaned and then ripped my panties off so he could bury his head in my pussy.

He climbed up on the bed with me, placing his knees beside my shoulders. That's when I did something I'd never imagined doing. I actually licked the brotha's ass. It was kind of tart, but you could tell that he was clean. Some of my friends have spoken about eating their men's asses, but the thought had always appalled me. Not that night.

The Lickmaster matched me tit for tat by moving his head even farther down so he could eat my ass out, too. He had the thickest tongue in the world and knew how to work it. He definitely deserved his title.

Through my peripheral vision, I could see the other two getting completely undressed. I almost gagged on the dick that I had put back in my mouth when I saw the size of the one on the Dickmaster. This wasn't a myth. His dick was really down to his knees. He was fine as shit, just like the other two. Caramel with a fade and dark bedroom eyes. His dick looked like two feet of smoked sausage. I couldn't wait to dig in, but I was a bit leery about him sticking it up in me. I envisioned it going in my pussy and coming out my mouth.

I didn't have to wonder long because he came over and tapped the Lickmaster on the ass. "Let me get in there, dog."

The Lickmaster sat up and wiped his lips. "Girl, you've got it going on. Some sistahs don't eat right, and let's just say, their pussies are kind of rank, but yours is on the money."

I took that as a compliment, even though his descriptions were kind of raunchy. For five thousand, I thought he would be more cautious about his choice of words.

The Dickmaster went around to the opposite side of the bed, spread my legs wider, licked all of his fingers in one swoop, and then rubbed them over my pussy. He stuck one finger inside and said, "Um, nice and tight."

The Wishmaster chuckled. "Not after you get done with it, homey."

Those words hit home, and I propped myself up on my elbows. "Listen, I'm not trying to get ruined for life. You can't stick all that in me."

The Dickmaster hooked his arms under my knees and pulled me closer to the edge of the bed. "Relax. You're going to love it, and you'll never forget me."

I started thinking way back to my sexual health class in high school. They always said that a woman's vagina could conform to handle large items and then pop right back into shape. After all, babies come from there, and most are about two feet long at birth.

That helped me out a little, but my thighs still started trembling when the tip of his dick hit my clit. I closed my eyes and braced myself for *the dick*. He eased it in a little at a time until he had it about halfway in. That was my limit!

"No more," I pleaded. "I can't take any more."

He held himself inside me for a minute, rubbing my ass cheeks and licking his lips. Then he started going for it, and all I can say is, it hurt, but it was a good kind of hurt. He pulled out before he came and exploded all over my tummy.

After that, we all took a shower together, which was a feat in itself. Three big-ass men and little ole me in a shower doing all sorts of freaky things. I sucked off the Wishmaster, who ate me out in return. Then the Lickmaster lifted me up against the tile wall and banged the hell out of me there. I was going to attempt to give the Dickmaster a blow job, but decided I was simply not up to the task.

After we got out of the shower, the Wishmaster kept his promise and made my wish come true. I could never describe the intensity of it, so I won't even try. It was the ultimate sexual experience to have a dick in my mouth, in my pussy, and in my ass at the same time. Miraculously, I was even able to walk the next day.

*   *   *

I called in to my job and told them I needed another day off. Much to my amazement, my boss didn't have an attitude for a change. He even wished me a happy birthday, and it meant something even though his was a belated one.

I went home and crawled into bed. Scott was at work, thank goodness. I had no idea what to say to him, so it was just as well that he was gone. I slept all day and woke up with Scott standing over me, staring at me.

"So, Laura, have you thought about it?" he asked without so much as a hello first.

"Yes, I thought about it," I lied. I hadn't been thinking about anything but other men's dicks since I had seen him last.

"And what's your decision?"

I didn't respond.

"Laura, I have been here for you for three years. If I haven't proven that I love you, that I live for you, that I would die for you, then maybe I don't need to be here."

"Scott, I—"

"Fine, just forget it. Just remember that no man is ever going to love you as much as I do. Not ever."

He was right about that. No one would ever love me as much as him, which is why I blurted out, "Yes, I'll marry you."

A huge grin spread across Scott's face. "Really?"

"Yes. Want to pick a date?"

Okay, so maybe Scott isn't perfect, but he's all mine. I love him, and he loves me. We're getting married in the spring, and I am actually looking forward to it. While the relationship might be lacking in certain departments, no one is perfect. This is as perfect as it gets, and if I ever feel like I need more, all I have to do is log onto *www.dickyoudowncrew.com*.